They swirled gloriously through the water, creating wide eddies that caught up the girl and sent her helplessly in whirl after whirl. Caro loved the feeling of being bandied about by these huge, gentle beasts and the water that was their medium. The carepies' fins, looking like fluid skirts, undulated in great waves that ringed their rotund bodies. The male abruptly dropped to the bottom of the tank, swam under Caro and rose just as suddenly, lifting the girl high above the water. She slid off his back and was shot off to the side by a circling wave of his fin. The carepie plummeted below the water again and Caro heard the thunderous slap as the new-formed eddy smashed against the sides of the tank.

She was again shot to the surface, and trying to keep her seat on the slick, bobbing back of the carepie, she grinned up through her faceplate at Dr. Lutes. The small man was dripping with brine, his thin hair clumped in wet tails, water running off his shoulders. But he looked exultant, as joyfully moved by the experience as the girl.

"Can you imagine their play in the spaciousness of the ocean environment, Caro!" he exclaimed.

Caro nodded, her eyes shining. When she was with the carepies she was whole. The creature whirled like a top under her and Caro laughed as the cool water closed over her head.

Fay S Lapka

Fay Lapka is a young Canadian writer, author of
DARK IS A COLOUR, to which this book is the
sequel. She has two degrees from Trinity Western
University and has also studied at Regent College,
Vancouver. She now lives in Vancouver, Canada.

HOVERLIGHT

Fay S Lapka

GOLD
BOOKS

HODDER AND STOUGHTON
LONDON SYDNEY AUCKLAND

British Library C.I.P.

A Catalogue record for this
book is available from the
British Library

ISBN 0-340-57074-1

Printed and bound in Great Britain
for Hodder Christian Paperbacks, a
division of Hodder and Stoughton
Ltd, Mill Road, Dunton Green,
Sevenoaks, Kent TN13 2YA
(Editorial Office: 47 Bedford
Square, London WC1B 3DP) by
Clays Ltd, St. Ives plc.

For
Joy, Hope, Mark & Holly,
who bring Light & Laughter
into the darkest of tunnels.

*Now faith is the substance of things hoped for,
the evidence of things not seen.*

*. . . and we beheld His glory . . .
full of grace and truth.*

Contents

March, 2456

Actaeon—

    I received my orders today and, soon after, stole out onto the roof of the Genetics lab building and waited for the night to arrive. I watched the late afternoon moon, a pale flat ghost, take on the sun's light and, in an instant, become substance. For the first time I noticed that stars appear slowly: at first one by one, then small clusters glow into view, and finally large choruses spring into being. I saw Venus glimmering low on the horizon like a dropped diamond.

    Somewhere, just this side of the glory of Saturn's rings, in Jupiter's fiery shadow, silently spins the planet Clytie: small, insignificant—thrown like a blob of excess wax during the giant's geological evolution. As though it senses it is nothing but Jupiter's leavings, the tiny planet has a stubborn streak: it is stuck in its revolutionary phase—the same side always faces the sun—and the resultant polar predicament spawns strange creatures. I am told that the wind blows with eerie precision, and the vegetation has evolved gaunt and bent. Birds and beasts are thickly skinned, scaled, feathered or furred to diminish the drying effects of either the fierce cold or eternal sun, and, always, the wind.

    Actaeon, soon I will be walking the alien soil of this contrary planet. Although it is what I have longed for, without warning my vision blurs and the stars meld together in a shining wash of light. Already I am homesick for Earth.

—Reginald

1

Friendly Giants

It was hot. Those three small words seemed to be the most repeated and least necessary words the summer of 2463 on Clytie's Main Base. The Atmospheric Officer was the only one in good humor; surely her name would go down in the Community History along with the record-breaking temperatures that she entered.

The sun, dimly seen through the thick atmosphere, radiated a fierce heat that penetrated the soil and shimmered off the porchlike roofs of the Main Base laboratories and housing units. In the brown hills, the Jonah trees, sculpted into gaunt arcs by the hot wind, appeared and disappeared behind curtains of thermal updrafts, and the round pools the trees ringed were glazed with oily muck. Clytie's lavender sky seemed to boil over the few scientists who dared to venture outside the cool of the stone labs, causing them to gasp and shiver with the heat.

Eleven-year-old Ricky seemed oblivious to the temperature; clutching his respirator to his side, he ran close to the parched ground, his mouth open, eyes narrowed, feet pumping, very aware that he could still be seen and apprehended by his Russian teacher.

Caro, from the window of the school library, watched him run. She shook back her dark hair, half wishing that she could be off with him, half wondering if it were her sisterly duty to report him. At fifteen—almost sixteen—she was used to weighing out the ethics of when to Tell and when not to Tell. Ricky's short figure blurred in the shifting heat waves and disappeared from sight. Caro craned her neck trying to see him, but he had moved beyond view of the window. She shrugged. What the teachers missed was their problem. She leaned back in her chair, automatically pushing the wisps of hair from off her damp face, and tried to settle back into her animal behavior assigned reading.

It was difficult to concentrate after lunchbreak. And the summer heat didn't help. The ceiling fans stirred sluggish air in circles around the school building; the whirr of the blades formed the background to every lecture, every lab. Tall jugs of ice-water, beading and running with condensation, rested on a desk at the front of each classroom. The water station provided a ready and welcome distraction for anyone—student or teacher—suffering from procrastination. And it was a handy meeting place to catch up on bits of hurriedly passed news.

Caro looked up as a group of preprimary students left the water station, tightly clutching their pastel-bright cups. The children marched raggedly in twos, a teacher before and after herding them toward the picture-book terminals. As they passed Caro's study table, one skinny girl stopped and stared at her.

Caro gave a tentative smile. The girl pointed a bony finger at Caro. "Look," she announced in high-pitched ringing tones, "an alien!" All the preprimaries stopped dead, cups sloshing, and gazed at Caro in morbid fascination, until the two teachers, their arms raised like wings, swooped down on the gawking children and drove them along. The teacher at the end of the line, smiling too brightly, looked back at Caro apologetically.

Caro heard the snickers coming from the table behind her. She felt one side of her face burn and the other side begin to itch; she tried to focus on the words on her monitor. *Just stay seated for a minute or two,* she told herself savagely, *then leave.* Caro forced herself to count to 100, and then 200. She glanced at the wall clock. Feigning horror at the time, she powered off her terminal, grabbed the magnetic bar, and hurried out of the library as though she were late for a class.

In truth, the only thing left on her day's schedule was a tutorial with her Biology mentor, Dr. Lutes, and that wasn't for another thirty minutes. Caro headed into the washroom, dropped her book bag onto the floor, gripped the side of the sink and stared unflinchingly into the mirror.

The surgeons had done the best job they could. "Time," they said, "just give yourself time to heal." Caro stared at this stranger's face in the mirror. A harlequin's mask. A ragged zigzag-marked fake face. Half her own familiar nut-brown complexion, half white plasti-graft with small patches of new-grown skin showing through. The hair at her left temple had been shaved for the graft; the regrowth was in the wild, wispy stage that shot out in all directions. Caro ground shut her eyes, catching the tears that tried to spill out of them and sending them back to where they originated.

"Hi-Ho," a voice boomed past her ear and footsteps crashed past her. Caro opened her eyes to catch in the mirror a tall girl in black leather shorts racing by. A stall door slammed behind her.

"I got my period in Computer Science—right in the middle of a sneak test—isn't that great!" Sheila's voice echoed off the washroom tiles.

3

"Your what?" Caro asked cautiously.

"My period. Time of the moon . . . Woman's season . . . ?" Her face shot round the door of the stall, gazing incredulously at Caro's puzzled expression.

"I'm menstruating, chump," she boomed. "They called it 'a period' in the 20th. Wow, what a mixed-up century!" Her head abruptly withdrew. "Yeow! Caught my earring on the door knob." The door carefully opened and shut. "Once I ripped it right out of my earlobe," she said cheerfully. "Anyway, what's the conversion factor for binary code? I was stuck on a question when I had to run for it. I was hoping someone smart would be in here."

"I thought you were ahead of me in Computer Sci—" Caro began.

"Yeah, yeah, but not when it comes to figuring out berserk stuff like binary code conversion—how stupid when a computer'll do it for you. But just give me a program to break into, I don't care *how* secure they make it—I can get into anything!" Sheila wound up excitedly. "Did you hear about the time I—"

The door opened and Dr. Menue entered, tapping her small foot on the floor. "Sheila? I trust you are ready to finish your test now?" Her staccato voice ended every sentence with an uptilt as if her words insisted on leaping towards the ceiling. She glanced at Caro, her eyes methodically skimming the girl's scarred face. Caro turned on the faucet and washed her hands, feeling every inch of the woman's scalpel-like gaze.

The toilet flushed and Sheila bounced out. She washed her hands as long as she dared, but Dr. Menue insisted on waiting for her. As Sheila followed the teacher out the door, she turned toward Caro, her eyeballs turned back into her head so that only the whites showed and her cheeks swelled out like two angry pufferfish.

4

Caro found herself grinning. For all of Sheila's bizarre fads—such as her obsession with 20th-century videos—she was a welcome relief from the rigid view most of her peers adhered to in regard to dress, language, and behavior.

Caro reached down for her book bag, caught a glimpse of her own face in the mirror, and her grin fled. Just a few short months ago, before the lumie incident at the End Base, Caro had fit in with all the rest of the high-school students. Now it were as if she and Sheila had traded places. Only Caro didn't merely look eccentric, she had become the freak.

She had never thought of herself as beautiful, for Caro lacked the classic bone-structure and pure complexion of what she considered to be true beauty. Nor did she have the startling dark eyes and fragile face of her best friend, Sherri. Yet Caro had moved easily within herself, had been at home with her body, feeling as rich and lithe and unique as a darkly golden deer in a wildflower meadow. Sometimes, when faced with a sudden reflection of herself, the girl had stopped, startled, as though seeing a stranger. She would have forgotten that her features tended toward squareness, that her brow was too heavily defined, and that her skin and hair ran together in a dull-brown blur.

Now, though Caro tried, she could not forget the false paleness of the plasti-graft through which the itching skin grew, nor the raw Z-shaped edge slashed from eye to jaw. This new image was branded too deeply within.

Throwing the bag over her shoulder, Caro wearily left the sanctuary of the bathroom and walked down the hall to Dr. Lutes' office.

There was a note waiting for her, written in Dr. Lutes' precise, old-fashioned handwriting: *Caro, please join me in the marine lab.* Caro smiled. How like Dr. Lutes to tape a handwritten note directly on top of the high-tech audio message minder mounted on his office door instead of using it to leave a verbal message for her. She picked up her pace and headed toward the stairwell leading down into the basement.

It was always cool in the lower labs. Caro pushed through the swinging doors into the marine lab and paused, pushing a wisp of hair back off her forehead, waiting for her eyes to adjust to the dimness.

This was her favorite place at school—perhaps in all of the Main Base. The softly lit tanks bubbled gently, and the mist from the fountain of the large corner pool released a cool, ocean scent into the air. Caro breathed deeply, feeling the tightness in her stomach releasing. There was no room for tension in the steady rhythm of the underwater world. She smiled as the round, inky-blue pair of carapace-fish bumped in a friendly manner against the side of the pool. Caro flattened her palm against the clear silicone-plate and the creatures butted up against it. These two were her special friends.

Carapacefish, or carepies, were the friendly giants of Clytie's warmer ocean, the Pantropic. Although quite capable of growing four meters in diameter in the open ocean, if they remained in captivity, these teen-agers would grow to only half that size. Their turtlelike faces seemed to beam with goodwill, and the circular fins that ringed their bowl-shaped bodies moved them gracefully through the water. For all their ponderous mass, the carepies maneuvered through the ocean like hummingbirds through air. Families of carepies could be seen hovering in the ocean, as though hanging in the depths, motionless except for an almost imperceptible wave in their banding fins. And they could rise straight up, or sink directly down like elevators.

Wherever carepies gathered in pods it was safe to swim. Although they were vegetarians, feeding on vast amounts of plankton strained from the water through their beaks, for some unknown reason, the terrors of the sea, the whip-thin snakefish, were never sighted in their domain.

"Ah, there you are, my dear." Dr. Lutes' preoccupied voice floated down from the deck above the carepies' tank. Caro looked up, blinking against the spotlight. The old, white-haired professor, wearing a damp-stained lab coat, trailed a green pole in the water. One end lay on the surface with a broad float. Clamped onto the other end, close by Dr. Lutes' hand, was a small screen. He peered nearsightedly into it.

"Do you want me up there, Dr. Lutes?" Caro called. There was silence while the professor adjusted the screen.

"No," he announced. "Please change into your gear and enter the tank . . . if you care to," he added, a quick gleam lighting his eyes.

Caro smiled. "I'll be ready in a minute. Or less." Another favorite thing.

A short wetsuit pulled up over her swimsuit was necessary to stay for any length of time in the water. Caro slipped into the weighted vest that held her air reserve and drew over her head the attached clear hood. She pulled on the mass-pockets, resembling stiff fingerless mittens and toeless socks, and then walked to the ladder.

Carefully she swung her body down the rungs leading into the carepies' tank. Each step was hard work. Clytie's briny ocean made buoyancy a problem unless you were heavily weighted.

The carepies surrounded her, beaming and bumping up against her, sending her flying through the water. Snug in her suit, Caro laughed, her voice sounding flat and tinny through the intercom speakers in the wall.

"It seems as though your friends missed you over the weekend," Dr. Lutes commented.

7

"I missed them." The girl smoothed her hands over the female carepie's rigid, rubbery back. The male hovered benignly beside Caro, his banding fin rising and falling in a slow wave pattern.

"What are you measuring?" Caro asked as Dr. Lutes gazed raptly at the computer screen.

"The usual—heart rate, cellular respiration, body mass." Dr. Lutes paused. "And an additional factor . . . "

Caro looked up through the water. Dr. Lutes' face shifted and blurred and grew grotesquely long through the restless currents. Caro shivered. "What factor?"

"The proportion of oxygen directly breathed from the air to that taken in from the water."

"I thought that carepies breathed air or water—that either was fine."

"There is every indication that breathing air or water is not a random activity." Dr. Lutes sounded uncharacteristically stern. "My immediate calculations seem to suggest that they breathe air approximately 43 times more than they breathe water."

"Isn't that stran—uh, surprising?" Caro chose her words carefully. "I mean, wouldn't it be easier for them to breathe water rather than rising to the surface all the time? A more efficient use of energy?"

"We've taught you well, haven't we child," Dr. Lutes muttered sadly. "Come, come, Caro!" he added sharply. "Has your experience of living led you to believe that Life is nothing but a simple totaling of pluses and minuses?"

Caro said nothing, but rebelliously thought that life would certainly be a lot easier if it were a straightforward column calculation.

Dr. Lutes sighed. "Yes, it is surprising—and strange," he said in his usual quiet voice. He began calling out orders to the girl to guide the carepies through various speeds and movements, and the tense moment was forgotten.

"Now, full speed, Caro—that is, as fast as this small tank will allow them to move," he called.

They swirled gloriously through the water, creating wide eddies that caught up the girl and sent her helplessly in whirl after whirl. Caro loved the feeling of being bandied about by these huge, gentle beasts and the water that was their medium. The carepies' fins, looking like fluid skirts, undulated in great waves that ringed their rotund bodies. The male abruptly dropped to the bottom of the tank, swam under Caro and rose just as suddenly, lifting the girl high above the water. She slid off his back and was shot off to the side by a circling wave of his fin. The carepie plummeted below the water again and Caro heard the thunderous slap as the new-formed eddy smashed against the sides of the tank.

She was again shot to the surface, and trying to keep her seat on the slick, bobbing back of the carepie, she grinned up through her faceplate at Dr. Lutes. The small man was dripping with brine, his thin hair clumped in wet tails, water running off his shoulders. But he looked exultant, as joyfully moved by the experience as the girl.

"Can you imagine their play in the spaciousness of the ocean environment, Caro!" he exclaimed.

Caro nodded, her eyes shining. When she was with the carepies she was whole. The creature whirled like a top under her and Caro laughed as the cool water closed over her head.

April, 2456
Actaeon—

*The month journey to Clytie is only half over but I feel
as though the years of research at York have never been. It
is my early years that, somehow, seem closer. Do you remember "Birdbeak"? Our absurd name for Dr. Robin Thrushton,
our mentor at the museum in Paris? I can see him clearly:
small, with tiny eyes, and a chiseled nose. We were eleven
then. He was nearly seventy and quite deaf, far more at
home with the old volumes of literature that he catalogued
than with small boys. I smuggled out all sorts of banned
literature and read it in the old bomb shelter that was my
hideout. Against all laws of childrearing and education, I
became acquainted with the Bobbsey Twins, the Bastables,
and the Hardy Boys . . . I marveled at the strangeness of
Fair Play and Owning Up in spite of being Sent to Coventry
or, what to me then seemed a far worse thing, To Bed without
Supper. I longed to use the old words, "chum," or "buddy,"
to have friends that I could "stick up for" and not "squeal"
on. I even wished for a "pesky kid-sister" to protect from the
neighborhood bully . . . but there wasn't even a neighborhood bully, was there, Actaeon? It was just the two of us.
Always, just the two of us.*

—Reginald

2

Becka's Browser

"He glared at me and said, 'Phah! You smell like fish,'" Sherri said, twisting her mouth into a tight prune face. "Phah!"

"Mr. Blake said, 'Phah'?!" asked Caro, laughing as they watched the stiff back of their principal march into the school building.

"Phah." Sherri nodded. "That is EXACTLY what he said—and how he said it—only worse. Phah!" She spat out the word yet again with great feeling.

"Which one of you was worse—Mr. Blake—or you?" Caro asked innocently.

"Very funny," Sherri said. "Mr. Blake, of course. I was speaking colloquially—it's quite correct to do so, you know, when you are communicating with 'peers'—as Blake calls us. Oh, my mistake," she added. "I forgot that I was addressing a mere scientist-type. Us artists aren't so legalistically biased."

"Actually, I think that should be 'we artists,'" Caro corrected. "Anyway," she continued loudly over Sherri's "Phah!", "Did you get some good sketches of the carepies?"

"Yes! The field trip was a success—even if I do stink of fish. I'll show you the rough sketches tonight. You're

11

going to adore them when they're finished. There were two babies in the pod."

Caro smiled, seeing in her mind the two babies: miniature carepies with film-delicate skirts and little beakfaces on periscope necks. They would be as round, bouncing, and cheerful as beach balls. And she could just imagine the mature carepies, rolling in the briny ocean like boats.

Ricky and Hal joined the two girls waiting under the overhang by the pickup lot. It was Sherri's mom's turn to drive the four of them home from school.

Ricky swaggered along beside the tall, lean older boy. Ricky's dark eyes were wide and snapping. His hair, black and bushlike—at the moment so bushlike that bits of curled leaves were layered among the spiky tufts—seemed to bristle with excitement. Grey dust, like smeared war paint, adhered to his wind-burned face, arms, and legs. Ricky had found it a highly successful afternoon. He carried within the pocket of his shorts a creature resembling a flaking, brown rock. He could hardly wait to show it to his veterinarian mom; Ricky was sure that the little toadlike animal was a new find.

Hal, as usual, was impeccably groomed. His khaki-colored shorts, the respirator neatly tucked into the narrow pocket, had held their crease through the hot school day; his shirt sleeves were still rolled up in matching precision.

At times—more out of habit than anything—Hal still favored his left leg when he walked. His other leg had compensated for the wound inflicted by the lumies; the right calf muscle bulged and seemed almost twice the mass of the injured one. But perhaps this was simply an optical effect due to the hairless, white plasti-graft that ran irregularly around his calf from ankle to knee.

Caro looked down at her rumpled white shorts, pushed the straying tube of her respirator back into their pocket, and sighed at the fluorescent-green dribble of laboratory dye splashed across her pink shirt.

Hal raised his glasses and peered at Caro. "I smell fish," he said.

"Don't look at me!" she wailed as Sherri burst out laughing.

"It's me," Sherri explained. "A few of us were out this afternoon observing carepies and other fishlike beasties. The boat we were in must have been rubbed down with dead fish. Long dead fish. I reek. I know it, I cheerfully admit to it, and I've reached the stage where I'm proud of it!"

"Well, at least it's your parents' crawler," Hal said, elaborately holding his nose as the yellow caterpillar-treaded vehicle roared into the lot. "Sorry, Caro," he added above the noise. "You are usually the one who plays with fish, you know."

"I prefer them alive," Caro said loftily.

Hal smiled and held open the crawler door for her.

"I prefer them cooked—with piles of deep-fried vegi-roots," Ricky announced. "I'm starving."

Sherri's mom looked with worried eyes in the rearview mirror back to Caro, Hal, and Ricky who had settled into the rear seat of the crawler. Sherri owned up.

"It is I, mother," she said dramatically. "Forsooth, I reeketh."

"Sherri!" her mom warned. "You know that just because your father encourages you to read old books doesn't mean that it is wise to start quoting them publicly. Other people have different ideas." She deliberately avoided looking in the mirror at Hal, unsure whether or not his father agreed with the Community's ban on old literature.

"Public! Ha! These here folks are down-homers. Family," Sherri explained, viewing the others' uncertain expressions.

"You don't need to worry about Hal, Aunt Miriam," Ricky said in the patronizing tone he often used when his "adopted" aunt began her worrying.

Caro smiled inwardly. That was the difference between Sherri and her mother. Although they both had gleaming warm-black hair and liquid dark eyes set like jewels in their smooth bronze complexions, their personalities were very different. Sherri had the rollicking, easygoing temperament of her father; her mom greeted everything in life, big and little, with equal alarm. She seemed to feel that it was irresponsible to view life otherwise.

Although Caro admired Sherri's nonchalance and sheer exuberance, she often secretly sympathized with "Aunt" Miriam's approach to life. Caro glanced sideways at Hal, seated tall and upright beside her. In this case Aunt Miriam was wrong. Hal was safe. As safe as family.

"Mrs. Silverton, have you heard from Lee lately?" Hal politely asked Sherri's mom.

Mrs. Silverton sighed. "Oh, you know Lee. He disappears for weeks on end and suddenly shows up on your doorstep as if he had been gone ten minutes."

The crawler jolted to a stop outside Caro and Ricky's home. The summer heat rose in waves off the faded roof of the box-shaped housing unit. Hal and his dad lived next door to the Hunters in an identical, two-story dwelling. The long row of clay-colored housing units along the crawler track seemed a part of the stark, breathless landscape, as if the rectangular objects had simply risen like anthills out of the grey-brown soil.

Hal absently patted the respirator tucked in his shorts pocket and climbed out of the crawler. That summer he had experienced few respiratory distresses, but he was still careful; the habit of checking to make sure the respirator was with him whenever he stepped outside the artificial environment of crawler or building was very strong.

Sherri's little sister, Meggie, catapulted out the front door of the Hunters' unit, her black pigtails flapping, dress flying up around her chubby thighs. She swung her school book bag dangerously. Hal jumped back to avoid injury.

Becka followed, a sturdy figure in a yellow sunsuit. She seemed subdued, but Caro noted the unquenchable fire in her six-year-old sister's grey eyes.

"Becka let loose a browser in the barn," shrieked Meggie, her words gasped out in an effort to be the first to pass on bad news. Becka stood mutinously with her feet apart.

"Oh, Becka," Mrs. Silverton exclaimed. "Was anyone hurt? Did your mom have to tranquilize it?"

"Aw, Aunt Miriam," Ricky growled. "The browsers in the lab barns are like pets. They aren't going to hurt anyone. Mom rarely has to tranq even the bull."

Caro refused to ask Becka anything about the incident in front of everyone; her sisterly instinct told her that Becka was experiencing too much notoriety over the incident. She could easily imagine the grade-section-one students on their orderly educational tour of the research barns, and the pandemonium that had broken loose when Becka let out the huge, dragonlike beast.

"What did it do?" Ricky asked Becka.

She shrugged. "It just stood wagging its tail, and then it wanted this girl's hair."

"She cried," said Meggie dramatically. "The girl cried."

"I guess she was scared," said Aunt Miriam in a soothing tone. "She wasn't hurt though, was she?"

"No," Meggie reflected. "But her head sure got dirty."

"It licked her hair all over. Down flat, like this." Becka demonstrated. Ricky chortled. Sherri bit her lip to stop the

15

laughter, but her eyes overflowed with it. Hal and Caro glanced at each other with deadpan faces, but Caro saw the muscle in Hal's jaw twitch with the effort.

"I see that you've been informed of The Happening." Mrs. Hunter joined them on the side of the track.

"Mom, how did it happen?" Caro asked. "I thought there were security locks on all the stalls."

"Apparently, at the exact moment that Becka tugged on the gate, there was a computer glitch. Don't even try to work out the odds of that happening, Hal."

Hal smiled. "No fear of that. I know when something is beyond the realm of material science. See you later," he added, turning towards his unit. "I have to go start dinner for Dad and me."

"Bye, Hal," Sherri and Caro chorused.

Ricky rolled his eyes at the two girls and called, "Later."

"That boy sure has changed," commented Caro's mom as they watched Hal enter his front door.

"He's growing up, Clare, like the rest of them." Mrs. Silverton glanced at Sherri and Meggie and sighed.

"It's more than that, Miriam," Clare replied quietly.

Caro, hearing the two mothers over Sherri's chatter, agreed with her mom. Hal was different. More sure of himself. He didn't even blush as easily anymore, and when he did redden and some silly comment was made, he laughed it off.

Caro felt herself grow warm, but this was with anger. The lumie incident had improved everyone it seemed: Uncle Lee had received a promotion, Ricky was treated as a genius by his teachers, Hal had become popular at school, Sherri was even more sought after. Everyone had benefited but her. Sure, her friendship with Dr. Lutes had grown, and in spite of everything, Clytie had truly become her home, but she felt more awkward, unwanted, unlovely than ever. And for the first time in her life, Caro was afraid of things.

Little things. Like whether or not she had remembered to turn off the hot air tunnel in the marine lab shower room, or if she had forgotten to write down her assignment in Post-Calculus. She was afraid of big things, too: what if her entomologist dad picked up a poisonous insect in his research? Or if a browser stomped her mom? But horrors such as these, like grey ghosts, came and went of their own accord, or so it seemed.

The worry about the carepies did not. A thin edge of fear for them intruded on whatever she did. She could not shake the powerful intuition that they were in danger. Yet there was nothing to base it on. Dr. Lutes looked after his research animals with great solicitude; she knew that he would return the carepies to the ocean when they grew too big for their pool.

It was only when she was laughing with Sherri that the nebulous cloud of fear thinned to nothingness. But even in the midst of Sherri's most absurd nonsense, every now and then, the laughter would catch in her throat, gripped tight by sudden fear.

Ricky chose to unveil his rock-creature at the dinner table. It sat next to the steaming pot of lentil soup and unsheathed one brilliant blue eye at Caro's parents as they sat rigid with surprise. The eye was quickly sheathed by folds of scales that moved as a stony unit when Caro's dad pulled out of his shock and into escalating tones of horror.

Caro sighed as she watched Ricky stomp off, banished to his bedroom to "think about what might have happened had it been a toxic-releasing creature." Ricky generally did the foolhardy, the outrageous, at times even the dangerous, but always seemed to land on his feet, comparatively unscathed. The rock-toad was carefully picked up with gloved hands by Mrs. Hunter and placed into a glass tank under the back porch overhang they called the outside lab.

That evening there was to be a church meeting in the Hunters' home. So far, only Sherri's family was a regular part of the church, though Dr. Lutes would attend whenever he could. Often Hal and his dad, Dr. Rokmanoff, would wander over, and occasionally, Sheila and her two friends, Mike and Jeff, would come by.

Sheila adored the underlying sense of danger of such meetings, but she thought they should have more of a political agenda. "Too much God stuff," she complained loudly, to Caro's great chagrin, in the school hall. "We need to fight the system that represses the freedom of the Clytians." Sheila, although her dad was one of the high-ups in the Community—the governing body of both Clytie and Earth—never seemed to have an inkling of the harm she could do with her mouth in under ten seconds.

"What Clytians?" Sherri had asked, bewildered.

"Us, neerds," Sheila had boomed back at her.

"What's a neerds?" Sherri had persevered. Caro was hot and sweaty with embarrassment, trying to blend into the walls.

"Somebody dumb. It's what they called people that asked stupid questions in the 20th century," Sheila explained, a sarcastic glint in her eye.

Sherri thought a minute. "I guess even dumb people should have freedom all right. I don't think God's against that. But why call neerds Clytians? I mean, the real Clytians are the animals here, right, Caro?"

Thankfully, or so Caro thought, it was time for class. But it had taken her most of the lunchbreak to explain to Sherri just what Sheila had meant.

It was funny, though, how right—in the oddest sort of way—Sherri usually was. It was true that the real Clytians were the native creatures of Clytie's air, land, and waters.

And it was equally true that some of those strange beasts didn't have much freedom anymore. Caro thought of the carepies bumping into the sides of their pool, so used to the open expanse of their ocean home.

"Mom," Caro ventured, as she helped clear away the remains of dinner before the meeting, "do you think that animals—all kinds—should be free?"

Mrs. Hunter paused while wiping the counter, little crumbs piled into her palm, the moist sponge held motionless over the polymer shelving. "Freedom ... is a relative term," she said with a little laugh. "At least that's what I've always been told."

Caro immediately sensed where she was headed. "You mean that freedom for one creature can cause others to experience a loss of their own freedom. I know that. Like the browsers being free to stomp on, say, the rainbugs."

"Or lick a child's head," her mother added. Caro laughed.

"But," her mom continued, "if what you're asking is what right have we humans, as foreigners, to start tampering with Clytie's ecology, now that's quite a different matter. Especially when we don't know what we're doing."

"What do you mean?"

"Oh." Mrs. Hunter sighed, then laughed and shook her head. "What I'm going to say is very unscientific and not too wise to admit out loud. But here it is: we've already messed up one planet. Now it seems as though we're simply moving on to the next ... "

"I thought that the 22nd century was called the Great Clean-up on Earth," Caro said.

"Oh, Caro, I know that over the years science and technology have tried to come to terms with the damage they do to the environment. It's just that it's always a mop-up job. After the fact. We can never truly predict the outcome—or fall-out—of our research." Mrs. Hunter bit her lip, staring at her daughter standing so still, her hair and face illuminated in cross-wise patterns by the warmth beaming through the slats of the shuttered window. "I mean, you know very personally some of the horrible effects of quite simple, innocent research," she added quietly.

No one had to say "the lumies" out loud; the words hung dark and cold, dimming the bright yellow kitchen. Mrs. Hunter leaned over the counter again and scrubbed at the impenetrable surface.

April, 2456
Actaeon—

In another three days we will land on Clytie's Main Base airfield. The orders granted me at York were incomplete: I will receive further instructions from the Community at Main.

Actaeon, thinking about "Birdbeak" put me in mind of other volumes I stole from his library to read in secret: The Knights of the Round Table, Ghandi, A Christmas Carol, St. Francis of Assisi, The Holy Bible. *Strange books, filled with compelling ideas of choices and changed lives. I wanted to believe them: that life was more than the survival of the human race; that an individual could transform a species. Looking back now, I wonder if that was the primary drive pushing me into the new field of genetic behaviorism. To learn what made creatures move in mindless swarms, or stand against the pack . . . Or perhaps, Actaeon, to discover why I am so different inside, yet resonate with every ebb and flow of the Community's whims.*

—Reginald

3

Quasar

T he church meeting drew an unexpected visitor:
Sherri's Uncle Lee. He bounded into the living
room, a grin of sheer delight creasing his face,
enjoying to the full the surprise of his entry, exulting in the
warmth of his reception.

"Uncle Lee!" Becka hurled herself at the tall young
man. Ricky beamed, jumping on one foot in excitement.

Sherri bubbled to Caro, "I nearly died when Hal asked
Mom whether she'd heard from Uncle Lee—I couldn't say
a word—he made me promise. He wanted to surprise
everyone tonight!"

"Well, he did!" answered Caro, smiling. It was good, so
good to see his kind, exuberant face. She waited for him to
untangle himself from Becka, to greet her parents, to wink
at Ricky and cuff him affectionately. Then her face was
buried in his chest and his arms drew tight about her in a
welcoming hug. In a kind of daze, Caro realized, horrified,
that she was near tears.

There was a tap on the door and Dr. Lutes entered.
With a comforting pat on her back, Lee turned to say hello
to the old scientist. Caro smiled through the mist in her
eyes; it always struck her as humorous when she saw Dr.

Lutes without his lab coat, wearing the Main Base uniform of khaki shorts. And the disparity in appearance between the two scientists was almost as amusing: Lee, husky, bristling with energy, wiry black hair, clean-shaven except for the strip on the side of his face that he always missed, bending over this small, frail man who nonetheless walked like a king. Distracted from her upwelling emotion, she thankfully gulped back her tears. Ricky was dispatched next door to tell Hal and his dad of Lee's arrival.

The routine meeting was forgotten. When Hal and Dr. Rokmanoff had greeted Lee, everyone settled down in a circle of chairs, cushions, or floor, depending on age and personal preference. Ricky liked to lie under the coffee table, staring through the transparent top. Becka curled up on the left side of Lee, while Meggie jealously moved in on his right. Sherri, Hal, and Caro leaned back on floor cushions.

They talked, sighed, listened. They relived the experience with the lumies at the End Base. They marveled that they could all meet again, that they had survived and overcome. They praised God.

For what? Caro sat, heart racing, but half frozen. She felt as though many forces, like invisible, powerful magnets, pulled at her from all directions. She brought her knees up and wrapped her arms about them, hugging them to her, hard. She bit the inside of her cheek; the sharp pain and heavy taste of blood startled and distracted her, but only briefly.

Soon the feelings spiraled again, shooting her mind down horrifying channels. The many Caros deep inside her strove and elbowed their way to the surface, pushing and being pushed by others in their turn. One resonated with the truth of their deliverance; a second self raged at the impotence of a God who would leave her scarred and others dead; a third, sepulchral voice shamed her for her ego-centric fixation. Such a selfish, small mind—surely she knew that God had a Plan, a Design, that he had a purpose in allowing the lumies to kill and maim?

Caro swallowed and heard the strangled sound she made in the room. She flushed and looked down at her knees.

The conversation swirling without and within her seemed to rise like a living thing and grip her throat. She tried to swallow again, but this time the muscles closed in a spasm.

Caro got to her feet, stumbled up the stairs and into the washroom and sat, fully clothed, on the toilet until she felt the nausea subside. Then, feeling old and shaky, she got to her feet. She avoided looking in the mirror and washed her face. Before she left, she remembered to flush the toilet for effect. Then she slipped back into the living room and rejoined the group.

The meeting was ending. Caro's dad closed the gathering by reading a prayer:

> I called out from my
> deep
> distress
> to the Lord
> and he answered me.

> ———

> From the depths of Hell I cried for help;
> You heard my voice.

> You had thrown me down
> deep
> an abyss
> in the heart of the sea.

The current surrounded me,
Your breakers,
Your waves,
over me they closed,
and I thought:
I have been thrown
far
from Your eyes,
but still I will look
toward You
toward Your holy temple.

Waters roared and circled me
up to my neck—
the deep was surrounding me.
Seaweed wrapped around my head
tying me to the roots of mountains.
I went down
deep
into the underworld,
Hell's bars clanged shut behind me
forever.
But You,
You brought up from the grave my life.

Oh Lord, my God.
When my breath was dwindling
the Lord I remembered,
to You I called,
toward your holy temple I turned.

Those who court empty nothings,
those who fawn on worthless wood,
their faithfulness they abandon.

But I, with a thanksgiving voice
let me sacrifice to You.
What I have vowed,
let me fulfill.

Deliverance belongs to the Lord.

Caro got up, pivoted, and headed back into the wash-room. In the hard glare of the mirror, she watched the sweat bead up on her half-white forehead and felt the rumbling churn in her stomach.

But in a family home, full of guests, with only one washroom, she could not stay there long. There was an urgent hammering at the door and Caro barely slid back the lock before the door shot open, banging against the opposite wall. Meggie and Becka stormed in, looking wild.

"I knew it," Becka excitedly puffed. "You're always in here." Meggie, her two black braids flung back over her shoulders, plowed her way through the two sisters and made straight for the toilet.

Caro went downstairs to find Sherri. She was still in the living room with a group surrounding Lee, listening to him as he laughed and exchanged stories with Dr. Lutes. Hal stood by Sherri, smiling at Lee's expressive face. Ricky gazed adoringly up at his "adopted" uncle.

"Caro, there you are," Mrs. Hunter called. "Will you please help me get some iced tea and sandwiches out?"

Caro nodded and followed her mom into the kitchen. She poured the tea, brewed from duck leaves and berries, over ice-filled glasses and set them on a tray. Mrs. Hunter cut melkin and prawb-jelly sandwiches.

Melkins were a new find on Clytie. On the bushy trees skirting the ocean, hanging like bright bottles, grew the cone-shaped gourds. The old ones became hollow and their orange color faded in striped yellowish patterns. They knocked together musically in the wind until they fell on the sandy soil beneath the trees.

The melkins used for eating were picked at the height of their brilliant orange color. When the gourds were sliced lengthwise and the center scooped of the red seeds, butter-yellow sheets of dense, squashlike fruit were found. If the layers were carefully separated and then chilled, they could be used to take the place of bread in rolled sandwiches. Caro loved the contrast between the melkin's sweetish, fruity taste and their surprising breadlike texture. And the creamy, exotic-tasting prawb jelly was everybody's favorite. *A true Clytie tea,* thought Caro, as she surveyed the trays of bright yellow and cream pinwheel sandwiches and the berry-colored duck tea.

Lee raved over the melkin and prawb-jelly sandwiches and, after disposing of most of one tray, demanded that Mrs. Hunter show him how to make them.

"Old Henry Melkin discovered them," Dr. Lutes solemnly informed Lee.

Lee laughed. "So that's how you get in the Community's good graces—find an edible treat for them!"

Dr. Rokmanoff, after glancing sheepishly about him, gave a hearty guffaw. "They must have a tea break in their meetings or no one would survive." He could not, however, resist a glance about him yet again, just in case a Community official had sneaked into the room.

Caro intercepted Sherri's delighted gaze. Sherri was fascinated by what she called Dr. Rokmanoff's paranoia. She would torment him by staring over his head with a startled expression, as if someone were behind him. The poor man would grow hot and horrified, the color flooding his large face until his beard seemed on fire. Finally, unable to stand the torment any longer, he would whirl his head around—but never would see anyone. Sherri would open wide her large eyes and innocently make some remark about bugs and bug swatters.

Although Caro found her lips twitching with unholy laughter every time Sherri caught Dr. Rokmanoff, she felt sorry for the poor man, and could not help but recognize the validity of his concern. For everyone's livelihood depended upon the emotional well-being of the Community. Very few mavericks such as Lee were allowed to survive on this world. Caro lived in fear that someday he would be sent back to Earth to, say, observe the courtship behavior of nuked slugs, or some other ridiculous activity. She knew, deep in her bones, that Lee could not live that kind of life, and if Community orders were not followed . . . well, they just *were* followed.

Lee leaned back after a regretful glance at the empty tray on the tea table in front of him. He turned to Dr. Lutes seated beside him and picked up his conversation with him. "So you really see the carepies as having a part in all of this?"

Caro perked up her ears. "Shh," she hissed at Sherri who had leaned over to say something to her.

"Yes," Dr. Lutes was answering slowly, "the carepies are proving to be very interesting creatures—of course there are many, many unanswered questions at this point. And even more paradoxes. For instance . . . " He leaned closer to Lee and their voices were drowned out by Meggie and Becka who ran shrieking into the living room to tell Ricky that they had named his rock-toad.

"What?" said Ricky, scowling into their excited faces. Reconstituted fruit juice ran down their chins in purple bands. Becka's hair was flat on one side, pushed up in a pompadour on the other side. "You'd better shut up," he quickly added. "You know you weren't supposed to go near it until Mom identifies it as non-toxic."

"We didn't touch it, we just looked," hoarsely whispered Becka. She shot a dark glance at her mother. So far, Mrs. Hunter seemed unaware of the topic of conversation.

"So what are you going to call it?" asked Sherri.

"Quasar," Meggie burst in triumphantly.

"Quasar," echoed Becka, glaring at Meggie.

Ricky hooted. Hal and Caro exchanged glances and hid their amusement. Sherri exclaimed, "That's perfect! 'Quasar.' It has a nice ring to it. I like it!"

"Why 'Quasar,' Becka?" Caro asked.

"I know what it means!" Becka shouted indignantly.

"Naw you don't," Ricky growled.

"We do, we do!" shrieked Meggie. Her face grew mottled.

"Well, I think we're heading home," Mrs. Silverton hastily announced, throwing a pointed look toward her husband who was embroiled in a discussion with Mr. Hunter.

"Right, right," he replied hurriedly, "I'll be right there." He winked at Caro. "Astronomy lesson is postponed until further notice."

"What astronomy lesson, Dad?" Sherri asked, bewildered.

"Quasers, Sherri," Hal said in an undertone, "are the brightest spots in space. They are a cluster of galaxies all interacting with one another without a collision."

"Wow." Sherri's face displayed awe at the picture Hal's definition had conjured in her mind. "Well, Ricky," she declared, "you now have the most brilliant toad in the universe."

"Ha, ha," coughed Hal. Caro smiled with great effort.

"Yeah, well, I already knew that," Ricky replied smugly.

Mr. Silverton laughed and swept up the moist Meggie in his big arms. "There, there, Princess," he crooned to her, "it was a lovely name that you and Becka thought up."

Princess! Caro, barely controlling her twitching lips, avoided meeting Hal's eye. Meggie assailed the room with fresh wails at such sympathy.

"Hey, I haven't shown you my sketches," Sherri exclaimed to Caro.

"Hurry up, Sherri," her mom said warningly. "Five minutes—five minutes. We are leaving in five minutes."

Sherri nodded and drew Caro over to her book bag leaning against the kitchen wall. "Don't you think it's hilarious how parents repeat themselves over and over—as if you can hear them better the third time around or something."

Caro rolled her eyes. "My mom does that all the time."

Sherri pulled out her sketchbook. She slowly turned the pages and Caro saw the smiling beaks of the carepies and felt their warmth. Sherri had caught the joy of the baby carepies in their swirling, non-stop activity. Their banding fins were a blur compared to the gentle wave pattern of the adults.

"They're wonderful, Sherri." Caro relaxed from the inside out, paging through the sketches of the pod. *If only*, she thought, *if only I could carry a carepie around with me all the time.* Caro laughed out loud.

"What," Sherri demanded. "Did I draw something wrong?"

"No, no—they're perfect."

"They're far from perfect." Sherri's artist-look came over her and she studied the drawings critically.

"You've caught their substance, my dear." Dr. Lutes spoke from behind her. "And that's the most difficult thing to accomplish. If you take care of the soul, the things of the body will follow," he added in an undertone.

Caro felt a strange peace descend on her from his incomprehensible words.

"Coming, Lee?" Mr. Silverton asked.

"Actually, no thanks, Gus," he responded. "Dr. Lutes has offered to give me a ride back to your place. I want to talk with Clare and Phil yet."

Mr. Silverton nodded. "See you later, then."

"See you tomorrow, Sherri," Caro called from the front door, blinking in the brightness. "Bye Uncle Gus, Aunt Miriam. See you, Meggie."

"Yeah-hoo!" Sherri chortled. "Last day of classes tomorrow for four whole weeks!"

"Shush, Sherri," Aunt Miriam reminded her daughter. "It's almost PM, people are probably trying to sleep. Bye, dear," she softly called. Uncle Gus waved broadly to Caro.

The crawler bounced down the track with Meggie looking back irritably from the rear seat.

"Ah, there goes Miss Meggie's carriage." Lee had come up behind Caro. He grinned at her as she turned to him and laughed.

"Princess Meggie, you mean."

"Even princesses have their off days. Although, as un-uncley as this may sound, Princess Meggie does have her share of 'em. Now," Lee continued, looking her full in the face, "how is Princess Caro—and I don't want a 'fine, thanks' response."

Caro laughed. Sighed. And laughed again.

Lee caught the thin edge of hysterics underlying the brittle sound, but he remained silent, waiting for her words.

"Sometimes it's pretty rough," she managed.

"Just sometimes?"

Caro grew stubborn. "Well, it's no fun being the freak of Clytie, but I do manage to have a few bright moments now and again."

"Like when?"

"Like when I'm with the carepies—and Dr. Lutes. And Sherri's a good friend. And so is Hal. We do stuff together all the time."

"Good," Lee responded quietly. "Lutes was saying how well the carepies respond to you."

Caro breathed a sigh of relief that the focus had shifted from her. "The carepies are wonderful, fascinating. I will really miss working with them during the holidays."

"Caro." Lee looked steadily at her. "How would you feel about working with some carepies at the End Base for a couple of weeks?"

Caro stared at him, speechless. The words "End Base" turned her stomach inside out, but carepies? What were carepies doing so far from the ocean?

Lee closed the door and led her to the now-empty living room. Hal and his dad, along with Dr. Lutes and Mr. and Mrs. Hunter were being given an exhibition by Ricky of Quasar the rock-toad.

"They've got a whole pod of them, Caro. Five adults— of varying maturity, three cows, two bulls—and two calves. They're kept in a darkened, sealed tank. That is, they can't get up above the surface."

Caro's neck muscles tightened and she rubbed her throat uneasily. "Why?"

Lee shook his head in frustration. "Some idiotic experiment trying to determine their physiological limits."

"You mean they will monitor them until they die," she said painfully.

Lee nodded unhappily. "Unless we can prove that Lutes is right."

"About what?"

Lee looked surprised. "I was sure that you already knew—I think I've just put my foot in my mouth again."

"You have, Levi," Dr. Lutes said as he entered the room. He sat down on the chair opposite Caro and Lee.

"Sorry." Lee grimaced. "I really thought that you had filled in your right-hand assistant."

"I had not for the simple reason of the control factor involved, Levi. Caro, it certainly was not because I don't trust you; I do. Please believe me. It was imperative that you not know . . . well, that you not know what you were doing."

"And just what *was* I doing?" asked Caro.

"Healing and being healed," answered Dr. Lutes, his tone almost defiant.

"Me?!" said Caro dumbly. Her voice seemed to echo in the room.

"Please believe me when I say that I was not using you or your infirm condition, my dear," Dr. Lutes gently continued. "It came as a complete surprise to me that the readings on the carepies stabilized with your presence— and remained so for a time after you left. And I don't think that I am far off in stating that you, Caro, experience healing when you are with the carepies."

Healing? thought Caro. "Joy," she said without thinking, without realizing that she said it out loud. "The carepies share joy with me."

Dr. Lutes' eyes beamed; he seemed very satisfied with her response.

"Darling, you really need to go to bed." Mrs. Hunter walked into the room briskly. "Ricky's cleared the washroom, Dad's reading him *A Quark in Time* for the one-hundred-and-fifty-third time, Becka's almost asleep, now it's your turn. I know that you've only got one more day of school, but you need your sleep."

Caro looked at Lee and Dr. Lutes. "Sleep on it," Lee suggested.

"I don't have to sleep on it; I'll go," she answered. It was her mouth that said those words; the rest of her shrieked fearfully or angrily, tearing at her throat and stomach, making her legs shake and her neck hair prickle.

"It is for you too, Caro," Dr. Lutes said. "Somehow, I know that, beyond any doubt. And, of course, Lee and I will be with you."

Lee nodded, his bright eyes warm.

"And the rest—Hal, Sherri, and Ricky," Caro stubbornly stated, her eyes dark with warning.

"What is going on here?" Mrs. Hunter demanded. She stood straight, tight as stone.

Caro skipped up the stairs. At the landing she turned and called out with authority, "I'm *not* going without them."

"Not going where without whom?" Her dad hugged Caro on his way past, brushing his lips across the top of her head.

"To the End Base," his daughter replied firmly. "With Hal, Sherri, Ricky, and Uncle Lee. And Dr. Lutes, of course." She squirmed out of his grasp, not quite meeting her father's shocked eyes, strode into the washroom, and shut the door with just a hint of a bang.

"Lee!" Mr. Hunter walked heavily down the stairs.

Caro, in the safety of the washroom, listened to the high-pitched soprano of her mother and her father's blustery, indignant tenor. Their voices rose and mingled and clashed, reminding Caro of a mock opera. The girl's face grinned, but her hand shook as she picked up her tooth cleaner. Incredibly enough, in spite of the racing fear that caused her hands to shake and the muscle in her right eyelid to twitch, she felt better than she had for weeks. A strange excitement was building; she could hardly wait for tomorrow to tell Sherri and the others the news.

May, 2456
Actaeon—

   We have arrived on Clytie. Quite a welcoming commit-
tee: men and, presumably, women in full suits disinfecting
the air and ground before, around, after me. I am hurried
into a little cell where I will live for the next twenty days.
The hardest part of the journey—they call it quarantine.

   Actaeon, what would I do without you? The days pass
slowly and I sit for hours with my fingers curled in the mesh
protecting the small window. I see yellow vehicles come and
go, small figures crawling the surface of the airship, and,
in the distance, the burnt hills against the changing sky.
When PM arrives, the shutters close like lids, and I am left
in the false night, writing in the small yellow circle thrown
by my flashlight.

   Only one visitor, by letter—the medical officer will
allow no one near. A Dr. Gerald Lutes, an animal geneticist
on Main, has introduced himself to me. The letter is full of
welcoming words, but, Actaeon, both you and I know the
code of the Community: one for all and each one watch his
own backside.

                                              —Reginald

4

Nightmare

aro moaned uneasily in her sleep. Her dream-mind clouded; again, the sickening sensation of impending doom...

It begins as always; her eyes strain to open, but Caro is snatched, thrust into the nightmare. The horrifying roller-coaster plunge down a tunnel of suffocating darkness. Left all alone, falling, falling. Ricky's jeering eyes flash red like a cat in the dark as he runs by; Hal's long strides carry him past her, unconcerned. Sherri's shrill, mocking laughter fills the night; she is dancing alongside Hal. The three of them march on, arm in arm, faster and faster, eyes forward, while Caro speeds down the black well. She knows with crystal clarity that unless she stops falling, she will drown in nothingness. But there is only nothingness, and how can it stop her plummeting body? It velvets her in a thick shroud. She cannot move, cannot stop moving...

Caro jerked awake and sat up, heart pounding, sweat streaming from her pores. Her clock said 4:17; it would be another three hours before her alarm would go off. She pulled herself to her feet and stumbled to the window. Drawing aside the heavy blind, she opened the sash, slipped her hand out, and slid open the catch holding the outside reflective shutters in place. They swung wide, and Caro, curled up on the floor, reveled in the brilliant sunlight, not caring that the heat blasted into the room. She sat there: not thinking, just allowing the light to fill her, to burn out the nothingness.

She didn't hear her father softly knock and enter the room. He called her name quietly and she turned, startled, looking up into his concerned face.

"I heard the shutter bang. Another bad dream?"

Caro nodded. No words.

"I'm going to make a cup of soup. Do you want to join me?"

The girl got to her feet, still silent. Her dad closed the shutters but left the blind open. Splinters of light ran over the room and played across their faces, so similar with their square chins and thoughtful, almost pensive expressions.

Caro followed her dad out of the room, down the stairs, and into the kitchen.

"Your choice: simulated beef, simulated chicken, or, everybody's favorite, vegetable without any vegetables?" he asked with a wry twist to his face, holding up the packets.

Caro cleared her throat. "Chicken, please." She sat on the kitchen stool, one leg curled under her, the toes of her other foot gripping the lower rung.

"Hey, I just thought of something. Let's mix the chicken and 'vegetable' and see what that tastes like," he offered.

Caro nodded, the faintest glimmer of a smile touching her lips. Her dad treated the kitchen like he did his lab: cooking for him was a series of experiments.

This experiment was a success; the chicken-vegetable mix was an improvement over either alone. Father and daughter sat opposite each other, drinking long, solemn draughts of the hot soup.

"You don't have to go." Her dad's voice shattered the silence.

Caro began shaking her head, shaking it firmly, trying to gain control of her voice, knowing in advance that it would be high and weak.

Finally, "I *do* have to go—no, not just for the carepies," she said, anticipating her dad's response before it reached his lips. "I have to go for *me*," she said, her words formed as precisely as glass bubbles and her voice just as liable to breakage. "I can't be free from it until I go . . . The real thing can't be as bad as my nightmare—I have to face the real thing." She looked up at last, desperately, into her father's face.

And saw only compassion. Her fifteen-year-old eyes could not read a father's pain at the tenderness of his daughter; nor could she even imagine that the light shining through his tear-glazed eyes was pride.

"You'll let me go?" she whispered.

It took every gram of strength he had to nod his head, once, and he felt the weariness of that action all day.

Caro never knew what her dad said to her mom to convince her that Caro be allowed to go. She had taken her mug of soup up to her room, leaving her dad staring into space. Curled up on her bed, she had fallen into a sleep beyond dreams.

In the morning her mom came in and turned off the buzzing clock Caro had slept through. By the long, wordless hug she gave her daughter, Caro knew that she would not stand in the way of her going.

"We talked to Lee this morning," her mom said softly. "He asked you please not to mention the trip to Hal and Sherri until he talks with their parents today."

"And Ricky?"

"I don't think that he should go, Caro. He's only eleven! And the dreadful time you all went through last time—I don't know why you think that even Hal and Sherri will want to go back."

"They'll want to go," Caro replied with conviction. "And I don't know how you think you're going to stop Ricky from stowing away."

"Frankly, I don't know how we are either," her mother muttered. "Just please don't mention it to him yet."

"I won't." Caro knew that she wouldn't have to; Ricky had an uncanny way of ferreting things out all on his own.

But it was very hard not to blurt out the news to Sherri and Hal on the way to school. Caro's mom drove silently, lost in thought. Becka and Meggie had no morning school, just a pre-vacation party in the afternoon, so only Hal, Sherri, Ricky, and Caro occupied the back of the multi-seated crawler. Sherri was excitedly planning their four-week vacation from school and Hal was asking the three of them if they wanted to go fishing tomorrow with him and his dad.

Sherri started giggling; she pretended to be Dr. Rok-manoff sitting solemnly, bolt upright, in a smelly fishing boat.

"My dad likes fishing," Hal protested. "He's really a very good fisherman—and fun, too. Caro, you'll come, won't you?"

Sherri became Dr. Rokmanoff reeling in a whale.

Caro flushed with anger. "Why is that so funny—" she began to ask Sherri when Ricky dropped his bombshell.

"Caro can't go fishing tomorrow, Hal," he said, his black eyes needle sharp with excitement. "And neither can any of us. We're going with Uncle Lee to the End Base."

Caro's mom swerved the crawler off the track, bumping up and over the ridge of dust on the side of the road. The engine gave a dying whine.

"Caro is going to the End Base to assist Dr. Lutes for two weeks." Mrs. Hunter emphasized her words. *"Caro, Ricky. Not you. Not anyone else that I am aware of."*

Hal and Sherri gazed in astonishment at Caro. "How come you didn't tell me?" Sherri demanded.

Caro opened her mouth. "She couldn't," Mrs. Hunter answered tersely. "She was specifically asked to keep quiet about it. I can only ask you all; for goodness sake, not to breathe a word of this to anyone."

Hal found his voice. "Sure, Mrs. Hunter, we understand. We know enough to keep our mouths shut."

"I know you do, Hal."

"I do, too, Aunt Clare!" Sherri exclaimed, looking hurt.

"It was Ricky that I was really thinking of, Sherri," Mrs. Hunter replied.

Ricky stared coolly out the window.

"Ricky?!"

"Yeah, yeah, I won't say nothing," he mumbled.

"And you fully understand that you are in no way included in this venture," his mother continued. "Caro is going for a specific purpose, for the very least amount of time necessary."

"I hear you," Ricky shot back.

"We will talk about your rudeness later" was his mother's cold reply after the shocked silence. She restarted the crawler and they jerked back onto the track.

They were already late for class, but they congregated around Caro in the drop-off lot anyway. Mrs. Hunter drove away, leaving Sherri pouting and Hal looking shyly at Caro through his glasses. Ricky was red and angry.

"I told Uncle Lee and Dr. Lutes that I wouldn't go without you," Caro weakly protested. "It's just that Mom thinks Ricky's too young and your parents won't let you go."

"Look, they need you, Caro. All you have to do is refuse to go until we're allowed to go, too," Ricky said with impatience.

"I think that my dad would let me go if I asked him," Hal said thoughtfully.

"Really?!" Caro asked.

"He thinks a lot of you, Caro. If I told him that you sort of needed me—kind of for moral support, or something." Hal's ears turned scarlet with embarrassment.

"I do," cried Caro, forgetting her usual reserve.

"You two can't go without me!" Sherri looked from one to the other. "We're a team; they can't split us up!"

"There's no way that Aunt Miriam will let you go, Sherri." Caro swiped back the hair sticking to her forehead. "She's more paranoid than Hal's dad."

"My dad's not paranoid," defended Hal. "He's just seen a lot of things happen, that's all."

"Well, my mom *is* paranoid," Sherri admitted. "Still, her baby brother Lee can get around her anytime. So there's hope yet."

"Not for Ricky, there's not," Caro replied, looking at her little brother suspiciously. His expression had become too smooth; his eyes were round, unreadable pools.

"We're going to be late for school," Ricky replied angelically, turning and leading the way toward the stairwell.

Hal grinned.

Caro usually loved the last day of school before vacation. The teachers were always slightly silly with the anticipation of no students or early mornings, and the day usually flew by, filled with lessons like games. But today Caro was in an agony of impatience and the morning dragged on and on. In desperation, she sneaked out of physics and headed for the marine lab.

The doors swished shut behind her and the cool serenity of the undersea world began to soothe her frantic spirit. She climbed up the ladder to the crawlway on top of the large tanks and walked down the hollow-sounding platform until she came to the carepies' pool. Lying flat on her stomach, she trailed her hands in the water. The carepies' smiling beaks bumped against her palms and she caressed the resilient smoothness of their hides.

The girl spent most of the day with the carepies. From her high vantage point, she could see when anyone entered the lab and could duck back into the shadows when necessary. What she didn't realize was that she was also trapped: if a teacher entered the lab, she could not leave without that person seeing her, or hearing her footsteps echo along the crawlway.

So when Hal came in and met Dr. Lutes, and when the two of them stood talking below, alongside the carepies, she could hear them clearly, but could not leave without attracting attention to herself.

"Dr. Lutes, I really feel, sir, that I should be along on this trip," Hal began firmly.

"Yes, I'm sure you do."

Hal repositioned his glasses. "What you possibly don't realize, sir, is that Caro is very, uh, afraid, of the whole dark region since the lumie incident."

"Aren't we all, son," Dr. Lutes gently replied. It was a statement, not a question.

Hal persevered. "Caro is a very sensitive person, Dr. Lutes, sir. She feels things more deeply than she says. And she has not recovered from the lumie attack. I need to be with her."

"Yes, yes," agreed Dr. Lutes, shaking his head. "I can well understand that you need her. Why don't you come with us, son?"

"It's not that *I* need . . . what did you say?" Hal asked, confused.

"You'll come then, son?"

Hal looked dazed. "Of course, sir." He started to go, paused, opened his mouth, closed it again, and then left the lab.

Caro, listening in misery, waited for Dr. Lutes to leave the area. So Hal knew her secret of how scared she was. At least Dr. Lutes hadn't clued into what Hal was saying about her; of what use would a neurotic, panic-stricken insomniac be to him or the carepies?

"Caro, perhaps you had better rejoin your classes," Dr. Lutes called without so much as a glance in her direction.

"Uh, sure, yes, Dr. Lutes," she stammered. How long had he known she was there?! Caro waved a quick good-bye to the carepies, wiped her hands dry on her shorts and clattered down from the crawlway. "See you later, Dr. Lutes," she said.

"Caro." He stopped her. "You would not be the deeply insightful person I know you to be if you had no fear of the dark. However, it is when we forget *why* we are afraid of the dark that we become unfocused and unhappy."

Caro stared back, feeling embarrassed and foolish. *So Dr. Lutes knew, too.* Dr. Lutes ducked his head courteously and walked toward the back of the lab. She saw his slight figure appearing and disappearing between the rows of buckets and nets. His reflection twisted and shifted, growing long and thin or short and wide, thrown by the restless water in the tanks like bent mirrors. She could not call out, "What do you mean?" *I fear the dark with good reason,* a sudden, bitter voice roared inside her. But even that voice could not tell her *why.* The carepies bumped against the side of the pool where the girl stood, but Caro turned and left the lab.

She did not know how she was going to face Hal. The others. If Hal knew of her fear, surely Sherri did as well— and who else? Caro slipped into her last class, Russian, a full forty minutes late. Sherri looked up from her desk and raised her eyebrows, her face one large question mark.

Dr. Balabanov had his typical last-day-of-class "fun" assignment on the board: make up as many words as you can from the letters of this word . . .

The list on the board grew by short centimeters as the wall clock ticked down the final few minutes of class.

"Well, Caro, you have been very quiet this hour, perhaps you would care to share two or three of your words with us?" Dr. Balabanov asked graciously.

Caro tore her eyes off the clock and glanced frantically down the row of words on the board.

The bell rang.

"It is my hope that your vacations will bring you health and happiness," Dr. Balabanov pronounced solemnly to his students. But the class had already risen to their feet and were clattering out the door. Only Caro heard his words.

Lee waited for them in Sherri's parents' crawler at the pickup lot. Meggie and Becka, candy smeared over their faces, were fighting over the front seat next to him.

Lee spoke in veiled terms. "I have had interesting talks with the senior members of those clans represented in this vehicle."

"Oh?" Hal asked guardedly. Sherri and Ricky sat in tense silence, while Caro glanced cautiously at Meggie and Becka, trying to gauge their reaction to Lee's words.

"On the whole, the reception was more optimistic than anticipated. I foresee a potential relaxing on all quarters," he continued.

"All quarters?" asked Ricky anxiously.

"All quarters save one," Lee replied. "She's pretty stubborn about it, Ricky. And I can understand her reaction."

"I can't." Ricky's face was mutinous.

"Well, there's an unexpected ally in your corner. Give the man time," Lee said lightly. Becka began giving him suspicious looks.

"I'm going," Ricky muttered through set teeth. "I don't care what Mom says."

Caro asked carefully, "Is the ally, um, the other half?"

"No—well, yes, but this is another one."

Her face grew puzzled. "You?"

"Another." Caro saw his eyebrow quirk in the mirror.

Hal spoke casually, looking out the window, as though mentioning an unrelated fact, "Dr. Lutes is an amazing individual."

Caro flushed, recalling the overheard conversation in the marine lab. She knew intuitively that it was because of her, and her fear, that they were all to be allowed to go. She should feel grateful that her friends would be along on this journey of facing the shadows of her nightmare. Instead she struggled to keep down the dry sobs that threatened to betray her shame.

Lee was nodding vigorously. "I agree wholeheartedly with you, Hal." He began rakishly whistling the Community song, "Brothers We Are All."

Becka looked up from her conversation with Meggie and fixed her eye on Lee. "My mom says that song has an iron in it."

"Irony, Becka," Caro corrected automatically, thankful for the distraction. "And you shouldn't always repeat what Mom says in public."

Lee laughed. "Your mom has a way with words—and so do you, Becka. That song is full of irony and, 'the iron enters into the soul' every time it's sung."

Becka pushed her loose tooth out between her lips at Caro in triumphant defiance.

May, 2456
Actaeon—

I received two more notes of welcome from Gerald Lutes—one extending an invitation to visit his lab as soon as I am released from quarantine. But he will have to wait: I've received my second set of orders. Actaeon, I have no time to explore the light side of the planet. I am being quickly and silently shunted to the secret End Base—set in the half-light zone of the End region. Unexplored territory. My research orders? Unknown. My research partners? Unseen.

. . . The air shuttle is empty but for me and the pilot and navigator. I experience a curious moment of blindness as we cross over the parched, clay hills into the twilight of the End zone. The navigator, a talkative woman, tells me that it is the most hazardous moment for pilots—many air accidents occur at the strange matrix of day and night. I note a rare sight as we leave the light—two burnt-out shells of crescent moons floating wearily in the boiling sky.

—Reginald

5

Mob Flies and Warples

There was no secrecy in their preparations this time. Packing was almost complete and Caro stood watching, holding her wind-blown hair off her face, as Sherri, eyes rich with laughter, climbed aboard Lee's crawler. She turned to help Ricky, his stocky figure hoisting high a bag for her to load.

"Are all the suits stowed?" Ricky demanded in an abrupt manner.

Sherri called out from the back of the crawler, "They're supposed to be in the container. Do you want to go through the tunnel to check?"

Ricky replied by eagerly jumping into the crawler. Caro watched him climb through the accordionlike tube that provided access directly from the towing vehicle to the box-shaped container unit attached to it. She heard him call out, "All here!" and felt the fever-pitched excitement reverberating in his voice.

Lee came up quietly behind her. "All set, Caro?" he asked.

"I think so . . . You scared me. Did you see me jump?" She laughed, half embarrassed.

"Sorry. You were deep in thought. Trying to remember what we're forgetting? Or just reminiscing?" he asked.

"A little of both, I guess. It's so different this time. I mean, last time the four of us, and Sheila, and Mike and Jeff, were all racing about trying to get our gear hidden in Mom and Dad's container unit so we could stow away in it. We were so scared that Security would find us and haul us back to the hospital." She shook her head. "Now here we are, right out in the open, packing as if we were going camping at the beach."

His kindly eyes studied her; they traced the pattern of her zigzag scar, and she felt his compassion like warm fingers soothing her patched false-face. Suddenly she couldn't bear it and looked away from him.

"This time *is* different, Caro. Just fun stuff, and the carepies. They're waiting for you." Lee looked up as Ricky yelled for him with eleven-year-old importance.

"But we're still going to the End region. That's the same, that hasn't changed," the girl whispered through clenched teeth as he walked away from her toward the crawler, the wind sending ripples through his shirt.

Strange, eyeless creatures. A still fungus-forest that rang with the unitonal wind. Cruel and cunning *Lumini lupus* with their large eyes in soft baby-faces and deadly teeth. But worst of all would be the cold, timeless darkness. Although Caro was standing in fierce full sun, she shivered. Soon she would be boarding the crawler and, in six hours or so, they would go from the full-light region, where the Main Base was located, to the End Base, situated in the half-light zone on the planet's dark side.

The dark side. For Caro, they were words with well-worn channels of fear: where light never came, where darkness dwelt and built its house. Dr. Lutes had suggested that Caro had forgotten why she feared the dark side; the girl felt that she remembered only too well.

A crawler pulled up with Becka's eager face plastered to the window. Mr. Hunter's glasses glinted in the sun, hiding his expression. Caro's mother's face looked drawn. Ricky scuttled back inside the crawler; permission for him to go had been hard-won.

"We're here for the send-off," Caro's dad called with a determined smile. Becka ran to Caro, swinging a small sack.

"This is for you," she said. "It's treats."

"Thanks, Becka," Caro felt a tightening in her throat as she took the bag from her little sister.

"Where're you going? Moscow?" Becka asked.

"No, no, no, Becka. Don't you remember? We talked about where Caro and Ricky are going yesterday at dinner," her mom repeated patiently. "They're going to the other science base here on Clytie: the End Base. That's where the sun shines very dimly. Where Caro and Ricky will have to wear their Zero suits outside."

"Where there's no daytime," Becka chanted. "Where you have to have little heaters in your clothes."

Caro smiled, remembering how her dad, long ago, when they lived on Earth, had explained to them about Clytie's half-light, half-dark phenomenon. He had, at first, stated that "Clytie's revolution around the sun was exactly equal to its pivotal rotation." They had stared at him dimly: the flow of such a sentence had barely separated into words for them. Mr. Hunter had picked up baby Becka and placed her in the middle of the kitchen table with a big flashlight. Becka had become the sun. Then, walking around her, slowly spinning Ricky's basketball to represent Clytie, the two older children had grasped the idea of it. But only later, when Caro experienced constant day and unending night for herself, did she really know the meaning of it.

Hal arrived with Dr. Rokmanoff. Both were silent, each one uneasy in relaying affection for the other. Although they were alike in personality, they did not look at all alike physically. More often than not, people thought Hal was Mr. Hunter's son. Both Caro's dad and Hal were tall, lean, and athletic, with cleanly chiseled features. Both wore glasses. Dr. Rokmanoff was burly and bearded, with a wide face and a rolling gait. Caro wondered again if Hal resembled his mother, and where she was, if she were alive. Hal never spoke of her.

Lee had the back gate of the container unit open. The fathers clustered around him, examining equipment, double-checking the list—hydrogen bipacks for water, portable wind generator and lights, dehydrated foods, cooking equipment, extra energy packs—triple-checking the energy ratings on each Zero suit. In spite of the fact that they were driving directly to the End Base, an environmentally controlled, fully contained science base able to house around two hundred people, any travel into the End environment was treated very seriously.

Sherri, glancing back from the group, left them and joined Caro. They stood a little ways from the unit, watching and listening to the men going over the list, smiling at Ricky's efforts to be a part of the group.

Caro's mom, Clare, was standing with Miriam, talking earnestly in the comparative coolness of the porch overhang. Meggie and Becka roared about the yard with their rag-babies. They alternately raged and giggled at one another.

Sherri smiled at Caro. "Do you believe we're actually going? All four of us—and Uncle Lee, of course."

Caro's mouth was dry. "And Dr. Lutes is flying up in a couple of days," she managed.

"We'll have already spent three PM shifts there by then," Sherri said, thrilled.

"Three long nights," Caro said without thinking. "It seems weirder, somehow, to talk about night in a place of darkness, than it is to talk about day here—where it's always like noontime."

Sherri looked at her searchingly. Caro laughed, a hollow sound. "I don't really know what I'm trying to say—I guess I'm just excited and chattering nonsense."

"I guess," Sherri said softly. Caro had not exactly been chattering since the trip had first been suggested.

Then they were ready to leave. The good-byes began, each family enacting its own homey ritual. Sherri was hugged and wept over by her mother. Her father held them both tightly, his jovial face somber, all wisecracking set aside for a time. Meggie burst into loud laments and refused to be comforted. In the din, Caro saw Hal and his dad, faces scarlet and solemn with emotion, shaking hands so fiercely that she wondered about the aftereffects of such a trauma to Hal's wrists. Her own mom hugged her hard, and Caro saw the tears edging past her tightly clenched lids. Her dad with tenderness smoothed her hair, held her face, and whispered in her ear that he was proud of her, that she was very brave.

Becka looked from one parent to the other. "Oh," she said, two large tears running channels through the dust on her face, two more following. Then, fiercely, "Will Caro come back?"

"*Yes!* Of course, darling, in just two weeks." Her mother seemed to will those words into being.

"Me, too," said Ricky, on the verge of panic.

"Of course," she responded, as Ricky allowed her to pull him to her briefly.

A part of Caro watched in detached amazement while she climbed into the crawler: walking calmly up to the vehicle, accepting the hand Lee held out to her, returning his joking remarks, feeling his eyes trying to read her. She sat down beside Sherri, opposite Hal. The other back seat remained empty; Ricky had claimed the front seat beside

Lee, clambering importantly into the "navigator's" seat, adjusting his own mirror so that he could see out the back.

The crawler roared to life, vibrating in the electrical engine's warmup stage. Caro slid into the safety harness, clicked the belt shut. There were the last good-bye waves, then the crawler yanked and jerked, and the container treads clicked into synchrony with the crawler's. The twin caterpillarlike treads, working in unison, cut deeply into the dust ridges and hauled them up and over the bank out of Sherri's back yard and onto the track that provided access to the housing units.

Caro saw Becka's face, a muddy smear of tears, grow smaller and then disappear altogether as the crawler turned onto the main track that ran the length of the base. Past the lab complexes, the Community offices, the hospital, all built from the same rose-colored stone, their adjoining roofs forming a canopy over the walkway. Last glimpses of their parents' labs. Now almost to the Security station; Caro blinked her eyes against the sun blazing off the agricultural complex with its tightly closed barns and high fences. Soon her mother would be back at work in her research area in the browsers' barn.

The officer manning the Security station looked hot and tired. He impatiently waved them through as Lee slowed.

"Do they ever make anyone stop?" asked Ricky.

"I don't think so," replied Lee cheerfully. "They'd have to put down their ice tea and wade through the paperwork that we're supposed to carry."

Then they were passing the Communication's Center with its tall weather beacons looming overhead like giant scarecrows.

In the distant airfield, Caro caught a glimpse of the shining airship for Clytie to Earth voyages. A row of yellow, dust-covered crawlers, some with container units, looked like toys parked by the huge vessel. A convoy of attached crawlers and containers clicked their way down from the airfield and turned onto the track leading to the shore.

"There's the windmill field," murmured Sherri. Row upon flashing row of turbine-shaped windmills planted like corn covered a square kilometer and provided power for the Main Base. "Look, Caro," she exclaimed. "Those ugly bushes—lining the airfield—they're covered with flowers! And they're gorgeous!"

Lee slowed the crawler. "I've never seen them bloom before," he said. "They remind me of orchids."

"Smell," said Caro, sniffing the air.

They stopped and opened the doors and windows. The fresh, herb-sweet perfume permeated the dull, heat-baked dust that the wind whirled along the empty track.

"Wonderful," Sherri said with her eyes closed, sniffing rapturously. Her eyes popped open. "Can I go pick some?"

Lee shook his head. "Nope. You'll have to admire these from afar. I'll bet they would wilt right away anyway."

"Why can't we pick some?" asked Ricky.

"The leaves and tendrils of the bushes are covered with a gluey substance. You'd be stuck tight in no time, and very sore when we yanked you out. The 'glue' is quite acidic."

"It sure is an ugly bush to produce such incredible flowers," mused Hal.

Caro nodded. "The leaves are really irregular—with knobs hanging off them, and holes torn in them. And yellow leaves are too weird. Especially that mustardy-brown yellow." The leaves looked as though chunks had been bitten from them by rapacious insects that had not found the meal to their liking and had spat back oozing wads in disgust. But the flowers rising above the foliage on long, single stems looked intricately carved: fold within fold of milk-white layers smooth as wax, with rose-pink stamens like feathers cresting from their centers.

"If I touched just one leaf, would I get stuck?" Ricky looked at the bushes longingly.

"You'd have to fight those for the flowers," said Lee, pointing to a fast-approaching, low-flying red cloud. Everyone scrambled to close doors and roll up the double windows. Lee shut off the outside air intake, not wanting to trust the filters.

"They're small, but scary," Sherri said reverently.

"Uh, huh," agreed Hal with conviction. "My dad was caught out here by a small swarm of mob flies. He covered his face, but they bit him on his neck and arms. He had to go to the hospital to have them removed."

Sherri shuddered.

Even Ricky looked impressed. "What did they have to do at the hospital?" he asked morbidly.

"They had to cut the flies out with lasers. They just hang on—even when they're dead. And the toxin is in their exoskeletons, so the pain and swelling is pretty bad," Hal answered. "My dad carries a full net-suit with him when he inspects the windmill field now."

"But aren't the mob flies only active for a really short time in the summer?" Caro asked Lee.

"Your dad would be the one to ask—he's the ento-mologist," he replied. "I think, though, despite all scientific reports, if I worked out here I'd carry a net-suit around with me, too. I have no desire to feel their tiny, but mighty, jaws on my neck. Actually, this is embarrassing to admit for a biologist, but I'm not all that happy about bugs, period."

Ricky looked incredulous. "You're afraid of bugs, Uncle Lee?"

"Well . . . " Lee stalled. "Yeah, I guess I am. Oh, not rainbugs, I like rainbugs—though even that took awhile. They're awfully big for me." Ricky's eyes were wide, tragic, betrayed. "Everyone's afraid of something, Ricky," Lee said, glancing at Ricky in amusement.

Caro looked back out the window. The flies had descended on the fragile white petals; they looked stained, as though they had been splattered with drops of blood.

"Let's go," said Sherri suddenly. "I can't bear to see the mob flies wreck the flowers."

Lee started up the crawler. "Oddly enough, without those insects there would be no flowers next season," he commented.

"That's really crazy," said Caro. "What's the point of flowers next summer if they're just going to be ruined by next summer's bugs?"

Lee paused, thinking. "That's not an easy question to answer. I don't think that it can be answered on every level—I mean, economically it wouldn't make sense on a ledger sheet, would it? The energy outputs of the bush and the mob flies would probably just cancel each other out. Still I'm glad that we got to enjoy the flowers, as brief as the experience was . . . "

"Would it be that simple—even on an economic, or energy output level?" asked Hal. "I mean, wouldn't the whole ecosystem be affected if the bush and mob fly were rubbed out?"

"Yes, I think you're right, Hal," Lee replied. He geared the crawler down as they began to climb the long slope into the hills that surrounded the Main Base. "There are probably a lot more organisms at least partially dependent upon that one interaction between the flowers and the mob flies than we have any idea of."

"Yeah, just think, the mob flies bit Dr. Rokmanoff, who provided employment to several doctors and nurses," Sherri said earnestly.

"Not to mention all the technologists in the field of laser surgery who owe their families' well-being to the mob flies' jaws—and Hal's dad's neck," added Caro.

"Hmm" was Lee's only comment.

"I think that my dad should have at least received a commendation from the Community for his part in all of this," Hal grumbled, his eyes laughing.

"I don't know, Hal," Sherri said, shaking her head. "It seems to me that the mob flies took the greater initiative in the encounter. And there's your dad's attitude to consider. We hear that he's taken to wearing a net-suit to prevent further transactions from happening."

"Treachery! Treason!" Lee joined in bitterly. "And he looks so innocent, too. I should have guessed the truth about him by his beard. You gotta know that beard is hiding something."

"Yeah," replied Hal, grinning. "A pink birthmark in the shape of a heart."

Everyone roared.

"Really?!" squealed Sherri.

Hal nodded vigorously, his glasses slipping to one side. "He's mortified by it. Everyone has to promise that they'll never let on that they know—he'd die," he added, suddenly anxious, righting his glasses.

"We won't tell," Sherri assured him. "Whereabouts is the heart on his face?"

"Right here." Hal pointed to his right cheek, just under his cheekbone.

The conversation swirled around Caro as she looked out the window and watched the landscape. She loved

Clytie's hills: the six-cornered, silvery flowers that rose up from the clay like shy stars, the low-growing succulent that ran in tendrils over the rose-colored stones and popped when she stepped on its seed pods, and the clover-shaped groundcover that the rainbugs lived under.

In her wandering, she would sometimes blunder upon wild browsers. The herd would be grazing, blending in with the khaki-grey foliage. Then, for a second, it would look as though the entire side of the hill had begun to move, until the outline of the animals leaped into shape before her eyes. But once she had recognized the large, six-legged herbivores, it was impossible to fool her eyes again; never could she move back to re-experience the startling thrill of seeing nothing but meadow one instant, and the dragonish browsers the next. That is, until she came unknowingly upon the next herd.

The crawler roared triumphantly as it topped the long grade and reached the crest. Before them lay grey-brown hill upon grey-brown hill, layered far into the horizon until the ridges turned to silver-blue smokecaps and folded into the purple sky.

Clytie's full-light region had become home for Caro. She drew comfort from the steadfast hills and delight from the beauty of the vacillating sky. A rich purple in summer, it turned ice-green in winter with altered hues in between the two seasons.

The oily ocean, with its running currents of hot and cold water, so briny that even her dad couldn't sink, she gloried in. The lapping, or crashing, of the waves on the rough rocks had initially made Caro homesick for Earth. Now they were Clytie's music—strange and with an unpredictable rhythm.

Caro still missed Earth's darkly green forests that rose into glacier-edged meadows, but Clytie's gaunt, twisted vegetation, growing in heart-rending weirdness, called out an underdog loyalty from her.

The musky-scented pools of water ringed with Jonah trees had become a familiar part of the landscape. Jonah trees reminded Caro of oversize horsetail plants on Earth, with their feathery foliage on single, brown-grey stalks. Up to ten meters tall, they always faced defiantly into the wind, and as the wind always blew, Jonah trees never grew straight.

One day, when Caro and her father were out traipsing the hills, Caro had asked him why they were called Jonah trees. He replied that he supposed it was from the Bible . . . from Jonah and the Whale. "Jonah was a prophet, remember?"

"Yes," Caro answered. "But he didn't want to be." She squinted in the sun, tracing the bowed stalk with her eyes.

Her dad pulled off a broken limb of the tree: bracing his leg against the slender, bent trunk and straining hard. "Look out!" he yelled as the frail-looking branch came crashing down. "It was bigger than I thought." He wiped the sweat off his face, replaced his glasses, and smiled at Caro's disbelieving face. "Go ahead, you pick it up."

She couldn't budge it. The branch was as heavy as iron. "It's wood all right," he replied to her question, "but very dense wood."

They stripped the bark and fronds off the branch and he pulled the remaining core to the edge of the pond. "Help me push it in." With a deep *kerthunk* that sent a single muddy wave over their clothes, the branch disappeared. "Just like Jonah," Caro exclaimed, and they both laughed.

Caro smiled now, thinking of that day, and another time, a few months earlier, when Hal, Sherri, Ricky, and she were lost in the End forest and a stumbled-upon cache of Jonah tree wood had been life-saving.

Jonah trees, in spite of their obstinate characteristics, were useful. A kind of paper could be made out of the thin layer of cork under the bark, and the fronds and bark were sometimes braided into mats, hammocks, and bags. The wood itself, too bent to be used for poles, and extremely hard to cut into lengths, was hauled to the End Base where it was used as a fuel supplement. But the horny-rinded apples the Jonah tree bore in sporadic profusion were as bitter as poison.

Caro turned in her seat away from the window and caught Lee watching her in the rearview mirror. He smiled and looked away, but Caro felt a spreading warmth grow upward from the pit of her stomach. Again she was faced with the knowledge that everyone knew the shame of her fear. But Lee would not leave it unaddressed.

"How are you doing?" he asked.

Sherri and Hal looked up startled. Realizing that he was not asking them, they looked at Caro and waited for her response.

"Okay," she answered, a shade defensively. "How are you?"

He wasn't easily fazed. "I'm questioning my sanity in bringing you four back to the scene of such a horrendous experience. Even though I know that all the lumies at the Base have either been destroyed or caged, now that we're really on the way, I'm wondering whether or not I made a mistake." He gave a short laugh. "I really put my neck on the line with your parents."

"You didn't make a mistake," Ricky declared. "I wanted to come back."

Sherri, with a sideways glance at Caro, nodded. "I think that seeing the lumies under control now and unable to hurt anybody will sort of finish the nightmare for us." She blushed when she realized that she had used the word "nightmare."

Hal agreed too quickly. "We never got to see the base working as it should. I think it will do us all good."

They all know, thought Caro miserably. Her face itched and she felt like throwing up.

"What do you think, Caro?" Lee persisted.

"I'm supposed to work with the carepies, aren't I? Help Dr. Lutes and you? Well, that's exactly what I'm going to do." Her voice rang out harsh, but firm.

Lee stared straight ahead, maneuvering the crawler slowly along a banking turn. His lips and the corners of his eyes relaxed. "That you are, sweetheart."

Sherri looked relieved. "When exactly is Dr. Lutes arriving?"

"He's air-lifting in after the big Community meeting on Wednesday," Hal informed her.

"So Caro will have almost three days off before she has to work," Sherri exclaimed. "Good! We can explore and have some fun."

"Uh, have you forgotten about me? I know I'm not quite Dr. Lutes, but I do have a little desk of my own at the End Base. In fact, I have a whole lab with my name on the door. Caro will have some time off, but we need to get to work with the carepies right away—before the Community meeting, to be exact. You don't mind, Caro, do you?" Lee belatedly asked.

"No!" Caro answered. "I'm looking forward to it." Focusing on the carepies was the one thing keeping her from bolting out the crawler door. *But how things change. It was I, not Sherri, who was so drawn to the End region before. I wanted to explore. It was Sherri who was afraid, and only going along because of the job we had to do.*

"Well," grumbled Sherri, "when your boss lets you off for a minute or two, look me up."

"You'll be busy sketching. Remember, you didn't exactly have time to do much drawing last time," said Caro.

Inside she was picturing the carepies, hanging onto the image of a listless carepie calf gaining strength and circling in joy around her.

"Da—Darn!" shouted Lee, swerving and braking the crawler. It pulled to one side, throwing Sherri onto Hal, and flattening Hal and Caro to the window.

Ricky yelled, "Hey! Get out of the way!" His arms were straight out and his hands clutched the dash bar.

"Those stupid, stupid birds!" Lee continued his tirade. "I should just run them all down!"

Sherri was giggling, feebly trying to regain her balance and get off of Hal and back to her seat. " 'Da—darn'?!" she kept repeating until they were all laughing—except Lee, who was red-faced and furious. She finally made it to her seat and said with great innocence, " 'Da—darn'? What does that mean? I've never heard that word before."

Hal kicked her. Lee's eyes were slits. The warples gathered cheerfully in front of the silent crawler; Lee gripped the wheel, his muscles tight.

"It's imitation swearing," Ricky explained to Sherri solemnly. Lee swept him an amazed look.

"You wouldn't have fallen out of your seat if you had been buckled into your harness like you're supposed to be," Lee turned and roared at Sherri. She made a face behind his back and mouthed, " 'Da—darn'!" Hal, in fear for her life, kicked her again.

Warples were extremely annoying. The adults were atrocious parents, running blithely over their youngsters if anything interesting happened by. They were so curious that they would let anyone walk right up to them. The babies, with voracious appetites, would lunge at anything that moved. A warple colony near a crawler track could be deadly; warples never seemed to learn that running up the track towards a moving crawler was a dangerous pastime, and the adults were large enough to cause a serious accident.

"That one looked like Warpalee, Ricky." Caro broke the silence.

"No, no," scoffed Sherri. "It looked much more like Warpalow."

"Ha, ha, ha. So funny," answered Ricky.

Lee quit muttering malicious threats to the birds. His neck and arms relaxed. He couldn't resist asking, "Who are Warpalee and Warpalou?"

"Warpalee and Warpa*low*," Caro corrected, "were Ricky's first Clytian friends. The day after we arrived Ricky took off, as usual, leaving the rest of us unpacking, and—" She continued over Ricky's protests, "and in his explorations, he came across two 'orphaned' warples. They were the first wild creatures on Clytie any of us had seen. Only Mom knew that they were birds, not mammals—"

"They were so young, they still had their 'fur' on," interjected Ricky.

"Right. Well, one of them seemed to have a broken arm—I mean, wing—and the other had raced up to Ricky, warpling like crazy. Ricky decided that it had come running to him for help, so he picked up the one he thought was hurt and proceeded to carry it home. The other one followed, of course, never letting up on its warpling."

"I can well imagine the racket," Lee commented, glaring again at the birds.

"Anyway," Caro continued, "there was nothing wrong with either of them. Ricky named them Warpalee and Warpalow—Warpalow had a lower voice than Warpalee. We all loved them—at first. Then we realized that everything that the warples touched reeked. Including us. For days we smelled of warples. I remember how embarrassed I was the first day I had to go to school."

"Dad decided that Warpalee and Warpalow had to go. They not only smelled horrible, they got out of every cage I built them and dug burrows all over," said Ricky.

"Yeah," Caro added. "That's what made me realize that warples are incredibly stupid. They dig a burrow, promptly forget where it is, and dig another one. Then they forget where that one is. Anyway, for the longest time after that, whenever we passed by a colony of warples, Ricky was sure he recognized Warpalee and Warpalow. It got to be hilarious—Warpalee and Warpalow certainly got around!"

"Before you kids arrived on Clytie, we had a warple invasion at the Main Base. Don't feel bad, Ricky, everyone initially falls in love with a warple. Until they smell them." Lee grimaced and shook his fist at the large, pasty-grey, full-feathered adult attempting to ingest the front end of the crawler.

The flat, triangular remnant of the bird's beak clacked against the headlight and Lee yelled. The warple rolled its green eyes at him and closed in again. Waves of warple scent began to waft in through the ventilation system.

"Now it's a sure sign that you're a rookie to Clytie if you pay the least bit of attention to a warple." Hal sniffed the air with a grimace. "If Caro hadn't warned me, I would have probably 'rescued' one, too."

"They look like they're coming apart at the seams," Caro said without thinking.

Lee laughed. "You're right. Like gnawed on, covered in drool, moth-eaten, stomped-on, stuffed toys. Maybe that's why humans are so easily suckered in by them." He turned on the ignition, giving a blast of the air horn at the same time. As the warples started back, he slowly began to inch the crawler forward through the clumsy birds. They flapped their skinny wings, as though they were trying to flag the vehicle down. The tall adults began to run alongside the crawler, stumbling upon their round, rolling babies, tripping over rooted snags in the ground, falling with shrieks down forgotten burrows. Anguished, warpling wails filled the air as the colony was left behind.

"Are you in your harness, Sherri?" Lee abruptly demanded.

"Yes, mother," she sighed, rolling her eyes.

The crawler began laboring up a series of switchbacks. Ricky yawned hugely, setting into motion a series of yawns from the rest, each more lusty than the one before. Between yawns, Lee burst out laughing.

"Everyone always starts yawning here—we're climbing so rapidly that the inner atmosphere gauges for oxygen mix just can't keep up with the changes in pressure. It's never happened to me yet, but if you feel lightheaded, you may want to use your respirators. We'll level off in about fifteen more minutes," he explained.

"Now he tells us," grumbled Ricky, rubbing his streaming eyes.

The crawler slowed, treads clicking, engine dropping in pitch to a low whine, moving meter by meter up the steepest grade yet.

Then they reached the top.

Sherri pointed out the front window, and cried, "Look!"

They saw the end of the sky. Or so it seemed. A black horizon stretched across the land of perpetual day. It was as though they were looking at the negative of a sunset.

Lee stopped the crawler and powered back the outside roof, uncovering the double-glazed, transparent ceiling.

Caro saw that even the sky above them looked different. At the Main Base it was always noon; this was a late afternoon sky. They sat still and silent, watching the black gash.

It held them there. Caro tore her gaze away from the hole in the sky. In the rearview mirror she studied the faces of the others. Sherri looked full of awe, perhaps a little apprehensive. Hal was tense, as if he were watching an unfamiliar animal. Ricky looked thoughtful, but eager. Uncle Lee? Lee was mesmerized. *Did he love it that much?* Caro wondered. This was so much more than scientific curiosity; this was passion. *What drew him here? He could be anywhere he chose—why the End? With us?*

Lee collected himself, looked around with a short, self-conscious laugh, and revved up the crawler.

May, 2456
Actaeon—

*There is a legend told of a dark island that floats
Earth's Arctic seas, luring ships to their doom. It is said
that a woman sits enchained upon its ruthless rocks. Dark
as night, cloaked only in her raven hair, she weaves it as a
shroud around the rocks. And weeps and sings a dirge so
sad that sailors stop their duties and, so enchanted, crash
upon her shores.*

*The spell of that story, read so many years ago, sits
strangely upon me now as I, encased within my suit, explore
the End Base. Perhaps it is the wind that draws it from my
mind; certainly it is persistent, ringing, and, yes, dirgelike
in its tone.*

Clytie's shadow side; a singing shroud . . .

—Reginald

6

Swallowed by the Sky

They were all quiet now. Sherri's eyes were closed; Hal fixed his gaze out the side window. Ricky divided his time between studying Lee's face and gestures and observing the instrument board in front of him. The kilometers ticked by on the odometer, and the various gauges calculated the atmospheric conditions. Ricky watched in fascination as the outer temperature gauge fell rapidly along with the photon meter, which measured the quickly decreasing number of light units received as they traveled the surface of the planet.

Caro sat still, barely breathing, gazing out of the transparent ceiling at the black smear across the sky. As the minutes stretched into hours, she saw the yawning blackness gape bigger and bigger. She closed her eyes and felt them sting, so dry were they from her petrified stare. When she reopened her eyes the dark gash had disappeared. *That's odd,* the detached, observer part of her mind mused. Then she realized her mistake; she could no longer see the gradation of darkness because they had now entered the yawning mouth. The cold seemed to descend with the dark deep into her, imprisoning the real Caro in a brittle casing of fear. She could not move, could not swallow the thickness coating her mouth and throat.

The crawler headlights blinked up into a brighter beam. Sherri stirred and shivered. "I'm cold, Uncle Lee," she complained, "and starving."

"I'm sorry," his hearty voice rang out. "I should have stopped for a break long ago. I'm so used to driving straight through, I didn't even think. But for once I'm not racing to make it in time for some useless Community meeting." Lee brought the crawler to a standstill, cut the engine, switched on the auxiliary power, and swung his chair around, facing the three of them in the back.

"So," he said, "what's on the menu?"

"Who knows? My mom packed the famous blue chest. Do you want to go in through the tunnel and hand it out to me?" Sherri asked Hal.

"Sure." Hal got up from his seat, flexing his arms and legs.

"No!" Ricky shouted eagerly. "I'll go." Hal shrugged, keeping his neck bent to avoid banging his head on the ceiling of the crawler. He flopped back down in his seat gratefully.

Ricky gleefully began working his way through the adjoining soft silicone tunnel into the container unit. The accordion-folds yielded with his weight and then rebounded, bouncing him up and down with every stride.

"Must be nice to stand upright—even in the tunnel," Hal muttered, rubbing his neck.

Lee nodded companionably. "I could do with an assistant that size," he said, smiling at Ricky's short figure and face so lit up with delight.

"Better hand out the suits, too, Ricky. Do you know where they are?" Lee called. "We really should have them on, in keeping with safety standards. It'll be warmer for you, too," he added to Sherri.

"I know where they are," Ricky answered confidently from the depths of the container. The white Zero suits began shooting through the tunnel and Caro reached to pull them out, happy to be involved in a task that kept her thoughts focused and off the descending darkness all around.

"I think this is yours, Hal," she said, yanking on the large, attached boot.

"Thanks, Caro." Hal began undoing the various fastenings and zippers so that he could, mummy-fashion, work himself into the inner lining of the suit.

Caro handed Lee his suit, and then she and Sherri examined the two remaining similar-sized suits, trying to decide which was hers and which was Sherri's. "Ah, ha! My initials," Sherri announced triumphantly. "Wouldn't you know that only my mom would think of the obvious?"

Caro smiled. She knew that in an inner pocket of each suit was a packet of nuts and dried fruit, placed there by her own mother—in case of emergency.

Caro wriggled into the body-hugging jumpsuit lining with the heating coils woven into the material and left the respiratory and excretory tubes hanging. The inner suit felt damp and chill; the girl shivered as she worked one foot and then the other into place, and then slipped her arms in and felt the warp and woof of the material draw close about her body. The high neck felt tight against her throat; she yanked at it, gasping.

"My suit's cold, isn't yours?" Sherri said. "It must be a lot cooler in the container than in here."

"Well, just wait for them to warm up—don't make the energy hookups yet." Lee looked at Sherri's frantic face. "Oh, go ahead. The suits will be cleaned and recharged at the Base anyway. And we're only a couple of hours away now."

Caro slipped the tubes and connectors into place. Immediately the coils began heating, spreading comforting waves through her body. She patted the inner pocket with her mom's supply of emergency rations tucked in it and felt a deeper, inner warmth. She folded down the detachable hood and unzipped faceplate into a tall, thick collar around her neck.

"I could use a hand here" came a disgruntled voice from the container unit.

"Sorry, Ricky," Hal replied. "Is the chest too heavy for you?"

"Don't bring the whole thing," Lee called. "Just hand out to Hal the food we need."

"Like what?!"

"Well, what is there?" asked Caro.

"Everything! You know my mother," answered Sherri. "Probably an entire spit-roasted browser is waiting to pop out of that food chest the minute it's opened."

Lee agreed. "Next to Plant Science, if there's anything Miriam knows how to do, it's pack dinner. Bring forth the browser!"

"No browser," Ricky replied. "But there're bags and bags of sandwiches. And something hot—OW!—very hot—in the round cookers."

"Stew, I'll bet."

"Browser stew?"

"Caro! Come and help me," Ricky commanded in frustration.

"Okay—hang on a minute."

It was fish and vegetable stew, full of rich chunks of Clytie's "tuna," the small, fat lobefish so easily netted in schools that circled the ocean bay. Round, red orcles, firm and peppery as mild radishes, gave an agreeable chunkiness to the stew. While the familiar Earth-style lentils thickened the juices, the native herbs and plants added wonderfully unique textures and tastes.

"Wow," Lee said through a mouthful. "It pays to have an agricultural botanist for a sister. This is wonderful."

"It's all from our garden," Sherri said with pride. "Well, except the fish."

"What's this stuff?" Lee asked, holding up a spoonful of lumpish greyish-green. "It looks like seaweed, but tastes like squash."

"Greens," answered Sherri.

"My, my," Lee responded. "How do they come up with the names for all these newfangled things?"

"Well, that's what my mom calls it," Sherri defended herself. "It's got some scientific name, but who can remember it?"

"That's its nickname, Uncle Lee," Ricky chimed in, spraying stew in his effort to explain.

"Thank you, Ricky," Sherri said, looking injured.

"Well, whatever it is, I like it," Hal pronounced, refilling his mug.

Caro leaned back in her seat with her leg curled under her, a cup of hot duck tea resting on her knee. *Safe*, she thought. *Safe. Talking with your mouth full, silly jokes, homemade stew, light and warmth. That's what all these things have in common. They're safe.*

But the problem was they couldn't continue eating Aunt Miriam's homemade stew forever. Caro felt her stomach churn as the crawler lurched along on the last lap of their journey. Her eyes strained in the twilight, trying to see—what? She didn't know; she only knew that she needed, desperately, to see it—whatever "it" was—before it saw her.

The landscape of the End hills rolled before her like a dark desert. The opaque sky, close about the hills, blended

73

into the ground; instead of opening the planet to the heavens, the End sky was smothering. To Caro, it seemed as though they moved in circles, trapped under an inverted bowl.

Clumps of vegetation, short and sharp, rose like unbending blades before them in the crawler's headlights. Frontons began to appear. First, one every kilometer or so, stunted and tumble-down, then a few more, entwined into bewildering branchings. Then the tall, precariously built towers that Caro remembered from the End began to loom up in the headlights as they traveled into the darker zones. And Caro remembered the music of the wind, constant, filling the dark forest.

The crawler's outside lights blinked up yet another power.

"We're now officially in the half-light zone!" Ricky announced, staring at the photon meter.

"So we're very close to the End Base, now, right?" asked Hal.

"Yep. We'll see it soon, when we reach the top of this grade," Lee answered. His black eyes flickered away from the track in front of him to the mirror reflection of the dark-haired, scarred girl sitting so rigidly, staring so intently out the side window.

He cleared his throat. "You all know how to read the photon meters I had mounted on your suits, right? Caro?" She tore her eyes away from the night with difficulty, fixing them, for a moment, uncomprehendingly on him. "You know how to read the photon meter on your wrist, don't you Caro?" he persisted, forcing her to focus on him.

She glanced down at the sleeve of her suit. A round patch of clear polymer coated a digital read-out. "Um, you just read it directly, don't you? In kilometers?"

"Yes. It's calibrated to Clytie's light zones. Look at the crawler's meter—the one on your suit won't read correctly because we have the light on in here. See? It tells me that I'm 3.37 kilometers deep in the half-light zone. With a photon meter you always know the direction in which you are headed—toward or away from light."

"If we'd had one of these last time," Caro began slowly.

"We wouldn't have gotten lost," Sherri finished for her, in a voice full of awe.

Lee nodded. "Photon meters are standard equipment for the End region. They weren't issued with your suits initially because no one dreamed you would ever be in this region."

"You know what, though," said Hal thoughtfully. "If we hadn't gotten lost, we would never have found you, Lee. And then how would it have turned out? Maybe the lumies would have slaughtered every one of us at the Base."

Lee stared solemnly out the front window of the crawler. After a long silence, he said, "You know, the older I get, the harder it is for me to justify all the accidental happenings that occur as coincidence. Even horrible things. Like you all getting lost in the End—I think you're right, Hal—who knows what might have happened if we five hadn't met up—by accident."

"What you're saying is that God decreed that the innocent people at the End Base would be killed by lumies, and that we would all be hurt trying to stop them." Caro's voice startled everyone with its raw anger.

Ricky turned horrified eyes on her. "You're cursing God," he said frantically. "Now you're going to die!"

"No, no, no, Ricky!" Lee's firm voice rang out. "Caro's *not* cursing God, and even if she were, I think that he's big enough to handle it without throwing a temper tantrum. Caro's asking some very big questions, that's all. God takes people very seriously when they're brave enough to face such big questions—we all should."

"But it's in the Bible," Ricky insisted, gazing fearfully at his sister. "Curse God and you die!"

Lee ground the crawler to a standstill and stared at Ricky with a baffled look on his face. "Where is it in the Bible?"

"I don't remember, but it is, I know it. If you curse God, you die." He licked his lips nervously.

"Do any of you know what he's talking about?" Lee looked around at the rest of them.

Sherri was gazing alternately at Ricky and Caro. "I remember something like that, too," she said uncertainly. "Somebody saying 'Curse God and die.'"

Hal spoke up. "That doesn't seem to fit. Caro has read me different poems from the Bible that complain about God an awful lot. Why would they be allowed in there if God killed all the poets off after they wrote those poems?"

Caro laughed. She couldn't help it—the laugh jerked itself up through the depths of her pain from some unknown, even deeper source. "They're thinking about Job's wife," she said, looking at Lee. She leaned her head back on the seat. "Her advice to Job when he lost everything was, 'Curse God and die.'"

"Oh." Lee thought a minute. "I should have guessed. Ricky, Job's wife was simply stating her rather bitter opinion of what Job should do. It was like she was saying, 'Go ahead, spit in his eye, you're better off dead, anyway.' Or something like that. The point is, she was just mouthing off; she wasn't giving us a clear picture about the way God is. Do you see what I mean?"

Ricky looked dubious. "Well, why does he kill people then? I thought that God was stronger than anybody or anything—I mean, isn't that what it means to be 'God'? Someone bigger than anyone else?" Ricky glared at Lee stubbornly.

"Yes—among other things," Lee answered dryly.

"Well, then—why does he let people die? And why didn't he stop the lumies from hurting Caro?" Ricky barged on. Caro flushed and turned to look out the window.

Silence filled the crawler. For the first time, they heard the wind singing outside, soaring above and below them, wrapping them in sound. "I don't know," Lee finally said. "I don't think there's ever a truly satisfying answer to a question like that, Ricky."

"Then what's the point of asking them." Caro's words dropped like stones.

"Because when you stop asking them you stop living," Lee replied, his knuckles white on the steering wheel, his eyebrows drawn together. "If you accept the silence of nothingness, you choose to serve nothingness!" They stared at him dumbly. "And you become a non-human. You might as well be a, a mob fly. No!" he yelled, pounding the panel. "I take that back! A mob fly knows its reason for being. You stop questioning the evil in this world, and you hand in your reason for being!" He suddenly looked and saw their startled faces. "Sorry," he said with a twisted smile. "I'm sorry, Caro," he repeated. "I'm not really yelling at you." But he began winding up again. "It just makes me furious when I look around at all the people who have truly laid down the essence of their humanness—the ability to choose life—however hellish the struggle for it is sometimes. But you haven't. I know that. And so do the carepies." The last phrase was said so quietly that Caro wondered whether or not she had heard him correctly.

She shook her head as if to clear it. His speech was strangely comforting: he emanated passion, life. But the words themselves meant little to her. Except the fear of nothingness—she understood that completely: it was the core of her nightmare. She knew, from the way that Lee

77

had spat out *if you accept the silence of nothingness, you choose to serve nothingness!* that he had come face to face with this enemy himself. And he had won.

The crawler labored, meter by meter, shuddering along in low gear up the last steep slope of the End hills. Then the dark forest seemed to drop away; they were at the apex and far below, like fallen stars, glittered the lights of the End Base.

"There it is," said Lee. "Only about a forty-five minute drive now. Downhill all the way."

"Downhill all the way," echoed Ricky, leaning forward and staring eagerly at the brilliant outline of the Base.

"Seeing it from the hill like this sure brings back memories," murmured Hal.

"It looks cold," Sherri said.

Caro glanced at her. "It does," Sherri repeated. "I'm not sure why—I always think of light as being warm—but the Base lights look like, well, like sparkling ice."

"You're right," Caro agreed. "Or diamonds: hard and cold, but flashy."

Lee was listening intently to the girls. "I think that you two have managed to come up with the best image yet of the Community: brilliant, but frigid and unyielding as rock-hard ice."

"The Community is like a glacier, covering everything over with a killing frost, destroying life, squishing all the queechies and warples, leaving nothing behind but rubble." Sherri paused, evidently trying to think of something even more dramatic.

Lee roared. "Well, let's let 'em get the warples, anyway!"

Ricky's wide eyes relaxed. "The Community does some good things. They gave us a new holiday from school this year—Achievement Day. We got to stay home."

"Well, that would certainly be an achievement, Ricky—for you. And did you stay home?" Lee asked.

"I don't remember," he replied, puzzled.

Hal adjusted his glasses. "Still, there has to be some kind of governing control. The Community may not be anywhere near perfect, but they're all we have. Don't get me wrong—I don't like their autocratic bureaucracy, either. But I can't really see any other way of working things. If you don't have a group of people sharing in the running of things, we could end up going back in history with one crazy man making insane decisions for everyone."

"Hal, what you're saying is right-on in theory. The problem is, we don't in reality have a representative group of people making decisions. We have a few hand-picked men and women who might as well be one person. Most of the Community Officials are nice people who are afraid of the risk of voting against the status quo. Anyone who does tends to get a transfer to the Arctic counting ice fleas," Lee said with conviction.

"So we do have one crazy man running things?" Hal asked.

"Yes—but I don't mean one literal person. It's more of a composite person conjured up from the minds of those in power over a period of centuries. Made up of what learned people decided should be The Person. But a composite person doesn't exist, so can't represent anyone, and you can't reason with a nonentity. We've ended up being slaves to a figment of the imagination—and, unfortunately, the people who had a share in making up this Person didn't have great imaginations." Lee snorted. "Becka and Meggie could have done better. At least the kids know that people are just as much riddle and rhyme as they are reason."

"I don't understand all of what you just said, but I can *feel* that it's true," said Sherri.

"That's the artist in you, Sherri," Lee said soberly. "Hang onto it."

Caro looked up and met Lee's eyes squarely in the rearview mirror. "The Person—the figment-ruler of the Community—it's another Nothingness, isn't it?"

"No, sweetheart." Lee said. "It's the same Nothingness. Just another guise."

July, 2456
Actaeon—

"Not for me the false, sterile existence of laboratory research. Grinning and scraping to half-wits who mete out grant funds like gumdrops to whomever amuses them best. Running research with an entertainer's eye to the spectacular." So I wrote in my journal, Actaeon, only seven short years ago, and here I am, center ring, in the greatest circus of them all.

Security is so tight that no one knows what anyone else is doing. We do what is in front of us, day by day, never knowing where we are headed or what it is we are looking for. There are only two rules: discover something—anything—that will excite the Community, and keep your head down and an arm shielding your work, for that friendly colleague may steal you blind.

Actaeon, it is a circus, and I am one of the clowns.
                                                    —Reginald

7

Behind Bars

The Security station at the End Base entrance was empty. They drove up to the gates, hedged in on either side by tall towers of blinding lights, and passed through the high meshed fence that surrounded the entire Base. The End Base activities took part mainly in the large, three-level white building; the crawler settled into the well-worn treads, following the track to the vehicle entrance by the airlift field.

"Why isn't there any Security person at the gate?" Hal asked in concern.

"Oh, I expected that," replied Lee. "Most of our people are at Main for the big Community meeting this week. You'll find the place pretty empty. The only people around are the ones who keep the thing running—a few engineers, a couple of Power people, and one or two die-hard scientists, I imagine."

"Like you?" Sherri suggested.

Lee grinned. "Yep. Me and Caro."

"I thought that we were going to get to see the whole operation in action," Hal said.

"Yeah," Ricky complained. "Now most of the labs will be locked up."

"There will still be plenty to see and do," Lee said. "Besides, I'm a director here—ever hear of universal passes? My security code gives me clearance throughout most of the Base. And who knows when I'll need to check on something or other?"

"Yeah, but you'll be busy with Caro," Ricky continued to grumble.

"Hey, I'm counting on you to check on some of the lab animals for me—to make sure that the automatic feeders are doing their job."

Ricky cheered up. "Okay! Hey—are those lumies?!" he shouted, pointing to a row of barracklike cages. The light from the beacon high along the fence line gleamed off the roof and diamond-mesh of the enclosures. Beyond the sheet of light, dark figures stood poised; it was impossible to tell what kind of creatures they were in the shadow of that blinding wash of brilliance.

"Yes," Lee said, his voice even. He glanced at Caro in the rearview mirror. She gazed, stone-faced, in the direction Ricky pointed.

"Three older females and two males," Lee continued. "That's the last of the surgically sighted lumies. They're a pretty sad bunch."

"How can you feel sorry for them, Uncle Lee?" Sherri exclaimed. "No one was hurt by them worse than you!"

"I think that you'll feel the same way I do, Sherri, when—if—you go out and see them," said Lee carefully. "They weren't created for scientists to mess with their eyes and then hold them for life in some tiny cage—and tiny it is when you consider the range that a pack would travel in the wild."

"I thought they were the enemy . . . " Hal said.

Lee sighed. "Yes, they were. Or rather, they were the destructive force that had to be reckoned with. We did—and are continuing to do—what we have to. But who made them the destructive force? Don't get me wrong, Hal. If I found out that there were more sighted lumies wandering around loose that we had overlooked, I would be after them—disposing of them or permanently caging them. It *is* what has to be done. But we also need to face up to our responsibility in making this mess."

They left the row of enclosures behind them and the track turned, skirting the windmill and power field. The airfield was empty. Only the crisscross of long marks cut deeply in the soil from the airlifts' runners showed where the long, double-bladed carriers usually stood.

Lee maneuvered the crawler toward a ground-level platform where two raised runners, outlined in a pulsing emerald-green, were positioned coincidental to the crawlers' treads. As the treads clicked into place between each runner, they felt the crawler lurch and begin to be pulled by the runners onto the platform. Lee turned the engine off.

There was another jerk as the container treads jumped into place in the runners. The crawler-container unit was slowly drawn along the platform. When they were in the center of the large square, they heard a thin whine shiver through the air, and the platform below them began to vibrate.

"What's going on?" Ricky demanded fearfully.

"We're on an elevator, Ricky. An elevator for crawlers," Hal explained, looking at Lee for confirmation.

He nodded. "This way we can unload your gear from the container directly into the cargo elevator. And all in environmentally controlled comfort . . . "

Caro felt her stomach hang in the air and then swoop down to rejoin the rest of her body as the floor began to drop. She looked above, through the transparent ceiling of the crawler, and watched the outside world of the Base recede. A short ride and then a soft clunk and it seemed, for an instant, as if they were headed back up. But Lee reached forward and restarted the crawler engine.

"Here we move off the platform and through these doors into the lock. That's the sealed room that acts as a vault to stop the extra oxygen and heat from being sucked out the elevator shaft," he explained. "From there, once the outside doors are re-sealed, we can drive right on down the tunnel into the Base."

"This is where you and Dr. Lutes thought the lumies were entering from, right?" Ricky asked in hollow tones.

"Nope," answered Lee quickly. "None of the lumies ever learned how to drive. Dr. Lutes and I speculated that they were coming in through a foot tunnel that opens out into the windmill field. It's built along the same lines but on a much smaller scale. And it doesn't connect with this tunnel at all."

The huge doors opened and a *woof* of air blasted out at them. Lee drove through the doors into a drafty, echoing box. He stopped the crawler in front of another pair of giant doors. A long beam of light stretching on each side of the doors and running their length glowed a fierce crimson.

The doors behind them slowly rolled shut, the thunder building until they met with a crash and various locks clicked into place. The red light changed to amber and began pulsing.

Bands of neon green spread in waves along the light bar. The doors in front of the crawler began to shake and roll open, revealing the brilliant white plasti-coated walls of the End Base. They followed the long tube of light set into the ceiling; it curled with the tunnel to the left.

"How do you get the crawler back out?" asked Hal. "Or, I should say, how does anyone else get in the way we came? Does the elevator automatically go back up to the outside surface?"

"Yes," Lee answered. "The platform returns as soon as the crawler is completely inside the lock and the doors close behind it. It's set into motion from outside when a crawler's treads enter the runners up on the platform and, from inside, when the sensor beam is split by a vehicle approaching the lock."

"Ooh," said Sherri. "I just thought of something. What if a crawler tries to drive onto the platform when it has already dropped to pick up a crawler from inside?"

"There's an electra-magnetic barrier that comes on when the floor is in use, Sherri. A crawler simply cannot pass through it. Didn't you see the way that the entire length of the runners is lit up? That's how a driver knows that the floor is available. When it has dropped, the whole square boundary pulses red with the electric barrier. It's a very safe system."

"What I want to know is, why are we still heading down?" Caro asked.

"I know!" Ricky said. "The basement is the lowest point—because of the ventilation and heating systems. Because hot air rises."

"Actually, cold air sinks, Ricky," Caro answered. "What I meant was, how come the lift doesn't take us level with the basement?"

"Ricky's right, Caro," Hal said. "In order to provide proper ventilation throughout all the tunnels without using extra power, they build them on a slope and use the natural inclination of cold air to sink and push the hot air up to provide air movement through the tunnels."

Ricky looked smug. "I read about it in one of my dad's Circulating Papers," he said. "Dad keeps them all in the bathroom."

Lee laughed. "Yeah, that's the place for most of 'em. Phil has a lot of discrimination."

"Actually, that's just Dad's favorite spot to read," Caro said, her mouth wry. The others laughed, but a picture of her dad's face with his sensitive smile swam before Caro's eyes and a wave of homesickness rose in her throat.

"Well, here we are," announced Lee. The crawler came to a shuddering halt, the engine noise dying, leaving a sudden hole of silence. Hal, Sherri, and Caro stared dumbly at the cargo elevator and Lee examined their faces.

"Brings back some things, eh?" he said.

"It just seems like yesterday." Hal laughed nervously. "I mean, not much has changed around here. There's where we came from engineering room 'G,' pushing the cart with the three tranquilized lumies that attacked you, Lee."

"There's even a cart there—right by the elevator," Sherri said, swallowing.

"Yep—the only thing missing is the lumies. And, remember, folks, there ain't no more lumies in this building—sighted or otherwise. The only ones on the entire base complex are the five wretched specimens sitting in that dismal cage outside. Okay? Okay, Hal? Sherri? Caro?"

They each nodded. Hal flicked at the damp hair on his forehead. "I really didn't think it would hit me like that," he said, half embarrassed.

"Yeah," echoed Sherri, her eyes wide and dark with emotion. She smoothed the legs of her suit with moist hands.

Caro was silent, the scars on her face etched whiter than ever by the glare thrown from the inset lighting; her eyes were hooded, unreadable.

"It was a truly horrifying time," Lee said in gentle and emphatic tones. "I live here. I've had to face this thing every day and I'm still not sure that I've sorted it all out. You three—four—are probably going to go through some emotions you never knew you had in the next few days. And so you should. You'd have to be a robot—or an unmitigated half-wit—not to."

"Fine—vacation with Dr. Lee Krisman for a truly unforgettable time of tears and fears," announced Sherri in a determined, but shaky, voice. Hal smiled at her.

Ricky looked puzzled. "I don't feel anything at all—am I an unmitigating half-wit?"

"Unmitigated half-wit. And no, you're not," answered Lee. "You weren't part of the lumie attack that took place down here. For you, the observation pit may bring back some funny feelings. Or maybe the bathroom wall. You can never tell about such things. And it's quite possible that you've already dealt with your emotions and will feel nothing but curiosity and a certain nostalgia. Maybe you'll break into 'Auld Lang Syne' at the sandwich dispenser."

Sherri and Hal laughed and Ricky looked relieved. "I wouldn't mind some sandwiches right now," he said.

"All in good time," Lee replied. "Now, let's unload. Leave everything that is not absolutely necessary to your existence. I'm hungry, too. Caro, let's unload, eat, and then you and I will check on the carepies, okay?"

She turned to him slowly, her eyes gradually focusing on his, her face warming by degrees, turning from carved stone to flesh. "Yes," she said. "That will be fine." Her voice, even to her ears, sounded computerlike, soulless. "Um, we all just need to bring our packs, right?" she asked the others in a more normal manner.

They nodded, perplexed and a little frightened by her fear. "Good, good," Lee's hearty voice proclaimed, driving the specters from the air around them. "We can get everything in one load then. Hal, you get the cart."

Hal paused for an instant, wildly startled. "Talk about déjà vu," he said. Lee roared, further banishing the ghosts. "I *promise* we'll load it with only our gear—no lumies!"

They entered the cargo elevator, Hal and Ricky pushing the cart loaded with the rest of the food that Sherri's mom had packed and Lee's new lab equipment and supplies. Everyone had a backpack.

Caro carried her lab book and her underwater gear. Her bulging backpack threatened to pull her over backwards, and her aud-vis recorder, which hung from her neck, had joined forces with her viewers; both seemed determined to strangle her. Already she ached with their combined weights and walked stiff and wary into the elevator.

Sherri's arms were full of drawing materials: several sizes of sketch books, thick three-sided pencils and all colors of flow-stick paints, most with their ends already squished up and the vibrant hues leaking through. Her fingers were stained azure and tangerine, and she had unconsciously rubbed her nose and chin with her violently colored hands several times already. She held out one elbow at right angles to her body, trying to keep her overstuffed backpack from sliding off her shoulder.

Hal's backpack, modestly loaded instead of bulging horrifically like Sherri's and Caro's, hung tidily across his back. A pair of clean tennis shoes, neatly knotted, circled his neck, and his viewers, snug in their unscratched case, swung decorously from one shoulder. He was holding back the cart from upsetting over the crack at the door to the elevator.

Ricky had both arms through the straps of his rumpled backpack; it flapped, half empty, with every thrust of his body as he pushed, head down, against the stubborn cart.

Lee whistled through his teeth at a furious tempo, checking to see whether the container was empty of all needed items. He accidentally discovered his own tote, wedged between a hydrogen bipack unit and a box of dehydrated food, and beamed, delighted by the luck of it.

They exited the elevator on the second floor. Hal bumped the cart carefully over the crack while Ricky raced ahead excitedly. Caro cautiously maneuvered her way through the door, avoiding Sherri's jutting elbow. Sherri, following Caro, dropped a pencil down the shaft.

"Great, Sherri," said Lee, hoisting his tote to his other side and peering down the crack in the floor. "Now the elevator will decide to short out over the lead in that pencil and we'll have to use the stairs."

"That was my favorite pencil," moaned Sherri. "Wouldn't you know it? Can you get it, Lee?"

"Sherri! It's probably at the bottom of the shaft by now," Hal exclaimed. "You've got at least a dozen pencils in your hand."

"I think it's long gone, Sherri," Lee confirmed. "Come on, unload your stuff in your room, wash the warpaint— and tears—from your face, and let's eat."

They walked along the shiny floor of the blinding-white hall. The only relief from the starkness was the pastel-colored doors of the housing units. "We were in the yellow wing," Sherri said, remembering.

"I am still in the same unit—number 220—in the pink wing," Lee said. "The blue doors, in the section right next to mine, are the units held open for visitors. So I'm going to put you in units 230 and 232. The passes are in my suite, so that's where we're headed." He stopped abruptly. "Actually, my unit's further than yours'. Just drop your stuff here and pick it back up on the way from my place."

They thankfully shed their gear in a heap where they stood. Caro flexed her arms and raised her shoulders. "I wish I had a lighter aud-vis," she grumbled, rubbing her neck.

"Of course the size of your backpack doesn't come into it at all," Hal said, nudging it with the toe of his boot.

"I just want to get out of these suits," wailed Sherri. "I feel half boiled."

"I think you mean 'half baked,' " Lee said. He added smoothly, "Come along, children."

Lee pulled out from around his neck a chain from which the pass bar to his room dangled. He leaned down and slipped the bar into the lock panel to the left of the door. There was a sharp click and he turned the knob and pushed the door open. "Welcome," he said with a flourish.

The living room was strangely still. At the base of the floor lamp, positioned over the easy chair, there was a tidy stack of Circulating Papers. The matching tan couch had two triangular pillows of exactly the same hue as the rose-colored lamp shade. They leaned at identical angles against the opposite arms of the couch. The walls were bare, but there was a faint mark in the soft rose plasti-coat, hinting that at one time a picture might have hung above the couch. The large double-glazed window was unblinded, and brittle rays from a beacon washed the pink from the opposite wall.

The kitchen nook, off the living room, was uncluttered. A white teakettle stood neatly on the inset hot plate, and both the oven and cooler were shining clean. The sink was devoid of dirty dishes and bone dry.

Sherri and Caro looked at each other. "This, this I did not imagine," Sherri declared, arms raised. "Indeed, could not imagine." Then, in normal tones to Lee, "How long have you lived here? You do live here? You?"

"What?" asked Lee in an injured tone. Then he exploded. "Why does every woman hold dear the totally outdated, biased, bigoted view of the single man as an idiot in his home?"

"Not an idiot," Sherri said sweetly. "A pig."

Lee was speechless with indignation. His neck muscles knotted and his eyes became dark slits as he stared down at Sherri who stood cool and unperturbed, unconscious of the absurd blue and orange paint streaks across her face. Hal looked worriedly from Lee to Sherri and back again. Ricky was dancing up and down in an effort to side with his hero and all men in general. Caro rolled her eyes and asked Lee for a glass of water.

"Oh, oh, sure, Caro," he came to with an effort. "The water dispenser is on the left side of the cooler. And there's ice—I'll show you where I keep my glasses."

Caro shot a glare at Sherri, who shrugged disdainfully and disappeared into the bathroom. "Hey," an escalating wail ascended from that room, "Why didn't anyone tell me I had paint all over my face!"

When Sherri emerged, damp, with shadows of purple on her nose and cheek and transparent streaks of orange like juice stains on her chin, Lee graciously offered her a glass of ice water.

Hal said comfortingly, "It doesn't look that bad, Sherri."

Caro turned and walked over to the window. Lee's suite overlooked the animal enclosures. Under the harsh glare of the beacons the cages seemed frosted with tiny splinters of glass. Caro watched as dark shadows moved restlessly back and forth, behind the shimmering bars. She pulled at the collar of the suit lining so snug around her throat. Her face began to itch in the sealed atmosphere of the building and she held her glass of ice water up to the ragged scar.

"Let's go," Lee broke in. "Take your stuff to your units, change your clothes, do what you have to do, and meet me in the dining room in twenty minutes. Okay? We'll eat, and then Caro and I need to get to work." He gave Hal the pass bar for unit 230 and Caro the one for 232. "You remember how to get to the dining room, don't you?"

93

"I remember where everything is," Ricky said. "I know where the blue units are, too." He pointed. "Just go back to the main hall and turn left and there they are. Opposite the stairs, right?" Lee nodded. "And the cafeteria is right there, too—beside the stairwell. I remember everything," he repeated smugly. "And I never get lost."

"Good," Lee replied, amused. "I appoint you navigator to the other three—who do get lost, occasionally."

Ricky took his new position as navigator very seriously. He herded Hal, Sherri, and Caro mercilessly first to the pile of gear they had left in the main hall, and then to the doors of their rooms. "I'll come and pick you up in twenty minutes," he informed the girls before disappearing into the next door unit that he was to share with Hal.

Caro and Sherri looked at each other. "Well, I feel cared for," Sherri announced straightfaced.

"I feel watched," Caro said. "It is *not* the same thing. Lee must be informed that such casual endowments of power can be dangerous."

Caro slid the pass bar in and out of the panel beside the blue door. At the click, Sherri yanked it open and stumbled across the threshold, scattering pencils and paints across the gleaming sapphire-blue floor. Caro stepped over them and walked directly into the bedroom and dropped her gear on the floor by one of the beds.

"Do you want to shower first?" she called to Sherri.

"No, go ahead. You'll be faster than me. And I'm still trying to pick up all these stupid pencils. Ooh. Now I've offended them—they'll never let me draw anything worthwhile now. Only joking—I really didn't mean it. Wow, can you all move when you want to. Look at you, way under the couch." Sherri's voice faded as Caro, smiling at her friend's bizarre chatter, went into the bathroom and turned on the shower.

August, 2456
Actaeon—

    I am being haunted by a molecular physiologist by the name of Marchenko. Everywhere I turn, whatever I do, he is at my elbow. He joined me at breakfast: "Dr. Coleney, can I get you more tea?" Later, in my lab, a knock on the door. Yes, Actaeon, it was Marchenko, ostensibly to borrow a stereoscope, but, as there are several scopes in Physiology, I knew it really was to try and get me into a conversation. It could be that he is a Community official, trying to trip me up, checking to see if I am doing my job; or it could be that he thinks I am on the verge of a research breakthrough. In any case, I am going to keep him loaded with work; perhaps that will stop his prying.

                                     —Reginald

8

Red Skeletons

he cafeteria, aside from a new frozen dessert dispenser, was unchanged. Ricky welcomed the machine with open arms, heaping high a soup bowl with the soft, fruit-flavored dessert.

The dining room was empty. Their voices echoed through the large room, their only accompaniment the hollow hum of cooler units and the whir of the drying fan in the steri-wash unit.

"So, what are you three going to do while Caro and I make ourselves known to the carepies?" asked Lee. He tilted back his chair, replete from two large bowls of Miriam's fish stew and several sandwiches.

"Can we just look around?" Ricky asked.

Hal offered, "I wouldn't mind going for a walk."

"Sure," Lee said amiably. "If a door's unlocked, consider it an open invitation. You all know better than to mess around with instruments and papers on desks. How about you, Sherri?"

"I would like to see the carepies, too." Lee shook his head. "Nope. Sorry, but at this point it's Caro and me only. I'd like to open it up to you all, but we have to have some kind of control factor in this."

"Just what are you trying to do with the carepies?" asked Sherri. Hal leaned forward, curious, his glasses flashing.

Lee opened his mouth, and then closed it again. He looked at Caro. "Let's just say that Caro and carepies seem to have an affinity for one another. They communicate on a very deep level—a non-verbal level. I want the Community to realize that the carepies here at the End Base shouldn't be subjected to such barbaric conditions. They are too intelligent and too sensitive—I believe they're experiencing psychological and emotional pain."

"So what does Caro do?" asked Ricky, baffled.

"Her communicating—and receiving communication from the carepies should indicate to the Community that they are dealing with a more complex animal than they realize. Then, hopefully, they will begin to treat the carepies with a little more respect and call off these physiological stress tests."

"What stress tests are they doing?" asked Hal.

Lee chewed on his lower lip. "This is highly confidential, you realize." He cleared his throat. "They're observing them to see if they can be used in the underground network of rivers to carry tracking equipment for map-making."

"But that's not salt water," Caro said. "Carepies are marine, not fresh-water animals. They couldn't survive!"

"That's right, but they're remarkably tough—they take a long time to die," Lee said grimly. "And it doesn't matter, you know—there are so many carepies out in the Pantropic ocean." Lee leaned forward, his eyes hard. "And this is for the good of humankind and the advancement of science. And, of course, it is not forever. Once they know what the conditions are like down there, and they have a rough map, they'll come up with a more adequate robotship

98

that will replace the carepies." He swallowed. "It makes me want to throw up."

Caro looked down at her plate and pushed it away. "I suppose, then, the few carepies that are left will be named a Class A species and kept under surveillance in an aquarium."

Lee snorted. "Probably. But you and I and Dr. Lutes are going to give them a run for their money first," he said, banging his hand on the table. "Are you finished, Caro? You haven't tried any of the browser ice cream yet. How'd you like it, Ricky?"

"B-b-browser?" Ricky asked through numb lips.

"Yeah, not bad, is it? Every once in a while I am brought face to face with the good of science. Browser ice cream is one of the truly useful things that we've come up with on Clytie. And notice that we at the End Base have it first. For once we got something ahead of Main."

"Browser ice cream," Sherri repeated, swallowing hard. Hal looked green.

"Browser milk is awful," Caro exclaimed. "My mom brought some home and we tried it. It tastes like—stewed cactus—and it's a horrible grey color."

"That's where the miracle of modern science comes into play," said Lee. "They color it, and take away the natural taste, and sweeten it, and throw in all kinds of fruit—whatever's in season. It's good—really. It is, isn't it Ricky?"

"Yeah. It is," admitted Ricky. "But I can't believe it's made from browser milk."

"Well, are you going to have some?" Lee asked Caro.

"I'm pretty full—and I want to see the carepies. Maybe I'll wait till tomorrow," she answered in a rush.

"Yeah, me too," echoed Sherri. Hal nodded in vigorous agreement.

"Okay . . . Let's go, Caro." Lee pushed his chair back and got to his feet. He began gathering their dishes on his tray. "Hal, you don't mind running these through the steri-wash for us, do you?"

Hal shook his head. "Not at all."

"See you three later—I hope." Caro grinned nervously.

"Well, this gang's dwindling in size, guys," said Sherri glumly after Lee and Caro had gone through the swinging doors into the hall. "Where should we go first?"

"Let's check out the observation pit. And try the doors to the labs," replied Ricky immediately. "And I want to go down to the basement, too."

"All the sights, eh?" Hal said with a wry smile.

"All at once?" Sherri asked. "Maybe we should break ourselves in gradually."

"Aw, there's no reason to be scared, Sherri," Ricky said patronizingly. "Uncle Lee's caught all the sighted lumies."

"Maybe there's just one more left," Sherri said in a weird whisper. "Just one more—with claws this long, and bulging, red eyes, and teeth that drip blood—right over THERE!" she shrieked, pointing over Ricky's head. Ricky sat petrified.

"Very funny, Sherri," Hal said. "Don't ever go into acting—you'd starve."

"Yeah, you'd starve," Ricky echoed weakly.

Lee and Caro walked in silence to the stairwell. "Oh, my gear," Caro said. "I forgot—"

"You won't need your wetsuit or airvest tonight. It's already late, Caro. We've had a long trip and you need to be well-rested for tomorrow. Tonight I just want you to get a feel for the conditions that the carepies are under." Lee spoke in a detached tone. Caro glanced at him, puzzled by his manner.

Their footsteps rang in the stairwell and Caro held back her hair from her face at the rush of warm air from the lower levels.

"The marine lab—the carepie tank—is located in the basement," Lee continued. "Obviously, it makes more sense to have it there with the extreme weight of water. Also, it's right next to the water recycling plant."

Lee's chattering, Caro thought in surprise. *He's nervous.* She glanced at his face: a serious, impenetrable mask.

Lee's pace was quickening, his long stride jumping the occasional step. Caro began to pant in her effort to keep up with him. By the time they reached the heavy basement doors she was hot and her face burned as perspiration ran along her scars.

Directly opposite the stairwell was a high-security red door with the Community logo imprinted at eye level. Lee strode up to the door and manually entered a series of numbers into the lock panel. The door went through several spasmodic shudders and slid open, disappearing into the wall. Lee motioned for Caro to go through and closely followed her into a tiny room. The door shut tight behind them; there was an abrupt cut-off of the light and wind that had followed them down the stairwell and across the hall. Before Caro could panic in the utter black, Lee pushed them through a second door.

It was oppressive. Dead warm. And dark—so dark that Caro stopped short, causing Lee to stumble into her. "Can't see?" he asked. "Your eyes will adjust—just stand still a minute." He placed his hand on her shoulder.

Gradually her senses began penetrating the stifling atmosphere. Caro felt, rather than heard, the familiar movement of water, but contained, hushed, velveted. A soft bumping sound, and then another. Under the dull red glow of the low-hanging lamps a non-reflecting wall stood two or three meters from them. It was higher than her head.

"The tank is directly before us," Lee said. His voice was hushed in the windless room. "It's about twenty by thirty meters—we're facing the longer side. The entire tank—top and sides—are blacked out with a thick polymer. Those red lamps are a control against any visible light entering the tank; carepies don't seem to be able to see much in the red spectrum. The reports vary, but all of them indicate that red light is seen by carepies as either gradient shades of grey or total blackness." He was slowly guiding her to the edge of the tank and she placed her palm against it. The side was rough: thick and sticky. But when she pulled her hand away it was clean; the material remained clinging tightly to the glass. She put both hands flat against the tank and felt the water singing behind it.

"Are they in salt water now?" she asked and wondered at the strangeness of the way her words stood still in this veiled room. She glanced at Lee, seeing only the outline of his face and figure airbrushed by the dark red glow.

"It's a mixture, really. More salt than fresh, but not an ocean concentration of salts. More like the ocean tributaries during the tidal shifts."

"So they're okay—in that way, at any rate—right now?" she asked hopefully.

Lee shook his head. "They don't choose to live in the tributaries, Caro. Their home is the open ocean—full salt."

"How do I get in?" Caro asked abruptly. "If the top is sealed, how does a diver get in?"

"Through the intake pipe. It's a little crude, but it works. Can you see okay now?"

"I think so," Caro replied doubtfully. The red lamps lit little; under their irradiation the dark shadows did not dissipate but were outlined. They moved under her feet and all around her, large and grotesque, with a life of their own. She stepped carefully.

"Here, take my hand. I'll show you where you'll enter the tank." He led Caro slowly along the side of the aquarium to where a tube sloped from the wall down into the tank. "The water treatment center is across the hall. You enter the lock in the water room and swim down into the tank. Of course, I'll turn off the circulation before you enter the tube—you won't need to fight the current."

"It's awfully small . . . " Caro looked at the diameter of the intake tube with alarm.

"I've been through it—it's really not all that bad," Lee replied. "I'm going to take you to the observation and control deck now. It'll give you an idea of the inside of the tank and you can get a glimpse of the carepies."

She followed him, ducking under the shadow of the intake pipe, down a short distance under what she assumed was the output pipe, brushing along the sticky side of the dark tank. The warm, strong grip of Lee's hand on hers was the only solid reality in this room of close, red-black shadows.

Lee paused. "We're going to go through two doors. The first will take us into a closet-sized room that is pitch black. Once you close the door behind you, it will activate the next door, which opens into the staircase leading to the control room. The staircase—and the control room—have normal white light. Although the light is kept dimmer than out in the halls, it will seem very bright until your eyes adjust. Okay? You ready? Remember, I can't open the door into the staircase until the door behind you is closed tight."

"Okay," answered Caro. She licked her dry lips and swallowed hard.

It was very dark in the tiny, airless room. Caro crowded close to Lee, hesitating at first to close the door, unwilling to shut out even the dull-red, eerie light from the aquarium room. She heard Lee try the door to the staircase.

"Caro, close the door tight—the lock has to click shut before this door will activate." She drove herself to do it, pulling the door tight against its jamb, hearing it click, feeling the utter blackness fall upon her, forcing herself to focus on Lee's hand so real and warm and human. It seemed an unaccountable length of time before the door opened before them and a spray of light blinded their eyes; Caro nearly sobbed with relief.

Lee stood there, one foot stumbling into the first stair. "I must have slow eyes—"

"Mine are slow in the dark, but quick in the light," Caro said, smiling, hearing their words echo off the ceiling back at them. Everything around her—the white plasti-coated walls, the narrow steps running in a semicircle to a windowed door, the exhaust fan grinding above them—seemed bathed in a brilliance that exorcised the terror from her heart.

"I take it you approve of the stairs," Lee said, his mouth twitching and his eyes, now adjusted to the light, gleaming impishly.

Caro laughed, not caring in her state of utter relief, that he addressed her fear. "Yes—an impeccable design," she declared in a most Sherri-like manner.

Lee smiled, and she followed him up the stairs and into the control room.

It was larger than she had imagined it would be. Again, it was dimly lit, but with softly directed white light that settled the shadows, rather than giving them form as had the red lamps. The one-way windows overlooking the tank ran the length of the room and before them stood a row of desks with large-screen monitors and computer entry boards. Although Caro peered through cupped hands against the windows, she saw nothing but a vague red glow around what looked like a large, black inverted hole.

Lee had settled into a desk and was rapidly entering a series of numbers into first one computer terminal and then another. The muted tapping of his fingers on the flat entry board and the respondent electric muttering of the computer filtered through the air. Caro stared restlessly at one desk and then another, running her hands over the tops of terminals, trying to guess what some scraps of paper tossed carelessly on a tabletop were about.

"Here," he finally called. "Sit down at this computer. I want to show you what the tank looks like."

She slid into the chair in front of a large monitor. Lee focused on the entry board in front of him. "Okay," he said. "Here are the pictures taken of the tank while it was being constructed—"

Caro saw an silicone-clear ark positioned in the middle of a field of wires, pipes, and ducts. Men crawled on the flimsy scaffolding around it. Computer lenses, like small portholes, were cut and mounted into place all along the sides of the huge shell. As she watched, walls grew tight around the ark, wires were tucked into the ceiling, plasticoat camouflaged the ducts and all but two pipes. From the other side of the wall, like two skinny arms, the pipes held the tank. Water, white and furious, began to gush from one pipe filling the ark until the spray rose and the air above it glittered with precarious rainbows.

"Now," Lee murmured, hitting his entry board, "this is in preparation for the carepies—"

The water circled easily in the ark: clear and clean, with just a hint of emerald. In the rush at the inflow tube, a soft spray rose. Caro licked her lips, half expecting to taste the sea salt. Two men came and initialized a set of robots that with mechanical eptness covered the top of the tank with a netting of thick silicone that grew tight and closed up the ark. Two more robots were brought into the room.

They sprayed a thick, black polymer onto every millimeter of the silicone plating. The ark disappeared.

"And, the installation of the carepie pod—"

Caro watched, sickened, as round packages—five large, two small—wrapped in water-soaked insulation, shot into view, carried on the platform-covered tines of the speeding log lifters. Down the End Base halls, from the tunnel by the cargo elevator, the lifters came swaying. They entered the double doors opposite the room where the ark lay buried under the manmade darkness.

One by one, the round, dripping bundles were tipped into a rectangular-shaped box high in the air. Infrared radiation pictures picked up the bundles sliding helplessly down the input tube and into the blackness of the tank. Unable to move, they sank, bouncing gently when they struck the bottom; a small round object tipped on end as a bigger bundle hit it broadside; it, in turn, was sent ricocheting off the side by another.

A diver climbed up a portable set of steps and entered the rectangular lock in the input tube. She wore an infrared radiation-sensitive hood, and a knife was strapped to her ankle. In one hand the diver carried a tranquilizer spear gun, and in the other a curved-toothed rake on a long pole. Caro saw the peculiar, reddish, three-dimensional outline of her figure photographed by the infrared detectors as she slid through the tube and into the tank. The diver hooked off the insulating blankets, tranquilizer ready, but the carepies did not move.

The screen went blue blank.

Caro still stared at it. Lee pounded on the entry board, reprogramming the computer at an angry pace.

"And here are the carepies now," he said.

The screen darkened. "Watch," Lee commanded, as Caro glanced at him, uncertain. His fingers moved as he scowled at the monitor, flicking to each camera, scanning the pool.

"There—see? Remember, the only way we can view them is through infrared radiation. Look—right there. When they're facing the camera it's harder to see them . . . Okay, here's a good one." Caro leaned into the screen, eyes peering where Lee was pointing.

"Yes," she said. "I couldn't see a thing, and now suddenly, there they are. It's weird, though. It's like I'm seeing their skeletons, only in red."

"That's all you'll see when you're in the water," Lee said. "You know that you'll have to go into the tank alone. Even if I didn't have to be outside to monitor you and operate the locks, I still couldn't for control purposes."

"I know," she said, not looking at him.

Three large carepies, heads together, hovered in the center of the tank. The two calves moved in slow circles around them, bobbing at each other, feigning bites, and then falling away, settling in the water. One baby swam on top of an adult and rested there, lowering his little beak-face on the cow's back. The other nipped at the tail tucked under the banding fin of the other cow, hanging on to it like a life line.

"I thought there were five adults and two babies," Caro said.

"Yeah," replied Lee, absently, tapping at the board and frowning deeply into his monitor.

Caro saw them before Lee said a word. The other two adults—an older cow and a bull—were on the bottom of the tank. Scattered like two husks, several meters from the others, they lay unmoving, their circular fins still.

"I want to go in," Caro said in a low, hard voice. Lee looked at her and then back at the screen. "I need to go in," her voice rose unsteadily.

"You're tired, Caro," he replied gently. "And I honestly think that we need to concentrate on the five that are still swimming."

"They're not dead yet," Caro said stubbornly. "We couldn't see them if they were dead—there wouldn't be any infrared from them—I need to see them tonight. Lee, please, it will be too late tomorrow, I know it."

He made a move to say something and then closed his mouth and looked away. Caro knew without a doubt that he had been about to say that it was too late all ready. "Lee, it's for me—not just the carepies," she lied. "If I don't go in right now, I won't be able to. I'll think about it too much, I won't sleep, and, and, I won't be able to tomorrow, that's all there is to it," she finished, grasping upon her mother's phrasing.

Lee refused to meet her eyes. "Tomorrow, Caro," he repeated. "You need to rest."

"Lee," she said deliberately, "if you don't let me go in tonight and those carepies die, I will not go in tomorrow or any other time. Those two carepies are the only things giving me the courage to go into that tank." She knew that it was true even as the words came out of her mouth, just as she knew that she would later quake with the shame of them. Caro's eyes, burning intensely through her patched, harlequin mask, forced Lee to meet their light.

She was going to the carepies.

August, 2456
Actaeon—

    I have set up a "permanent" field camp and take research teams there for as long as our supplies hold out— four, maybe five days at a time. It is the longest field research to date in the End region.

    Large, silent beasts surround our camp; we see the reflected purple glow of their huge eyes. They comb through the garbage pits, their jaws slicing through the so-called invincible polymer sacks that hold our supplies. One of the team members taught one of the bearlike creatures to feed out of her hand. We have, of course, killed several for further study at the Base.

    Actaeon, it is not the beasts, but the wind that will never be tamed here. We cannot block its chill whine from our communication channel; it fills our suit intercoms until, nearly maddened, we snap them off and sign to one another. Marchenko has taken to shaking his head sporadically, even when inside the Base building, as if the wind still fills his ears.

                                 —Reginald

9

Giants in the Dark

She was going to the carepies, lying still as death at the bottom of the ark. Going to do—what? Just be with them, put her hands on them, let them know they were not alone.

Caro stepped into the heavy silicone suit, pulling on the resilient material, sliding her arms through the thick sleeves. Lee handed her the air vest and then checked the fastenings after she had hauled it on. "This suit is a little big for you; you're likely to feel some dampness creep in." They hadn't bothered to get Caro's gear; she was using the same suit the diver in the computer pictures had worn.

Lee drew the transparent hood over her head, carefully joining it to the air vest, asking her if she could breathe easily, adjusting the volume on her inner intercom. He double- and triple-checked the seal around the hood, and then attached a safety unit of compressed air to her outer vest. "Your suit is rated good for ten hours . . . you're going to be in there maybe twenty minutes, Caro—no more—I mean it, you must listen to me when I call you out. The safety unit will kick in if the oxygen level in your hood drops below the regulation minimum. It alone is good for sixty

111

minutes. It makes me feel better to know that—how about you?" He flashed a lopsided grin.

"How would I know I was using the safety unit of air?" Caro asked, more for Lee's sake, to let him know that she was listening. Although his words were sinking in, the forefront of her mind was occupied with the carepies. *I'm on my way, I'm on my way,* she sang to them.

"The computer would tell you. If by some bizarre event the computer failed, a truly dreadful alarm would go off and you'd have no choice but to get out of the tank and out of the suit before you went deaf or mad. Okay—here are your weights," he said, handing her a small belt.

"It's so light . . . "

"Remember, this water's not full brine like you're used to. You'll sink easier, and you'll work harder swimming. Now, it doesn't matter what tube you come back through— I'll be here and have both locks ready, okay?"

"Wait—how can I find the tubes after I'm in the tank?" Caro panicked. "It'll be all dark except for the carepies, and me!"

"The tubes are clearly marked. There's a ring of in-frared sensitive bacteria around each tube. I'm sorry—I should have showed you that on the computer. Caro, go through the input tube, and the second you find yourself through, turn around and look. If you can't see the ring, come back out, right away. Don't risk trying to find it later. Caro, look at me—do you understand?"

"Yes. I'll remember to look."

"Okay," Lee acknowledged grimly. "Now, this goes on your right shin." He knelt down and wrapped a short spear gun around her leg. "I take it you know how to use it?"

"I won't need it," she said absently. *I'm on my way, carepies.*

"I said, I take it you know how to use it—do you?" Lee repeated forcefully. "Do you?"

"Yes! I know how to use it—but you don't know anything about carepies if you think I may even have the vaguest possibility of needing it!" she burst out, stung from her reverie.

"Good," said Lee, an odd quirk illuminating his mouth. "Prove me to be an ignoramus." He got to his feet. "I'll hand your fins to you after you climb up the ladder."

Caro walked awkwardly up the ladder, the silicone suit legs alternately sticking together and tearing apart, sending out rough notes of protest. She waited on the little platform. Lee, with precise determination, tapped commands into the entry board mounted on the side of the octopuslike structure from which the intake tube and lock grew. From her perch alongside the lock, Caro gazed at the three large screens set into the wall: one monitored the five carepies hanging subdued in the water; one screen displayed the older cow and bull lying motionless on the bottom of the tank; the third, Caro knew, would be fixed on her.

Caro instinctively shrank from the appearance of the lock, choosing instead to look at the carepies, Lee, the blank screen—anything but the coffinlike box she must find herself lying in very soon. *Lock.* What a horrible term, but how perfect: she would be locked from light and warmth and wind . . . Again she tore her mind from fear and focused on the carepies. *I'm on my way—almost there.*

In the end it was Lee who was strong enough for both of them. The top of the lock popped open, water dripping onto the tiled floor. Lee held out her fins to her, holding Caro's terrified eyes in his steady gaze, meeting her fear unflinchingly. He never said a word, but Caro took with her a measure of his calm, unable to cognitively understand, but convinced down to her bones and sinews that somehow she would not be alone.

I'm on my way, carepies. Caro lay flat on her stomach in the lock. The double click of the lid sounded like rifle shots. *No more light.* "You'll feel the water entering from behind you now, Caro." Lee's solid voice filled the darkness. She saw the hazy red outline of her hands and arms stretched before her. Lee had shot the tunnel full of infrared; Caro would not be in absolute blackness.

The water swirled around her, knocking her on her side. Caro began gasping in gut reflex to the unseen cold assailing her from all sides. "Caro, count with me," came Lee's firm voice. "The lock will fill in 35 seconds. Count with me: one . . . two . . . three . . . " Desperately conquering the spasming muscles in her throat she forced herself to croak: "four . . . six . . . seven . . . eight . . . " She began to breathe easier, concentrating on the pulse of his voice and the red glow of her hands. *Almost there, carepies.* "twenty-three . . . twenty-four . . . twenty-five . . . " The water was heavy, pushing against her, creeping insidiously between her suit and her body. She shivered; her eyelashes brushed her faceplate as she blinked. "Thirty-three, thirty-four, okay, Caro, the gate in front of you should be open—" And it was and she was sliding through the dark, following the red of her hands. The tube bent slightly to the right—was she past the hall now? It sloped more steeply but Caro, having lost any sense of up and down, only knew that she moved more swiftly, cutting through the dark with her glowing fins. *I'm almost there, carepies.*

"Caro, you're almost to the end of the tube—slow down—remember to look for the ring of light around the entrance to the tubes. Slow down!" Lee's voice thundered, shocking her from her senseless rush. Her glowing hands stretched out to the sides to slow her descent; instinctively Caro curled her legs in towards her body, slowing, slowing. Too late, she shot into the tank.

But turned and saw the pulsing glow like a red ring of stars in the night. "I see it," she called, her voice high. "I see the entrance."

114

"Good girl." Relief sounded in his voice. "Now, the five carepies are to your right, at about the same level as you. The two on the bottom are almost straight ahead, a little to your right, and down," Lee directed. "Caro, sick animals do not always know what they're doing—use that spear gun if you have to. It'll just knock them out; it won't kill them."

Caro gave no indication of having heard him. She was gliding down, down, scissoring with her fins, cutting through the darkness, flying to the fallen carepies.

"Remember, Caro, they can't see you—you can see them only because of the infrared radiation sensors on your faceplate. They can smell you and feel your movements in the water, but approach them carefully; they will not be able to recognize you as a diver," Lee warned emphatically, his voice close to her ear. "And for goodness sake, slow down! You can't judge how close you are to the bottom—and you're very close."

Caro, getting her vertical cues from the carepies, twisted around in the water, drawing herself into a standing position. She wanted to approach the carepies from the side rather than above, so she was still several meters away. She tread water, trying to guess how close to the bottom she really was. Then she saw the water worms coiled in a heap, gleaming like thin ropes of living rubies on the velvet floor. Thankful, she kicked back into a swimming position, skimming low past the water worms, on to the carepies.

"Good!" Another outburst of relief came through the intercom from Lee.

Caro treaded water in front of the smaller of the two downed carepies. The cow's neck was stretched out, flat along the bottom; her beak was open and there was a fluttering movement along her throat. Caro moved to its side, put out her hand and gently touched the broad back of the creature. One emerald eye opened, glowing crimson

115

in the infrared, but the old carepie did not move. Caro reached out her other hand and touched the round knob of a head, thrilling to the silky feel, sorrowing with the too-quick, too-light breaths. The carepie rolled its eye but remained quiet.

Caro continued to stroke the frail-looking neck and the rubbery dorsal surface, watching the puzzled eye of the carepie search the darkness. The old cow raised her head and Caro hardly dared breathe for fear of frightening the carepie into a deadly flight against the invisible thick sides of the tank. Gently, so gently, she slid her palm under its nostril holes. Surely the carepie could smell her goodwill?

The carepie cautiously examined Caro's hand, exploring it in tentative whiffs of water, the long, tongue-like gill protruding, growing scarlet, wandering over the girl's palm in an effort to read her.

The large bull, two or three meters away from Caro and the cow, raised his head. Caro, glancing up, wondered at the misshapen beak and face; the bull could not open his eyes. Caro spoke softly through the intercom, trying not to move her hand from before the cow's beak. "Lee, the bull's head looks beaten up—why?"

"He kept trying to find a way out, Caro. He was the older bull—the navigator—the one that would have led the pod through their migration pattern."

The cow seemed pleased with her findings. She didn't budge but stared around her in an interested fashion. Caro drew her hand back, stroked the cow's dorsal surface again, and then circled her, moving towards the bull.

"Caro—be *very* careful," breathed Lee.

The old bull reared his head back at her approach. She glided to the side of him, but he spun around facing her. His fin began a slow wave pattern and he hovered centimeters off the floor of the tank. Caro stayed where she was, slowly offering him her hand. It was a long, tense while before he relaxed and wafted water through his nostril holes at her. Then the many-folded, narrow gill came out exploring Caro's palm.

Suddenly she felt a bump from behind and found herself sailing over the old bull, kicking desperately in an effort to avoid crashing into him. She felt one fin brush across the top of his back.

Lee's laughter filled her hood. "It's just a curious baby, Caro. I'm sorry—I couldn't warn you—I didn't see it approaching until too late. Are you okay?"

"Yes." She giggled in nervous relief. "I almost crashed, though."

"The whole pod is closing in," Lee blurted. "Oh, mamma! Just stay still where you are, Caro." He held his hand poised over the underwater sonic alarm that would scatter the pod—just in case.

"I'm not going anywhere," Caro said firmly. "This is the whole point of me coming here, remember?" She tread water, holding out her arms at right angles, waving them in the water, trying to spread the essence of herself and telegraph to them that she was safe.

A baby came straight toward her, butting into her arm in bewilderment. Its bright eyes searched the darkness for this strange, soft creature that could not be seen. The little beak-face was joined by the second baby, busily wuffling its gill in Caro's general direction.

The younger bull hovered in the water a few meters off while the two mothers circled closer like matronly tugboats, their necks outstretched and beaks half open. Again Caro noticed the fluttering tremor at their throats. Caro smoothed the back of the smallest baby and it bumped closer in response.

"Caro, it's time to come out—past time, actually. You've been in the tank for almost twenty-five minutes.

117

Turn around and look to your left and up. You should see the ring of bacteria around the intake tube."

Caro ran her hands over the baby, who was lipping her shoulder familiarly. She spun around, swimming carefully around the young bull who turned in response to this benevolent shadow gliding by. The babies raced after her and a cow followed them a short distance behind. *I'll be back, carepies.*

Caro frog-kicked up, her legs aching long before she reached the red ring around the intake tube. She slipped through the mouth of the tube and felt the grate slide back into place, shutting the babies out. *I'll see you tomorrow, babies.*

It was a long, weary swim back up the tube. There was no room to frog-kick, though she banged her knees on the sides trying. Caro forced her legs to move steadily, evenly, utilizing the power of her fins. She was trembling when she reached the lock, scrabbling along the sides to draw herself up and over the ridge of the gate.

"Okay, I'm closing the gate behind you, Caro." She felt the motion of the water cease as it shut. "Now, just thirty seconds or so while the water drains and then the lid will open. How are you doing? You're pretty quiet," asked Lee with concern.

"Fine," she gasped wearily, automatically. *I will be back, carepies. Tomorrow. Wait for me.*

The lid flew open and Lee was there, his arms pulling her up, half carrying her down the step ladder, seating her, swaying and dripping, on the desk chair. He frantically ripped the seal off the hood and pulled it off her head, staring into her face, his concern flowing like a current into her. "I'm fine I said," Caro replied to his eyes, a trifle irritated to be yanked so thoroughly from the still under-water world of the carepies. Her eyes, just half open, hurt in the light and she closed them completely. *Wait for me, old cow. Wait for me, old bull. I'll be back, babies.*

Lee pulled off her silicone suit, leaving it in a heap on the floor. Caro, her eyes still closed, began trembling in her damp clothes. "Caro," Lee said, his voice distant to her, "Caro . . . " He picked her up and carried her on his back, hurrying up the two flights of stairs to her suite.

Sherri, Hal, and Ricky, lounging in the living room of the girls' suite, were drinking duck tea and talking. They leapt up in alarm as Lee burst through the door with Caro slumped across his back.

Sherri's mouth flew open, but Lee cut her off. "She's fine, she's fine. Shut up, Sherri, and make some good, strong tea—" Then he was through the living room and into the bedroom, carefully depositing Caro on the nearest bed.

"I said I'm fine," Caro said crossly, her body quaking.

"Of course you are, of course you are—didn't you just hear me tell that to the others?" Lee said soothingly, heaping blankets around her.

"Sherri! Where's the tea?" he barked. Her eyes wide but her mouth firmly shut, Sherri came in with a steaming cup of duck tea. Lee took it from her.

"Here. Drink it, Caro." He closed her hands around the hot cup and she bent forward over it, soaking in the steam, the warmth. Her hands trembled as she lifted the mug to her mouth, but she drank and drank. "Bring in the whole pot, Sherri," Lee said quietly, not looking at her. "And another cup, please."

Sherri wordlessly disappeared and almost immediately came back with a tea pot and empty cup. Lee refilled Caro's mug and poured a cup for himself. She drank down another mug and stopped shaking quite so violently. Suddenly she began to cry.

"Close the door on your way out, Sherri, please," Lee said. Sherri turned and left; the door only banged a little.

Lee took the cup from Caro's hands and set it on the table by the bed. He held Caro against his chest, drawing the blanket up around her shoulders, silently holding her while she wept like a worn-out child. In the middle of a half-sob, half-sigh she fell asleep. He set her gently back on the pillows and tucked the blanket around her.

Lee stepped out of the room, pulling the door shut behind him. Three pairs of frantic eyes met him, one pair still with the attached mouth firmly shut. Lee relented. "Sorry, I'm sorry, Sherri, but the last thing she needed was to have to talk—or listen to chatter. Thanks for getting the tea ready so quickly."

"Actually Hal did," Sherri admitted. "Is she really okay?"

"Yes, yes—she's just totally exhausted. Will you please go in there and try to take those wet clothes off her? And, listen to me—leave her alone! Don't make her say a word to you that she doesn't want to! And, if she wakes up in the night, upset, for any reason, COME AND GET ME. Do you understand?" Lee demanded, hoarse with the effort.

"I am not an idiot," Sherri said in an offended tone. She got up and disappeared quietly into the bedroom.

Hal and Ricky stared up at him. Lee slumped down on the chair opposite them. "Ricky, Caro is fine. She just got overtired and chilled in the water. After a good sleep she will be as good as new. Really," Lee said earnestly into the black, worried eyes.

Ricky nodded, relaxing. Hal leaned back on the sofa.

"Maybe you two should call it a night," Lee suggested.

Hal cleared his throat. "That sounds like a good idea. What time should we be up tomorrow?"

"Sleep as late as you want," Lee replied. "You're on vacation, remember? See you tomorrow, then." He got up, stretched wearily, and left the suite. However, he didn't head in the direction of his housing unit; instead he began to sprint down the hall toward the stairwell.

Sherri peeked her head around the bedroom door. "Is he gone?" she whispered.

Ricky panicked. "He just left—should I go get him?!"

"No, no, no. Caro's fast asleep—she barely moved. I just didn't want to talk to Lee when he was in such a horrible mood. Honestly, you'd think I had no sense to hear him talk!" she exploded in a harsh whisper.

"I think he was just concerned about Caro," Hal said comfortingly. "He probably feels responsible for her getting so exhausted. He doesn't know Caro—she never knows when to quit."

"Mom says she's as stubborn as Dad," Ricky announced. "And Dad one time sat beside an insect burrow for fifty-four hours straight waiting for whatever lived in there to come out."

"Did the bug ever come out?" Sherri asked with interest.

"Nah—a snake did—it turned out not to be an insect burrow at all. That was way back on Earth, when Dad was young," Ricky explained.

Sherri and Hal stuffed their fists in their mouths to keep from laughing out loud.

In the Aquatics Lab control room, Lee glanced at the clock, waiting impatiently for print-outs from the computer's data banks. He tapped his fingers on a terminal and stared hard at the dataprint. Finally the last was through. He grabbed up the stack of paper and the magnetic bars he needed to run the computer pictures on his private terminal. Then he rushed out the door, violently pulled it shut, and raced back up the hall, taking the stairs two at a time.

Caro slept on. No nightmares or visions of any kind invaded her rest, although the mattress beneath her seemed to move as though swaying to the call of the tides. And somewhere far beyond the realm of dreams, she felt the soft caress of the water stirred by slow-waving fins, and the curious wuffling beaks of the baby carepies on her fingers.

September, 2456
Actaeon—

The large beasts that surround our field camp have strangely peaceful faces. They have a natural wariness of us, but never flee in cringing, abject fear. There is a nobleness that clings to them, bringing to my mind the mountain-ranging bear of North America, in early times a deity of the indigenous peoples. The Clytians, were there ever such a people, must have worshiped at the shrines of the Endregion sculpted trees and held the bearlike giants as their totems.

We have bagged several more; Marchenko and I are slated to dissect one tomorrow.

—Reginald

10

Unseen Presence

L ee sat hunched over his computer, whistling tensely through his teeth. The red-etched pictures moved across the monitor, their ruby glow flashing enigmatic messages along his bedroom ceiling and wall. He broke off whistling. His hand shot out and froze the picture, then enlarged a small section of it. Lee squinted at it, chewing his lip, frowning. Then his face cleared. He reached over to page through the pile of print-outs that ran ribbonlike along the side of the desk and flopped in piles around his chair. *There it was!* He drew a wide circle first on the monitor and then on the print-out sheet. He flipped back several wide pages, whistling again, tracing the columns of figures with two fingers. He stopped and drew another circle around the time of entry and the corresponding read-out.

A slow-growing smile appeared, lighting his tired face, and he thumped the page appreciatively with his fist. Lee leaned back, the chair creaking companionably under his weight, and stretched, flexing his cramped muscles. He laughed, shook his head, and laughed again. "We got 'em!" he declared to the humming computer, shaking a gleefully defiant finger at the screen. He leaned forward, the back of the chair snapping into an upright position, and pulled the entry board out from under his open journal. A few quick taps and he had sent the first of a series of reports to Dr. Lutes' private terminal.

Lee smiled again and reached for his mug of tea. It was stone cold and with a grimace he turned and dumped the remainder of the duck tea into a small holding tank full of soil from which grew an ugly, sinewy vine with greyish-brown leaves shaped like conch shells. The leaves snapped shut, and Lee laughed again. "I love it when you do that," he announced to the plant, silly with lack of sleep and an abundance of good news. He powered down the computer to standby mode, yawned widely, and threw himself across the bed for a couple of hours sleep.

Caro awoke with a feeling of well-being. She yawned and stretched and turned over in her bed to meet Sherri's bloodshot eyes peering at her over her blanket. Sherri didn't say one word; she just kept watching, wary, struggling to keep her eyes wide and alert.

Caro pushed the hair out of her eyes, waiting ... Sherri remained silent, her eyes trained on Caro.

"Are you okay?" Alarmed, Caro raised herself up on one elbow.

Sherri nodded. "And you?" she inquired politely, undemandingly, of Caro.

"I'm fine. Hey, what's the matter—oh. I made an awful idiot of myself last night, didn't I?" Caro fell back on her pillow. "I must have been totally out of it. Oh, Sherri—what did I say—did I cry? What happened?"

Sherri thought a minute. "Well, Uncle Lee says you're just fine, but exhausted," she said reassuringly.

Caro turned and propped herself up on one elbow, staring incredulously at the stranger in the next bed. "Are you sure *you're* okay?" she demanded.

"I'm fine!" Sherri said indignantly. Then she remembered herself. "You had a good sleep," she said soothingly.

"Sherri!"

"Wouldn't you like some duck tea?" Sherri asked with desperation. "I'll make us some, okay? Or would you prefer something cold?"

"Sherri!" Caro leapt up and hugged the sheets to herself when she realized that she was not wearing anything. "Sherri, listen—I'M FINE—just tell me, did I make an awful fool of myself last night?"

Sherri's eyes wandered around the room evasively. "I'm glad you're fine. Should we get up and go meet the boys for breakfast? Or would you like me to bring you something here?"

"I know what I'm going to do. I'm going to get dressed and call your uncle—you've been invaded by an alien or something. You are definitely scary," Caro announced, struggling to wrap herself in a sheet.

"No, no, no! Don't call Uncle Lee," Sherri said frantically, rising to a sitting position. "I'll talk! I'll talk! Lee laid down the law last night and told us that we weren't supposed to bug you with a lot of questions. Well me, mainly. He told me to keep my mouth shut." Her face darkened and her eyes flashed. "As if I didn't know how to talk to my best friend!"

Caro grinned. She vaguely recalled hearing Lee order Sherri to shut up. "I must have looked a fright."

"Like you were dead." Sherri had thoroughly put away her reassuring, 'safe' manner now. "Lee came roaring through the door, carrying you limp like a corpse across his back. He yelled like a fiend for me to make tea—"

"I remember drinking tea—did *you* really make it?" Caro broke in unbelievingly.

"Are you kidding? You know me and cooking of any kind. Hal did," Sherri said candidly. "Anyway, I was going to ask you what happened. My dear uncle sent me out of the room."

"I think I wailed like Meggie." Caro gulped in shame. "That's the last time he'll let me see the carepies, I'll bet you anything. How embarrassing. He probably is sorry he brought me here—and Dr. Lutes will be so disappointed."

"Oh, well—you did your best. And just think, now we can have some fun instead of you working. I mean, Uncle Lee won't take us back right away," Sherri said, looking on the bright side as usual.

"You don't understand, Sherri. I really want to go back and visit the carepies again. You wouldn't believe how miserable they are."

"You mean it wasn't awful?" Sherri asked, baffled.

"No! Yes!" Caro laughed. "It was excruciating. But wonderful." She paused, her jaw set. "I am going back—at least once more. I told them I'd come back and I will. I don't care what Uncle Lee says."

"Did you ever hear the story about your dad and a certain insect burrow some years ago on Earth?" Sherri asked slyly, watching Caro dig through her pack for clean clothes.

"What?" Caro muttered, yanking at some unseen article of clothing deep in her pack. "Do you mind if I shower first?"

"Not at all," Sherri smiled, leaning back on her pillows. "I think I'm going to have a nap."

Caro emerged from the bathroom encased in a thick towel. Her face itched from the shower and the hot air tunnel and she sat on the bed, rubbing her scars absentmindedly. For all her newfound courage and genetically determined stubbornness, she was rapidly wilting on the inside at the thought of facing Lee after what she felt was her miserable failure with the carepies. Sherri was curled up in a ball sound asleep. No help from that quarter.

Caro dressed slowly, pulling on her blue cotton shorts set, leaving her feet bare. She brushed her hair, avoiding looking at herself in the mirror as usual. She picked up her damp clothes from last night—Sherri had left them in a wet clump on the floor—and hung them to dry on the towel rack in the bathroom. She knew that she was simply stalling for time, hoping that Sherri would awaken and come with her. Sherri, happily equipped with a lively personality and spontaneous mouth, had always helped shy, tongue-tied Caro find her way through tense situations.

Sherri turned over and sighed loudly. Caro brightened. "I guess I'd better get up—it's a wonder we've been left to sleep peacefully this long. I'll bet I have you to thank for that—or, rather, your state of exhaustion and Uncle Lee's tirade. Ricky wouldn't have dared to bang on our door this morning." She sat up. "Oh, wow, you're already dressed—I'll be quick—will you wait for me? Then we'll both go to the cafeteria together, okay? I mean, without you, or navigator Ricky, I'd be sure to get lost," she added, starting to grin and ending up in a loud yawn.

Caro smiled. "Of course I'll wait," she said, her voice cracking.

It was still hard, even with Sherri bouncing in beside her, to walk through the dining room doors and join Lee, Hal, and Ricky at the table. They had finished eating and immediately three pairs of eyes zoomed in on her: two of them gently concerned, searching her face and glancing away again in relief, one small black pair frankly curious and leveled like scopes on her.

"I'm FINE," Caro heard her voice state in no uncertain terms as she banged her tray down on the table. She vaguely seemed to recall saying that several times already . . .

"Of course you are, of course you are," Lee said hurriedly, and then paused, his words also sounding reminiscent.

"So am I," said Sherri. "I'm fine too, in case anyone is interested." This was directed away from Lee. "Are you fine, Ricky? How about you, Hal? Oh," she turned and chirped falsely, "and how's Uncle Lee this fine morning? Fine? Good, good, good. We're all fine."

Lee laughed. "I can see that I haven't been forgiven yet, eh, Sherri. But you're right—we're all fine and it is a fine morning. Even if there's never any sun in these parts."

Caro looked cautiously at Lee. He seemed in very good humor. How could this be after her dreadful fiasco last night? Surely he cared about the carepies more than that. Lee caught her looking at him and smiled at her.

"So," Lee said, addressing Hal, "what are you three going to do this morning?"

Caro stopped chewing. He had said "you *three*." Had he made a mistake? *No*, her realistic side corrected her before she could even start to think that Lee was going to allow her to continue working with the carepies. *He just wants to talk with you alone. Let you down easily. Explain to you in his own kind way that he and Dr. Lutes cannot risk working with a sniveling coward.*

"No," Lee was saying with finality to Hal. "If you want to go see the lumies, I am going to be along. I don't even want an argument about it."

Hal glanced sideways at Ricky, and Caro knew immediately who really had been the source of that request. Ricky glared, but the fire in his eyes quelled when Lee turned to meet them. "Ricky, I promise you that I will take you to look at the lumies if that's what you really want. But Caro and I will be busy for a while yet. And if you even attempt to leave the building, that's it. I'm packing you up and sending you straight home, carepies or no carepies. Understand?"

Ricky mouthed "yes."

"Why don't you go up to the third floor? The guy in Communications is all right—he does his job and doesn't feel any compulsion to open his mouth to the Community officials about anything that doesn't concern him. He'll show you around, if you ask him the right way. There are no Community people around to bother you now, so it's a good time to do it. How does that sound?"

Hal looked pleased. "Sounds good. I'd like that. What's your friend's name? And what's the right way to ask him?"

"I just want to know how old he is," asked Sherri, eyes narrowed in a great show of being a manhunter.

"He's just your type, Sherri," Lee said mildly. "His name is J-32. And I'll tell you what buttons you need to push to get him to talk. Or, in your case, to get him to shut up. Just think—a date that you'll never have to listen to rattle on and on—you can do all the talking."

"Sounds wonderful," she responded with a wry smile. Ricky was screeching with laughter, and Hal tried, unsuccessfully, not to join in.

Lee said, shaking his head sadly, "You're slipping, Sherri. You set that one up for me all by yourself." He sighed, looking pleased with himself. "It's getting too easy—no fun at all—the challenge is gone."

"Yeah, well, I had a tough night," she said, swinging her hair back. "Anyway, tell us. How do we get my date to speak?"

"Here is the key to his heart. I'll write down the series of commands you need to enter into the main entry board. J-32 runs along a track behind the manual boards. There— I hope the two, or rather the four of you will be very happy. Caro and I have to go to work."

"Do you want us to take care of your trays for you?" Hal asked politely.

"No, Caro's still eating. In fact, I'll take care of your trays, just this once, okay?" he replied.

"Boy, you must really want us gone," Sherri said. "Well, we're on our way. Don't let this slave driver keep you busy all day, Caro. See you for lunch?" she asked, looking at Lee questioningly.

"Of course, honey. We'll be here," he affirmed cheerfully. "Of course, *you* may have other plans . . . "

Ricky's loud guffaws and Sherri's forced "Ha, ha," seemed to hang in the air after the three of them clattered out of the dining room. Caro pushed back her tray and met Lee's gaze squarely. Again she watched him turn into the serious scientist as he had yesterday when they first walked down the hall and entered the Aquatics Lab.

"Look," he said, kindly but emphatically, "we're working for a common cause here—the carepies. But I don't intend to lose sight of you in all of this. For us to work well together, we need to be straightforward and honest with each other. I need to know *really* how you're doing. I can go into a thousand and one apologies and self-beratings about how I should never have let you into that tank when you were so tired, but that's not going to get us anywhere. Suffice to say this: I get excited—too excited, maybe—about what I think are crimes against animals, against humans, well, against God. The situation of the carepies here is one of those crimes—against all three: the carepies themselves, the boomerang effect the crime will eventually have on humans—and it will, someday—and the disdain with which we are treating God and his creation in all this. Now, I could make this thing become a crime against you if I pushed you into this in any way. I need to know, Caro. How do you feel about being a part of this? Have I or Dr. Lutes unwittingly coerced you—made you feel somehow obliged to help out because of your natural affinity with the carepies?"

Caro looked hard at him, uncomprehending at first. He wasn't doing a very good job of firing her. Suddenly she smiled and tears welled up in her eyes. "No, don't worry. I won't cry again." She laughed shakily.

"It's all right if you do, you know. It's altogether a very human characteristic." He smiled, his eyes tender.

"I'm here for two reasons," she began, her voice low and intense. "I'm here for the carepies and I'm here for me. But what's funny is I can't really sort out what is for me and what is for them. It's like both are twined together somehow. I'm not making any sense, am I?"

"You're making a whole lot of sense, sweetheart," Lee replied soberly. "And you're answering my question at the deepest level that it can be answered—in words, that is. Go on—"

"Last night I knew I had to go to the two carepies on the bottom of the ark—tank. And yet I was fighting my own fear of the dark, of being all alone, to get to them. And when I was actually there with them, it was just the carepies, not me, not my fear, just them. When it was just them, I didn't have my fear anymore . . . "

"Are you afraid right now?" asked Lee quietly.

"Yes. I could throw up, actually." She half laughed. "But no, too. I *have* to go back to them—not for you or Lutes, or even for me—I just have to go to them. I know that I just contradicted myself," she said, looking openly into his warm eyes, "but that's the whole problem—both things are true: it is all for the carepies and it is all for me." She shook her head, baffled by her words but knowing the truth of her heart.

There was silence after her words. Lee searched her eyes and she met his gaze unflinchingly.

He smiled and swirled the tea in his cup. "Well," he said. "That's okay, then." He added, "That's the paradox of love, Caro. It's all for the other, yet, somehow, it's all for us, too . . . "

Caro tried to puzzle out what she could only feel to be right.

"Exactly what physical state are you in?" Lee asked. "Do you need a rest this morning? Do you want to wait until this afternoon to go into the tank?"

"No," Caro answered without hesitation. "I want to go in now. I want to get something done today—maybe after this morning with them, when I go in again this afternoon you'll see some results. Yesterday we were just starting to get acquainted. I'm sorry that it's going so slow . . . "

Lee shot up in his chair. "Caro," he roared excitedly, "you little idiot! No, I'm sorry—I didn't mean that—it's just a term of affection, anyway, no matter what Sherri says. Listen! I've been up most of the PM going through the data from your 'nothing' visit with the carepies last night—it was wonderful. Very promising. I sent Dr. Lutes a report already. He will be—" He choked over his words. "—beside himself. Unable to contain himself. Very happy!"

"Really?!"

"Really."

"Well. That's okay then," Caro said, and grinned.

"Ready to go?" Lee asked. She nodded, and pushed back her chair.

The babies took to the invisible presence of Caro with total, immediate abandonment. Caro found herself laughing out loud at the antics of the two in their near sibling rivalry over her. If one seemed to be tucked too comfortably under an unseen arm, the other grew jealous—even though he was, until covetousness grew, happily perched on Caro's back. The baby bull would then fall upon his sister-cousin, beak bared, skinny neck outstretched, and the two would streak around the tank in a furious frenzy of bubbles. When they grew tired they would begin to tilt to one side fearsomely and wobble about in an uncertain course back to Caro. And then the whole thing would start again.

Caro had to be careful in their mad rushes. Unable to see her, and forgetful in their baby-fury, they were quite likely to head straight for her. She barely escaped the catapult of one and then the other—Lee abruptly cutting short his laughter and shouting, "Look out! LOOK OUT!" so loudly that her ears rang for hours. A baby carepie, even at slow speed, was quite capable of knocking the wind out of her, a dangerous enough thing to occur underwater with the pressure of the water pushing against her chest cavity; a baby at full speed was a deadly missile.

The three younger adults were friendly but far more dignified in their response to Caro. After Caro's second visit, they began to loiter around the intake tube where this strange, unseen presence would first be sensed.

A routine began to emerge. On each arrival they would respectfully surround her and the visit would begin with Caro greeting each adult carepie by running her hands over their backs. As familiarity grew, Caro would touch each knobby head, their hoods of eyelids winking down and lifting in sudden amazement. *Hello, carepies, I'm back.* Then the babies would push forward for their more exuberant welcome. *Hello, babies, did you miss me?*

It was her fourth visit with the carepies, and Caro, after going through the ritual greetings of all the younger ones, began, as usual, the swim down to the bottom of the tank to visit the old cow and bull. The babies were joyously swimming alongside, around, and above Caro. The little bull, his beak set in an expression of near-human smugness, caught a short ride on Caro's back, until the female calf in a fit of spite tumbled him off ingloriously.

As Caro neared the downed carepies, the babies faltered in their headlong rush, circled once over the old navigator bull, dipped low over the cow, and returned to the three younger adults. Caro continued alone, slowly approaching the cow, who held out her head to the girl. Caro, keeping her balance by gripping the almost motionless fin, stroked the old matron. For the rest of her time in the tank she stayed with the two downed carepies, gliding from one to the other.

The girl, concentrating so completely on the old couple, at first didn't see what was happening a few short meters behind and above her. When she did glance up, wondering where the calves had gone, she saw only their beaks, thrusting out from under and around their parents' fins.

For the three adult carepies had penned the impatient, eager babies in their midst. Like a three-cornered playpen they stood vigilant, keeping the heedless babies away from Caro's ministrations.

September, 2456
Actaeon—

Well, Actaeon, congratulate me. I have found the new amusement for the Community. Yes, it is the giants of the dark—recently named Lumini lupus. *A commission for me, more grant credits for the End Base—everyone is happy. Except, of course, the scientists who are not part of the research. We have several live specimens at the Base now. However, from a behaviorist's standpoint, it is difficult to observe them in the half-light conditions to which their eyes are adapted.*

—Reginald

11

Friends

"I just don't think I'm doing any good at all!" Caro exclaimed miserably, grinding her face into her hands as she sat in the cafeteria, her elbows on the table. "Worse—I don't think I'm doing *anything* at all," she corrected herself morosely. Her scars and the white area of the plasti-graft itched worse than ever after being trapped so frequently under her faceplate.

"Well, why don't you ask him how you're doing?" counseled Sherri. "Doesn't Lee tell you anything about how it's all going?"

"Sometimes. He says that Dr. Lutes is pleased—that he considers what Lee sent him 'hard evidence'—"

"Caro, that sounds great!"

"But it's not anything I'm doing. How could it be? I'm not doing anything scientific at all! I'm playing with them! Petting them! What kind of 'hard evidence' could there be?" Caro exploded.

"I suggest you tell my uncle that it is high time—after all, you're his partner in all this—that he let you in on what's up. Make him tell you what evidence he has." Sherri rapped the table with a stale muffin. "Then you'll know whether or not you should feel miserable."

"Thanks—I think. But I can't demand anything. He's the boss, I'm just the peon playmate of the carepies. Besides, you know me . . . chicken to my gills." Caro grinned inwardly at her interesting biological mix of metaphors.

"Well, I'm going to ask him, then," Sherri decided. "As soon as he gets here. And as soon as I figure out how to eat this muffin."

"With plenty of tea," Caro said with a straight face. "Dipping frequently." She scratched her face, scrinching up her eyes with the pleasure of it.

"Should you be doing that?" Sherri asked sternly.

"No, she shouldn't." Lee's voice broke over their heads. "You're going to infect yourself again, Caro. Remind me to get you some cream from the clinic. So, where are the boys?"

"Mesmerized by the display of giant ticks in the parasitology lab. What an inspirational way to make a living. Anyway, never mind the boys. I want to ask you something," Sherri announced, shaking the muffin at him.

"Ask away," he responded cheerfully. "You have twenty minutes of my undivided attention before Caro and I disappear again."

"Which is exactly my point," Sherri said, making no sense at all. Lee raised an eyebrow, an amused expression on his face.

"What is Caro doing? And what are you up to? And is it working?" Sherri pressed on determinedly.

"Caro, will you translate for me?" asked Lee.

Caro swept Sherri a look of disgust. But, to her surprise, all at once she was able to clearly and unembarrassedly ask Lee what she wanted to know. "I was just saying to Sherri, before you got here, that I felt as though I were doing nothing, just playing with the carepies, and I couldn't imagine what 'hard evidence' you could have sent Dr. Lutes that would help the carepie situation any."

"Yeah," interjected Sherri.

Lee looked at Caro gravely. "I don't mind telling you now. We have safely passed the point where I'm going to worry that your 'knowing what you're doing' is going to affect your performance. In other words, I didn't want to make you self-conscious in your play with the carepies. Your relationship with them will now safeguard our talking about it. Do you know what I mean?"

"Yes," answered Caro. "It's like if you talk about being friends with someone, or decide you should like somebody, all of a sudden you can't. You can't even talk to them naturally. To become friends you have to spend time together just being silly or doing stuff—not thinking about trying to be friends at all—and then, there you are. Friends. After that, it's okay to talk about it."

Lee smiled. "That's exactly it. Now it's okay to talk about your friendship with the carepies. So, first of all— that is what you are doing—you're 'just' being friends with them. That's all—and that's way, way more than we ever figured it could be. Somehow, in really being friends—and you have a natural ability to make friends deeply, very quickly—you and the carepies are helping each other. Now what I'm doing, which was Sherri's number two question, is monitoring the only thing that the Community will consider 'hard evidence.' That is the 'material' aspects, the measurable physical condition of you and the carepies during your visits. The carepies are constantly being monitored; even when we're not with them the computer is recording blood pressure, respiration rates, metabolism fluctuations. Every physical statistic that we can record on them is being recorded. And the hard evidence is this: when you touch the carepies, their respiration distress diminishes. And their respiration distress is lessening for longer and longer periods of time after you've been with them. I think that is very impressive work."

Caro found her voice slowly. "Has Dr. Lutes presented any of this to the Community yet?"

"No. Tomorrow's the big meeting, sweetheart."

"Do you think they'll listen?"

"I think we'll shake them into slowing down this particular research here," Lee said cautiously. "Other than that—I don't know. It's the Community we're talking about; they're not always the easiest to predict."

"So you think that they won't send these carepies down into the tunnels?" Caro's eyes shone.

"I don't think so. But stranger things have happened," Lee admitted. "But I cannot fathom them ignoring this data." He laughed shortly. "Of course, I thought that way about the lumies at one time, didn't I? But no, the Community had far more invested into the lumie research. This is comparatively new—they can easily justify cutting their losses."

Lee glanced over Caro's head at the wall clock. "Our twenty minutes are up. Caro, how do you feel about going in one more time before the big meeting tomorrow? Say no if you're at all tired. We really do have enough evidence for Dr. Lutes to go in fairly confidently." Lee looked at the girl searchingly.

"I'm fine" was her immediate response. She laughed at his raised eyebrows, remembering that that was her stock answer. "No, really. I'm ready to go in again—as long as I get some cream on my face," she added with a grimace.

"It's a deal—let's go to the clinic on the way down. So, one last time before the big meeting—but we'll make it a short one. No longer than fifteen minutes, okay?"

"This is really something," Sherri said, looking at Caro reverently. "I sure wish we could see you with the carepies."

"Well, why not?" Lee said expansively. He pushed back his chair and stood up, leaning on his hands over the table. "I have to get my final report in tonight. But tomorrow morning, after breakfast, why don't all four of you come to my place and I'll run some pictures on my terminal?"

"Oh, pictures," Sherri spat out in disgust. "I meant really see her. Go into the lab with you—right now."

"Sorry, honey. Can't be done. Besides me being a little busy when Caro is lazing around with the carepies . . . " He grinned at Sherri, avoiding Caro's anguished expression. ". . . there is the whole control factor of the research to consider—as well as the breachment of security. One violation is about all I can justify—all our credibility would be thrown to the winds with all four of you trooping around in there."

Secretly Caro was very glad that Lee would not allow Sherri or anyone else in to watch when she was with the carepies. Not that she would have minded when she was actually with the carepies in the tank. When she was face to face with the carepies, nothing else really mattered. It was as though her own fears and insecurities ceased to be: you cannot see shadows in a room without light.

Every time she drew on the sleek silicone suit and fitted the infrared sensor into her faceplate, a strange sense would resound in her that she was, somehow, outfitting herself for combat. Yet combat, or any aggressive form of confrontation, was the last thing she wanted, and in no way described what actually took place every time she shot out of the lock, through the tube and plunged into the tank.

No, it was not the tank that was the trouble spot for her; it was the lock. And it grew no less fearful to her with every dive. Each time that Caro suited up and Lee checked over the fastenings and instruments, the tension grew. Each time there came the moment when she wondered whether or not this time she could actually do it. Each time there came the second of flat denial: she could not crawl into that coffinlike box and hear the lock snap shut on all light and warmth and wind.

It was Lee who carried her through the black death of it. Caro knew that he saw the animal struggle, the tooth-and-claw-fight to overcome fear, and the sudden, over-whelming instinct for flight. But he continued on. Never a pause in his sure movements; never a check in his voice. He moved with certainty when she stood paralyzed; he held her faith when her hands flew wide with horror. And each time it was his voice that forged a life line that took her safely through the dark of the lock to the carepies. From death to life.

It was the same again. "Caro, count with me—remember—thirty-five seconds." Her voice obedient, " . . . twelve, thirteen, fourteen . . . " Then, after what seemed an excruciating length of time, " . . . thirty-three, thirty-four, thirty-five." And she was out of the lock and speeding through the tube. In her rush through the enclosed channel she was always witless for a time, never remembering or feeling anything but the mad relief of the flight. Then came the surprising drop into the tank; the uncertainty of direction. No "up," no "down," only utter blackness—but a strange, singing blackness full of warm, blind, giants. She reoriented herself when she saw the carepies.

After the customary greetings, she allowed herself five minutes of play with the babies, their reckless glee sending joy rushing to her so that her throat ached with the holding of it. *Thank you, babies, thank you.* Then she was swimming down, down, skimming over the matron, calm as a queen, so serene in her exile. She gently stroked the tired old navigator, who had dropped in his traces for a time but was still singular in purpose, loyal to the wild pulse of freedom. *Thank you, old ones, thank you.*

It was time. She turned to face the upward journey, searching for the ring of red light hanging in the black that guided her like a constellation in the night.

"Hold on a bit, Caro. Stay where you are—the automatic feeders are going to come on in just a few seconds—the calves will be rushing around like mad." Lee's tones startled the girl. "There they go," he added quietly.

The night was transfixed. Through Caro's infrared sensors, the jets of plankton released by the feeders lit up the tank like tiny fireflies, bursts of light that shot through the black and then were no more. And the babies, in joyful rushes, chased through the tiny organisms, their beaks open and gill-tongues quivering. Caro wondered at the sureness of their scooping mouths; they fed blindly in the dark in utter faith, certain of their portion. The old cow, stiffly stirring her fin, rose from her throne and hovered, a meter or so from Caro, her mouth open and receiving.

It was another fifteen minutes before Caro could maneuver around the feeding carepies and begin the swim up the intake tube to the lock. Her muscles were beyond mere tired soreness; they trembled and flabbily refused the orders of her brain. She collapsed into the lock, breathing hard, hearing Lee's worried reassurances. The water drained away, leaving her body heavy and sodden.

The lock clicked open and she turned her face, looking up into Lee's anxious eyes. "Sorry," Caro gasped out. "I'm really all right, just winded."

"Stay where you are," Lee commanded. She saw the anger in his face. "I'm the one who's sorry. I should have remembered that we were going to conflict with the feeding schedule."

Caro's breathing grew less ragged and the color in her hands deepened. She made a move to get to her feet and fell back, laughing. "They won't work—I can't get up yet," she said, giggling in a strange release of tension.

"Here," Lee said, attempting to grin companionably with her. "Give me your hand, sweetheart. You are going straight to the dining room for a meal and then to bed. And I'm going to lock Sherri in the parasitology lab and chain her to the giant tick display if she bothers you."

"Sherri doesn't bother me!" Caro snapped. "Sherri's my best friend!"

"Okay, okay—I won't chain her to any giant ticks, I promise. I just want you to get lots of sleep," Lee replied soothingly.

Caro glared at him. "Okay," she finally said. She allowed him to carry her out of the lock and down the stepladder, and stood shakily, leaning against the computer desk. Lee helped her pull off her hood and airvest.

"Let's take the elevator up," he suggested tentatively.

Caro, blinking wearily, said, "I think that might be a good idea."

Caro slept well. She awoke almost eleven hours later, and when she stretched and got to her feet, there was just a hint of remembered soreness in her young muscles.

They all gathered in Lee's living room, Lee yawning and rubbing his bloodshot eyes. It had taken him most of the PM to send Dr. Lutes a thorough, well-documented report.

"So, let the show begin," he announced. "Caro and the Carepies—how's that for a title?"

"This place, this place," muttered Sherri, looking around. Hal looked at her in alarm; was she again going to offend Lee with some comment about his surprisingly clean suite?

"This is not you," Sherri finally said in a baffled tone. "There is no sign that you live here. And I find that troubling." Lee looked at her levelly, a twinkle fighting for life in his narrowed eyes. "Really," she continued, "this place is sterile—and that's not you at all."

The twinkle won. "Well—I don't spend a lot of time in here. And I couldn't stand the 'assigned' wall picture for this room so I flung it far away. I'm waiting for you to paint me one, Sherri. Anyway, my terminal is in the bedroom; maybe you'll feel less troubled when you see that room."

Lee solemnly led the way down the tiny hall to the bedroom door. He flung it open with a grand sweep of his arm, gesturing Sherri inside. The others shuffled into the small room after her.

Strange plants potted in a variety of double-duty containers stood tall, or drooped languidly, lining the walls. A row of silicon-based fungi, resembling lacy ocean coral, shot in frozen sprays from the top of the cluttered bookshelf. Photographs of family and friends lay scattered in piles, competing for floor space with stacks of scientific reports, moldy tea mugs, and unlabeled computer bars. There was an uncertain path from the desk to the bed—the evidence of this being an old set of tea stains overlaid with shiny, new drips. Dead leaves crunched underfoot and curled in grey heaps against the bubbling aquarium on the floor under the window. There was nothing in the aquarium.

Sherri looked around her with a fond smile. Opening her arms wide as if to embrace the whole room she said with a sigh, "This, this, is my Uncle Lee!"

Lee replied with a straight face, "I cleaned it up just for you, honey."

Hal moved in a daze, trying not to stare obtrusively at the mess. "Where's your computer terminal?" he asked faintly.

"Right there on the desk," Lee replied; the sideways wrinkle appeared between his eyes.

Ricky was crouched in front of the brown, algae-encrusted aquarium. "There's nothing in it," he said in disappointed bewilderment.

"Sure there is!" Lee strode over. "It's just hard to see them. They blend in so well." He squatted down, took the handy stick from across the top of the tank and poked it in the muddy depths. "There! Did you see that one?" he asked Ricky excitedly. Ricky nodded, well pleased.

"What are they?" Caro asked, unable to resist peering down over their shoulders.

"Tarangoas," Lee replied. He reached in with his hand, made a sudden motion, and pulled one out. The small, brown, arrow-shaped creature squirmed around on his palm. Ricky bent close over it. "Watch it," Lee said. "They spit." Ricky backed away a fraction of a centimeter.

"See, Caro?" Lee asked.

"Yeah. They remind me of squid—only tiny, and without the tentacles. And no eyes." Caro paused. "Well, maybe they're not too much like squid after all—" Lee grinned with her.

"Where are they from?" Hal asked. Sherri peeped cautiously around him.

"Very deep in Jonah pools. You come up with a multitude of them when you dredge the bottom. When they cleaned the pump here they found a whole bunch of these little guys plugging up the first filter. So I thought I'd keep them for a while," Lee explained.

"What do they eat?" asked Ricky, breathing heavily over Lee's hand. The tarangoa suddenly squished itself into an accordion and sent a thin, dank stream toward the hot tornado of Ricky's mouth. Everyone howled. Ricky ran to the bathroom and spat repeatedly, furiously, into the sink.

"It's just a little muddy water, Ricky," Lee called, weak with laughter. "It won't hurt you." The tarangoa was released back into the aquarium and Lee dried his hands on his coveralls.

"Well, that was the warm-up show," Lee announced in good humor. "And now for the main event."

Lee powered up the terminal and with computer pictures went through a brief history of the carepie's tank, showing them where Caro entered the tube and the control terminal where he monitored each encounter.

"That's a horribly tiny tube," Sherri said with a shudder. She looked at Caro with respect.

"The worst is the lock," Caro admitted. "That's where I wait in this little chamber until it fills with water. It's a control so that no light or unmonitored oxygen gets into the tank," she explained.

"I would just die," declared Sherri. Caro inwardly smiled. She did die—every time the lock lid clicked shut on her.

"Now, these red blobs are the carepies," said Lee, tapping the screen with a fossilized bone. "And this red streak is Caro. Here, I'll power it up. Now you can tell."

"Sort of," said Ricky doubtfully. "How come they're not real pictures? These look like red X-rays or something. I mean, I can tell from their shapes what they are supposed to be, but they're sure not very clear, are they?"

"Remember, there is no light allowed inside the sealed tank. Caro, because of the sensors in her faceplate, can see only wherever the infrared radiation is being absorbed and released by living organisms that are sensitive to the wavelength of radiation with which we bombard the tank. You're right—it doesn't compare to full-light photography, but you get used to it after a while. Don't you, Caro?"

"Yes—and it's far clearer when I'm actually in the tank than it looks on the computer."

At first, Caro, after she got used to the different perspective of standing outside of herself, watching a strange red figure greeting the carepies, enjoyed hearing her visits explained by Lee in their scientific context. But then, unaccountably, the presentation bored her and made her restless. It was as if by some gross mixup in files Lee was telling the wrong story. As if her friendship with the carepies had been a contrived, temporary thing.

But that's exactly what it was, a cold voice inside her stated. She tried to distract herself from it by getting up and looking out the window; the shifting shadows of the lumies behind the glittering bars below only intensified her restlessness.

But it was Ricky who first suggested going to see the lumies.

October, 2456
Actaeon—

Lumini lupus *tame easily. Like dogs, they will do anything for a bit of meat. I set up a real show for the Community officials here yesterday: the finale had three specimens sitting up begging, and a fourth climbing onto their backs with a Community flag in its mouth. It didn't even occur to the idiots that someone might be making fun of them. But, of course, my paw was out just like everyone else's. Actaeon, how we have progressed . . .*

—Reginald

12

Lying Beauties

T he "Caro and the Carepies" show on Lee's computer was over, and Lee, Caro, Sherri, Hal, and Ricky were seated around a table in the dining room. Lunch was finished: plates had been pushed away and half mugs of duck tea were growing cold. The conversation had lagged to the point of waiting for someone to put forward "the next thing to do."

Caro, oddly enough, the cold voice still ringing in her ears telling her that she would soon leave the carepies forever, could not face the thought of another dive just then. She would have gone into the tank if Lee had said, as she expected him to do at any second, "Well, what are you three going to do while Caro and I go to work?" but he didn't.

"I guess you and Caro are going to disappear again, right?" Sherri said, tapping her fork on her tray. "And the three of 'us children' will have to amuse ourselves again?"

"Nope. I'm waiting for a communication from Lutes. I don't want to risk missing it. He may need to clarify something in the reports with me during the meeting. But even if he doesn't, I can't settle to do anything until I hear from him about how it's going. If Caro wants to visit her friends, she'll have to wait until this evening, okay?" He lifted his eyebrows at Caro. She nodded, the strong feeling of relief mixed with disloyalty and shame. "So, Caro and I are ready to amuse you kidlets. What's on the menu?"

And it was then that Ricky said stubbornly, "I want you to take us to see the lumies."

Hal and Sherri, in one motion, turned to look at Caro. She had her eyes fixed on Lee; the plastic seam on her face itched fiercely and she longed to reach up and scratch it, but found she couldn't.

"Ricky," Lee said, observing him levelly, "I promised you that if you wanted to go see the lumies that I would take you. So I will—" He drowned out Ricky's victory shout. "But right now we should do something all together. The time we have right now should be for all of us, and I'm sure that the others prefer to do other things. You and I will go alone another time."

Ricky scowled. "It's because of Caro that you won't take us. We all want to go but Caro," he burst out in frustration.

Caro turned on him. She watched herself in faint surprise as she did, but she swung around in her seat and stared at her little brother coldly, the soul in her eyes hidden far, far away. "I don't mind." She shrugged. "If everyone else wants to go see the lumies, that's fine with me—it's better than nothing." She could feel Lee's eyes willing her to look at him, trying to read her, but she did not turn to him.

"What Sherri and I told Ricky was that if he really wanted to see them we would go along," said Hal, fingering his mug uneasily.

Lee's eyes seemed to be boring holes through her dark head, but still Caro looked away.

"I'll go if everyone else wants to," Sherri said uncertainly. "But don't you have to wait for a message from Lutes?" She brightened.

Lee swung around, reorienting himself toward Sherri. "There's a message minder in my suit—it's not like the marine lab where I can't leave if a message comes through on my terminal. Look," Lee said with a ring of finality. "If anyone—regardless of any previous agreements or whatever—has any reason for not wanting to go—stated or unstated—let him speak now. We're all solid enough friends simply to say 'no, I don't want to go.'"

In the silence that followed, Caro knew that all four of them were waiting for her to form those words. But she, caught in this impermeable, cold cocoon of rage, could not, and did not. Caro drained the last of the lukewarm tea from her cup and her hand did not shake.

"Well, then," said Lee, breaking the tense stillness. He closely scrutinized the dregs of tea in his mug. "Let's go get our suits on."

Sherri got up from the table with a troubled look marring her lovely face. Hal began to stack dirty dishes onto his tray, sorting out cutlery into neat rows, arranging the mugs into the most strategic space-saving arrangement. Ricky was impatiently jumping from foot to foot. "Hurry up, Hal!"

Lee put his hand over Hal's and Hal stopped, looking up, startled. "I'll do it—you go help Ricky," he said. Caro began to hurry, grabbing plates and setting them haphazardly on her tray. She did not want to be left alone with Lee.

"Sherri," Lee said steadily, "will you do me a favor and go check the message minder on the kitchen door to see if it's leaving any instructions to reset or refill anything?" Sherri nodded, the dimple between her eyes deepening. She sent Caro a compassionate look that Caro felt rather than saw.

Caro reached over to pick up Ricky's tray and Lee grabbed her wrist. "Look at me," he said.

"What?" Caro turned and stared at him, her eyes hidden.

"Why are you doing this? You don't need to—nobody will think any less of you, Caro." His eyes were full of deep sorrow, for her.

"I don't know what you're talking about" came the voice that bypassed the real Caro. "It's no big deal—going to see a few animals in a cage. You said yourself that you felt sorry for them." She couldn't feel her lips.

"It is a big deal—for you. You're not Hal or Sherri, and you're certainly not Ricky." A hint of humor ran unexpectedly through his voice like a warm breeze. Her muscles cautiously relaxed under his hand. "You're a deeply sensitive person who has been greatly hurt by these creatures. It will be a very big deal for you to see them—and that is how it should be."

Sherri, loitering in front of the message minder by the kitchen door, shifted uneasily. Caro yanked her arm away from Lee and picked up her tray. "Are you ready to go, Sherri?" she called in a tight, hard voice.

"If you change your mind at any time, Caro, let me know," Lee said quietly as she walked away.

"Nothing here, Lee," Sherri called to him from the message minder, her tone forced. She waited by the door of the dining room for Caro to send her tray of dishes along the treadmill into the steri-wash, looking back and forth from Caro to Lee, unhappily tapping her toe to the floor.

Caro pulled out their Zero suits from the bottom of the closet where Sherri had stuffed them. Sherri was tunneling through her pack, tossing several cotton tees to the floor in disdain.

"Do you dress up or do you dress down when you visit the beasts that tried to kill you?" she asked tongue-in-cheek. "Mother never told me that piece of etiquette."

What Lee's stern compassion had been unable to do, Sherri's garish humor almost did. "I'm appearing in traditional white," Caro answered, holding up the brilliant Zero suit. They giggled in high relief, but Caro, catching a glimpse in the mirror of the fake white graft masking half her face, choked on her laughter.

The five white-suited figures marched solemnly toward the cargo elevator. "Too hot to take the stairs in these things," Lee had proclaimed.

The shortest figure wore a studied air of importance through which his barely controlled excitement shot through. Caro watched him, half in contemptuous amusement, half in tender compassion; she often felt the equal compulsion to both smack and hug her little brother. She wondered if Ricky had any real interest in seeing the lumies or was just wanting a chance to dress up and play at being his hero, Uncle Lee.

They rode in silence down the elevator: Ricky leaning with his back against the wall, beating his hands against it, Hal nervously clearing his throat, Lee whistling softly through his teeth.

"My mom says that when you were little you got your head stuck between the doors of an elevator in the largest Community Complex on Earth," Sherri suddenly stated, gazing at her uncle.

Lee stared and then laughed. "Yep—maybe that was the start of all my troubles with the Community. It was an ominous beginning, anyway. Miriam should talk—it was her fault—she was my big sister, she was supposed to watch out for me." He drowned out the cries of indignation from the two big sisters currently in the elevator. "No—it really was her fault. Just as the elevator doors started to close, she said, 'look!' and pointed out somebody Mom and Dad knew. So I looked." The four howled. "Yeah, thanks," he added wryly. "My ears rang for days."

"Just the same," Sherri said when she could speak, "you shouldn't blame older sisters. How would you like to have to stop Meggie from terrorizing the entire Main Base every living minute you're not in school? It's a thankless job, as Caro well knows, having to watch Meggie's number one partner-in-crime."

"Yeah, you both do have handfuls with those two. But Miriam had it lucky. I was a saintly child—" Lee replied, loftily, looking toward the heavens.

"Hold on, I feel the Judgement coming," Sherri announced to the others. When no lightning bolt fell, and the elevator door opened prosaically into the basement, she added, "You better be careful, dear uncle. I have lots more little tidbits like that from Mom that I could tell."

"Yeah, well, just remember, dear niece," he replied, grinning, "I have some rather, um, interesting baby pictures of you somewhere about my place." Sherri's eyes grew round and she shot an inadvertent, horror-filled glance at Hal. "I thought so," Lee nodded in satisfaction, throwing his arm about her and guiding her out of the elevator.

They cut across the hall and into the lot where Lee's crawler still waited plugged into the wall, the panel lights blinking green, juiced up, ready to go. "Do you think it missed me?" Lee asked, giving the crawler a meditative pat as they passed it on their way to the foot tunnel. Hal looked at him in amazement.

Lee led them to a door and tapped his security number into the entry board. The door slid open and Ricky rushed through. "Wait," Sherri cried, "Ricky's hood isn't done up."

"It's okay, Sherri," Hal explained. "The tunnels are heated and ventilated same as the rest of the Base building."

"Oh," she said. "Well, why the security door, then?"

"It's just a precaution," Lee replied. "They are a recent—"

"Because that's how the lumies got in and killed everybody," Ricky broke in.

Lee looked at him. "The doors are a safety precaution, Ricky. Against a lot of things."

They followed the long ribbon of light inset into the tunnel ceiling. The solid walls of a grey rocklike material only allowed them to travel in close pairs, and the ceiling, with its inset bar of light, closed in from above.

Sherri swallowed and swallowed again, walking with her head ducked away from the low ceiling. She fell back and Caro moved alongside of her. The two girls walked in a green-tinged silence several meters behind the others. The short, quick strides of Ricky and the longer, ground-eating paces of Lee and Hal began to leave them further and further behind.

Lee noticed the two trailing along behind them. He began to deliberately slow his steps and Hal, glancing back, accommodated himself agreeably to the slower pace. Ricky forged on ahead.

As they rounded a slow-banking curve, Caro saw, in the distance, a red bar of light over a door and down one side of it. "Hey, wait for me, Ricky," Sherri shouted. "Come on, Caro," she called back as she dashed toward the door.

"Wait for all of us, Ricky," Lee yelled. He grabbed Caro's hand. "We better catch up to them, Hal. Ricky's quite capable of trying to open the lock."

Both Ricky and Sherri had pulled on their hoods and had zipped their faceplates. They were hopping with impatience, frantic in their eagerness to go outside. Hal and Caro stared at Sherri in surprise.

"Okay," Lee said firmly. "Before I open the door into the lock, everyone needs to have his hood in place and have checked the read-out on power." He double-checked Ricky's, looked at Sherri and Hal who nodded, and then at Caro. "I'm fine," she said automatically, and then flushed at his look.

Lee entered his code into the first door of the lock. Caro watched as the pulsing bar stilled to a steady crimson; the edges faded to amber and the color spread until the bar gleamed a warm orange-yellow. After a few seconds the process began again, the bar turning to an electric green from the outside edges in. The door slid open.

The lock was small, no bigger than the elevator. When all five of them were safely inside, Lee entered his code in the entry board beside the next door. The door behind them slid shut, and Caro saw the pulsing of its bar stain the backs of the others' suits blood-red. The second door flicked through its color-changing process quickly—more quickly than Caro anticipated. The door slid open with a rush of wind and they were outside the End Base building, their faces silvered by the cold glare of the beacons.

"We're right in front of the outdoor Animal Science lab," said Lee, watching Caro's impassive face. "I thought we might walk along here and you could see the lab animals on our way to the other side of the building where the permanent animal enclosures are. Then we'll go back in through the main doors instead of the tunnel."

"Queechies!" Sherri screamed, running over to a long, tight-meshed enclosure. Hal hurriedly turned down the volume on his intercom. "Ricky—remember the queechie that ran over you when we were all flopped down by the fire—when we were lost?"

The queechies responded to Sherri's ecstatic greeting in typical fashion—running in blind panic, ricocheting off the sides of the mesh, finding by trial and error their burrow entrances. The small, madly dashing creatures, resembling animated feather-dusters, sent out alarm "queeches," shattering the frozen stillness with their thin wails.

"Oh," said Sherri sadly, kneeling down and peering through the mesh sides of the enclosure. "They're gone."

"I'll say," muttered Ricky. He had rushed to the cage with Sherri.

"But what an exit," said Hal. Lee laughed.

Caro stared at the label on the door of the cage, *Ochotona leucinerea*. Such a large official name for so small and unimposing a beastie.

"What's the official name for the carepies?" Caro abruptly asked.

"Well, you know that 'carepie' is short for carapacefish, and they're called that because their dorsal surface is rounded like a turtle's shell, or carapace. But their scientific name is *Dermocarepae delphi*."

"That's pretty," Sherri remarked. "Say it again."

"*Dermocarepae delphi*," Lee obligingly repeated. He paused. "Actually, maybe 'carepie' comes from the Latin name after all."

They walked past a long, blacked-out enclosure, which Lee said was a quarter-light environment for another cage of queechies. It was silent except for a faint scrabbling sound.

"Probably digging a burrow," Lee commented.

"And this," he said, coming to a full stop before a fine-screened darkened enclosure, "houses our two very cherished *Lepidonotinus leucrubi* specimens—relatives of Caro's infamous 'white worm.'" Lee nodded vigorously in response to Caro's look of surprise and Sherri's "Really?!" "I was holding out for the name *Lepidonotinus caro,* but I got voted down—some scientists have no taste," he complained, grinning.

"Were you really going to name the worm after Caro?" Ricky screeched, overwhelmed by the honor of having a sister who almost had her name go down in history.

"Yes—she's the first one who was recorded as seeing one," Lee declared. "So why not? I submitted it, but, as I say, it got turned down."

"Just for the record, Lee, don't do me the privilege of naming any worms after me, okay?" Sherri said, her mouth twisted in horror.

Caro laughed. "It could have been worse, I suppose," she said to Sherri. "I could have found some horrible lethal virus or something."

Lee looked baffled at the two.

"I think *Lepidonotinus caro* has a nice ring to it," Hal said, repeating the name to himself.

"Not when it's attached to a huge, ugly worm!" Sherri retorted.

Ricky looked at the two girls in disgust. He said earnestly to Lee, "Name something after me—anything, okay?"

Lee patted him on the shoulder and led them to the next enclosure.

"You can't see anything in this one, either," Lee began. "But it—"

Sherri laughed, interrupting with, "Whatever do you mean when you scientists say 'you are holding an animal for observation'! Except for the queechies in the first cage, we haven't observed *anything.*"

" 'Observation' is a much bigger word than just 'seeing,' " Lee explained. "It means that we're trying to capture a slice of life of that creature, or colony of creatures.

Now, what you're not going to see, but what we are observing in this cage, is a clutch of eggs found in the early quarter-light zone. We've been holding them for several weeks now, but nothing's happened yet."

"Where are they?" Ricky asked, his faceplate pressed against the mesh.

"They've been dug almost a meter down—they were found below ground," he replied. "Oh, wow," Lee suddenly said, "there's a message coming in from Main on my terminal—my minder is blinking. Wait—it's gone off—so he's obviously not needing an immediate response. Do you want to wait and see the lumies another time, or do you want to see them now, just for a couple of minutes?"

"I only wanted to see them for a couple of minutes anyhow," Sherri said. "Let's just do that and get it over with."

"Okay by me," Hal agreed.

Ricky frowned. He kicked the dirt, marring the white toe of his boot, but he nodded.

"Caro?" Lee asked.

"Yes—but I do want to hurry up and see what Lutes had to say," Caro blurted.

"Right." Lee set his lips firmly. "Let's skip the rest of these and cut across the track to the permanent holding enclosures. Remember, Ricky, we only have a couple of minutes."

"Yeah, yeah," Ricky muttered, still scuffling his feet in the brittle soil.

They passed the main entrance and turned left, following the long side of the End Base building. Although most of this front area was undeveloped, there had been a gradual accumulation of enclosures, holding areas, and outhouses. The smaller, secondary windmill field was at the far end along this side. Against the backdrop of the Soil Science lab outbuildings that lined the high fence a startling display of natural flora grew in odd contortions out of the half-moon section cut by the returning crawler track. The permanent enclosures for animals ran almost one-quarter of the length of the building. Its only occupants were the five sighted lumies.

Caro, walking toward the enclosures with the others, stared dispassionately at the distant dark forms, crouched against the shimmering mesh. As she drew nearer, the shadows seemed to gather together in one leap of recognition and she began shaking.

One large male reared up, balancing a heavy paw on the second lumie's back. It was the size of the massive beast that seemed to strike the four like a physical blow. Caro vaguely heard Sherri gasp and felt Lee spin around to look at her. Ricky inadvertently jumped nearer to Uncle Lee. Hal and Caro stood still, Caro's mind running with melded memories of fur and blood and pain.

The thick chestnut-coated lumie slumped on all fours again, joining the second in its vigil against the wire that separated the two males from the females. The black and white face of the second lumie whirled around for a tenth of a second, but Caro saw the white-ringed, huge eyes and round baby-face like a burning imprint on her mind.

A spasm passed through Caro, then a volcanic rush of rage that quaked up from her depths and sent her reeling closer, closer to the bars and that hateful, smug, lying beauty. She stopped by sheer force of will, her teeth cutting through her tongue until salty, warm fluid filled her mouth. But still she shook, aching to feel a sharp stick, a long bar of metal, anything, clenched in her hands, and to prod and poke and drive it through such lovely eyes.

Lee, moving alongside her, looked up in the direction that the two lumies were gazing. The merged shadows of the three females were several meters away, but Lee stiffened, uttered a low exclamation, and pushed past Caro.

His pace quickened until he was running along the fence toward the three lumies. The others followed, dazed, uncertain of anything but staying near Uncle Lee.

Lee came to a dead stop on the other side of the enclosure opposite the three lumies. Not taking his eyes from them, he hurriedly unzipped his chest pocket and pulled out a small tranquilizer gun. He leveled it and shot: once, twice, and then a third time. The sharp pop of the pistol startled Caro so that she jumped each time, her body surging with adrenaline.

The two lumies had begun eating the third, oldest female; she was still alive. Her pain-laced eyes slowly closed in response to the tranquilizer darts, and the lumies settled in closer to their meal, nuzzling into her side like two grotesquely oversized kittens at their mother's teats.

Caro's faceplate clouded, misted, iced. In distant surprise she became aware of the flushing course of tears, rinsing warm over the patched skin of her face.

October, 2456
Actaeon—

Everyone at the Base, from the lowest engineer's assistant to the highest Community official, has jumped on the Lumini lupus bandwagon. Meterologists are trying to determine whether or not climate changes can be predicted through their hide thickness; medical physicists have theorized that the creatures should not be able to stand, much less walk, due to the low density of their femurs; geologists are trying to correlate substrate and their habitat. The botanists are sulking because the physiologists have "proven" that Lumini lupus cannot digest vegetation . . .

And my work, Actaeon, has been frustrating. My behavior studies go slowly because it is impossible to duplicate the conditions of the half-light zone and still observe the subjects. Dissections of the creatures' eyes were beginning to prove interesting, but it has all ground to a halt: Marchenko, my molecular physiologist, is exhibiting signs of space fatigue and has been ordered to complete bed rest. For the last forty-eight hours he has been batting at his ears as if there were angry bees buzzing around his head. Who knows when he can be replaced?

—Reginald

13

Command Performance

hy, why did they kill her, Uncle Lee?" Ricky's plaintive wails echoed through their intercoms as Lee shepherded the four through the main entrance doors.

"She was old, and sometimes animals turn on one another when they're caged," replied Lee simply, evenly. He had one hand on Ricky's shoulder, keeping him moving, guiding him as quickly as possible inside the heavy doors, through the airlock.

Sherri and Hal, closely following, were silent; a shiver quaked Sherri's body every few seconds, and her dark eyes registered the shock of horror they had received.

Caro's eyes still flowed; a deep well of sorrow had been tapped and there was no staunching the cleansing stream until it ran dry. She walked like a child, her hand in Lee's, trusting him to lead her, for her faceplate was opaque with frozen tears and warm mist.

Again, it was Lee who unzipped her faceplate so that she could see, and feel the warm, circulating wind inside from out of the darkness. They walked down the hall, up the stairwell, their footsteps echoing, crashing, deafening, but not touching the silence of Caro's mind.

Then down the second-floor hall to their housing units, walking dutifully like automatons, and Sherri was startled from her trance by Caro's tears. Caro heard, from a great distance, her frightened voice repeating, "Oh, Caro! Oh, Caro!" and Lee's reassurances that all was well and would be well.

Caro climbed wearily out of her Zero suit, curled up on top of her bed and slept and slept and slept. And sometime during the night, the tears ran dry.

Caro awoke to a new world. The End Base was bustling with returned personnel, the halls busy with scientists in white lab coats and khaki coveralls. Dr. Lutes was with Lee at their dining-room table, rising when he saw her, holding out his hands to her in greeting. His warmly lit eyes and quiet "Well, well, my dear" flowed through her like a benediction.

Somehow Caro could not feel embarrassed about the day before, and the others, sensing this in relief, treated her naturally.

"The carepies are going to be fine," blurted Ricky importantly.

"Ricky! That's not what Dr. Lutes said—" Lee exclaimed. "Sorry, Caro, we haven't really discussed this in detail without you, just the bare facts. Which are: that our work was met with great interest, and that Dr. Lutes and I are to meet in a special closed conference with a few Community leaders. We imagine it will decide the outcome of the seven carepies here. And we're guardedly optimistic."

"Once burned, twice shy," murmured Dr. Lutes, eyes gleaming. "We are, however, extremely happy with the outcome to this stage, Caro. And much thanks is due to you, my dear."

Lee smiled proudly at her. "Without her we would have had nothing."

"When is the meeting?" Caro asked, blushing. It was Sherri's and Hal's foreign looks of respect that were the most difficult to handle in all this praise.

"This afternoon. Not everyone, by any means, is back from Main yet," Lee replied. "Say—how do you feel, Caro? Do you want to visit the carepies one last time before the big meeting? Give a special command performance for Dr. Lutes?"

Caro smiled. "I'd love to."

Lee and Dr. Lutes left the four of them in the dining room to finish their breakfast.

"Caro," Ricky said, spraying crumbs at her, "I've thought of a plan. Get the carepies to talk, like dolphins or something. Then I'll bet the Community would listen. Why don't you try?"

Sherri hooted. "Caro and her trained carepies!"

Hal smiled at the look on Caro's face. "Ricky, how do you think the carepies could talk—physiologically, I mean? Dolphins make sounds naturally, carepies don't—do they, Caro?"

"No," she managed faintly, staring at Ricky in surprise.

"Well, Uncle Lee said that you talked to them and they talked to you," Ricky said indignantly. "I just thought that if you could make them say something to the Community then they would let them go!"

"I don't talk to them verbally, Ricky," Caro said, wondering how Lee knew. "I sort of talk to them in my head."

"Do they answer you in your head?" asked Ricky bluntly.

"Yes—no, not in words." She fumbled around trying to explain what she could only feel. *That was it!* She closed

169

her eyes and felt the carepies warmth flow to her. "They talk to me through my feelings—my heart, I guess you would say." Ricky stared at her suspiciously, his mouth ringed in juice.

"How do you know it's them?" asked Sherri, curious.

Caro laughed. It was such an outrageous question. "The same way I know it's you and not Hal talking to me right now."

"Huh?" said Sherri, looking from Hal to Caro and back again.

Hal leaned back and waved his hand at her. "Don't look at me, Sherri. I'm just as confused as the rest of you. I have a feeling that this is one of those things that—"

"—is beyond the realm of material science," Sherri and Caro chanted together, grinning at one other. That quote of Lee's had become a favorite part of Hal's vocabulary whenever he came up against anything that he couldn't immediately understand or put in terms of scientific "matter."

"Well, this time, it is," he muttered goodnaturedly in defense.

"Well, *Uncle Hal,*" said Sherri, "I think it's time—if everyone has finally consumed enough tea—to deliver Caro to the carepies. Then perhaps you can entertain us two remaining 'kidlets.' Don't you hate that word?" she bit out, slapping her hand on the table. "If Lee says that to us one more time, Caro . . . I'm going to pick up this tea pot and, and—"

"And what, Sherri?" Caro led her on. Lee had entered the room and was striding toward them, coming up to their table from behind Sherri. Hal covered his mouth with his hand.

"And I am going to throw this teapot—full to the brim of hot tea—for all I'm worth at his self-satisfied, smug face!" she wound up, eyes glaring.

"Who's the recipient of all this wrath, Sherri?" Lee asked from behind her. Sherri jumped, eyes wide, sending an accusing look to Caro for not warning her.

Lee didn't wait for an answer. "You ready, Caro?"

"Yes!" Caro leapt to her feet. "And not a minute too soon!"

The torment of the lock was, as always, barely to be endured, but the rush through the dark tube and the joyous plunge into the tank washed away the taste of death from her soul. *I'm here, carepies!*

The babies seemed more rambunctious than ever, chasing around Caro in dizzying circles, tilting like small, wind-driven boats into her, sending her flying against the resilient side of an adult. Caro laughed; the cow stayed still, and the girl felt as though she were amused by the babies' show-off performance. The second cow came in close by her other side, guarding her from the calves' reckless behavior. The young bull seemed to trade tolerant looks with Caro, winking his thick lid down over one bright eye.

The old cow had remained a short distance off the bottom of the tank. She hung in space, her fin undulating evenly around her, and stretched out her neck as Caro drew near. *Hello, old cow, I'm glad to see you.*

The navigator bull still rested on the dark floor, but to Caro's joy she saw that he had turned around and was facing in the other direction: at some time since her last visit he must have risen. Caro pictured him in slow, careful motion, blindly maneuvering through the darkness, his battered fin creaking and straining with the immense effort. He must be better to have moved, she thought exultantly. *It's good, so good to see you, Navigator!*

"Okay, Caro," came Lee's voice. "We're going to have to cut this short—I want a chance to edit some of this for the conference. Just a couple more minutes."

Caro swam up to the babies, smiling at the two quickly extended beaks; they bumped against the three adults, longing to be turned loose to play with Caro's warm, unseen presence. Suspended in the soft velvet, she paused for a moment, drinking in the ruby stars floating, flickering through the strange night. A red gleam of escaped plankton glittered by the corner of her eye. Unaccountably, a sweet sadness welled up within her. Of course Caro would be thrilled to have the carepies returned to the ocean, free, but she would miss this comrade sharing between fellow prisoners. *Thank you, carepies, thank you.*

Only a few minutes of play with the calves, then the long swim up, the babies straining beside her, necks out, beaks open with the effort. Up through the center of the glowing ring, feeling the swish of the grate sliding into place behind her, and the calves' disapproval at being shut out yet again. Then the awful unbidden words: *Good-bye, babies, good-bye carepies. Be well, oh, be well. Why?* she wondered as she labored up the tube into the lock. *Why?* as the lock drained of water around her. There were many more days of her two weeks at the End Base left; surely she would visit the carepies again.

The meeting was going well. Lee had given an updated report, showing pictures of Caro's most recent encounter with the carepies. The change in position of the old bull was duly noted and eyebrows were respectfully raised. Dr. Lutes, clearing his throat, began a final appeal to the three Community officials, summarizing the main points of the research at the Main Base and the more dramatic results here.

Lee sat back and observed the panel. They seemed to be concentrating with careful interest on Lutes' summary. The older woman, with iron-grey hair clipped short to her head, gazed over her half-glasses at Lutes in deep scrutiny. The middle-aged man, tapping a computer wand against his teeth, narrowed his eyes at the picture of Caro and the old cow still on the screen. The younger man, now, the younger man . . . the sideways wrinkle appeared between Lee's eyes. *What was he doing here?* He was no senior member of the elite. Lee was familiar with both other officials; they had been on the Board of Inquiry into the lumie affair when he had been commisioned to take charge of hunting down the surgically sighted lumies at the End Base. But what was this junior man doing here—and why was he so blasé about being in this high-level meeting?

The young man, in an immaculate lab jacket, sat there: glancing at the wall clock every few seconds, shifting in his chair, swirling a mug of tea, glancing knowingly, condescendingly at Lee and Lutes. As Lee watched, he looked again at the wall clock and, with a gleam of satisfaction, tapped the chest pocket of his white jacket, turning off a blinking message minder. Swiveling his chair, the young man caught the grey-haired woman's eye and nodded. He relaxed, sat back, and again swept both Lee and Lutes that look, that superior . . . pitying . . . look. . . .

Lee leapt to his feet, sending his chair spinning against the wall. He planted his hands on the table before him, leaned over the young man, now racked with panic, and glared deep into his eyes. Then Lee knew. He turned, kicked the chair out of the way, and slammed his fist against the door, sending it crashing against the outside wall. He ran, still glaring, a roar in his head, pushing his way impatiently through the wide-eyed men and women who stopped to gaze at him in amazement. Down the stairs, two, then three at a time, he reached the level of the basement, breathing harsh and deep. Another door smashed against the wall. In three strides he was across the hall to the Marine lab door.

It stood open; the security panel was disconnected, the wires hanging down, swinging. A blaze of white light lit the previously closeted room. The carepies' tank stood huge, open, empty. Strips of black insulation were peeled away in thick curls from the sides. The top had been cut open; the sections of silicone were tipped against the walls and the sides of the yawning tank. Water pooled along the floor with bits of black polymer floating in it.

Lee beat his fist on the side of the door, swearing cursing the young man who had known that the meeting was a set-up, an effective means to keep the two trouble-makers out of the way while the carepies were being transported into the End-region tunnels.

Lee took a step forward and tripped over Caro, huddled in dry-eyed pain against the wall. The others were with her: silent, horror-struck at the desecration.

"We tried to get in to tell you, but they wouldn't let us anywhere near the third floor," Hal said dully. "They started right away—as soon as you and Dr. Lutes left for the conference." He shook his head and rubbed his eyes behind his glasses. "I just can't believe they'd do this."

"At first we thought they were taking them to the ocean," Sherri said, her voice shaky. "Then Caro said no. And Hal said that you and Lutes would be here if that's where they were taking the carepies."

"They wrapped them in this thick stuff," Ricky said gulping, "and picked them up with log lifters. And they wouldn't quit—even when one of the carepies fell off—they just reloaded it and kept going."

Lee looked at Caro, who sat rocking against the wall hugging her knees to her. He opened up his mouth—and closed it again. No words. She turned and looked at him burning him with her eyes.

"We're going after them," Caro stated. "We are going to find them, aren't we." It wasn't a question.

"We'd better hurry," answered Lee.

They wore their suits—all five of them. Meeting the stubborn, united onslaught of Hal, Ricky, and Sherri, Lee had grabbed his face in despair, beside himself with anxious haste to be off before his security clearance was revoked, but desperate to leave the three behind with Dr. Lutes. "No," he said through gritted teeth. "No, I'm not going to risk taking all four of you. Caro needs to come— that's bad enough. I *cannot* answer for all of you."

It was Hal who won the day. "You've got it wrong," he said in a rough voice. "*We* are not going to let *you* answer for Caro alone—we're her friends and we're going to see that she's all right."

Lee had stared furiously, helplessly. In vicious impatience he snarled, "Jump in, then—I've got no more time to argue absurdities with idiots who haven't got a brain between them."

The drive leaving the Base was a silent, tense one. Waiting for the vehicle elevator, Lee sat sullen, tapping his fingers impatiently on the dash. They roared along the Base building, swerved around an incoming crawler, and sped down the track past the animal enclosures where the four remaining lumies stood watchful as cats. Security waved them through.

Caro sat in the front with Lee. In her lap, she cradled her wrist, on which was strapped a small, flat disc with a blinking red light. With each pulse it monitored the powerful signal waves from the equipment that would, by now, be mounted onto the carepies. Lee had his own, but Dr. Lutes had secured another for Caro. The small man had pressed it gently into her hand, saying, "Go carefully, my dear. God will be with you—in spite of evidence to the contrary. This instrument may help you in your search, but it is not to be relied upon. You have a far greater way of hearing. Listen; listen for them, my dear. You will hear."

The engine droned on, pulling them deeper into the eternal twilight, away from the piercing rays of the light beacons guarding the End Base. The crawler dropped down a steep slope and the lights winked out.

Out of sight of the Base, Lee turned off the track and began blazing a course through the End-region forest.

October, 2456
Actaeon—

   A short time ago, while going through Marchenko's files, I found something rather interesting. He had been theorizing that Lumini lupus *had adapted to half-light conditions by eliminating most of the neural connections between the bright-light sensitive cone cells of the retina and the optic nerve. Today I submitted a paper proposing that if a series of surgical connections could be made between the cone cells and the optic nerves* Lumini lupus *could be made to see in bright-light conditions . . .*

   My paper was well received. Marchenko would have been the man to head up a team to attempt it but he has disappeared. One day he was simply gone from the Base. The security people could find no trace of him—no trail of used supplies, no suit, no body. Again my research will have to wait.

                                        —Reginald

14

She-Who-Talks-with-Carepies

hey drove through the dark forest with **Lee** hunched solemnly over the wheel. The crawler and container unit jolted over the uneven soil, dodging the sinuous frontons, maneuvering around the wide "donut" structures formed from silicon plates. To Caro, staring out the front window, the frontons and doughnuts seemed to rush at them, leaping into the view cut by the four swaths of light from the crawler's headlights.

Lee ground the crawler to a halt. The silence in the vehicle deepened.

"Look," he said, "I'm sorry. I'm sorry, Hal and Sherri, and Ricky. I shouldn't have talked to you the way I did and I apologize. If anyone is an idiot in this group, it's me. You three are loyal friends, and we're a team—all five of us. I'm really sorry. It's just that, besides knowing the score out here better than you all, and, rightly being concerned at the risk we're all taking, I . . . well . . . I have to answer to your parents. They trusted you to me. And right now, if they knew what I was doing—" He chewed on his lower lip. "Well, I can already hear Miriam—not to mention Caro's and Ricky's mom, who has, by the way, an incredibly extensive vocabulary when she's angry. It is quite likely that I've just given up my welcome in both their homes . . . and that's if everything goes well—"

"Only for a little while," Sherri said, trying to comfort him. "You know that Mom can never stay mad at you for long."

"And you don't need to worry about my mom," Ricky put forth eagerly. "When she's as mad as she's going to be at you, she can't say a word—she just turns purple and sends you to your room."

Lee reluctantly laughed. "I won't even have a room to get sent to, Ricky," he said soberly.

"My dad will understand," Hal said with conviction.

Lee paused. "Yes. I believe he is the one person who will."

"We have to go; that's all there is to it," Caro said.

"That's about the size of it, isn't it," Lee muttered, turning back to the wheel.

And they were off again, further into the night, but the cloud inside the crawler had lifted; they were a team once more.

"Where are we going?" Hal asked.

"Lutes and I figure that the most likely place they'll dump the carepies is at the newest field camp. I've never been there—the big push in that camp is Geology, although Soil Science have digs there, too. And it's the geology people that have been trying to push the mapping of the deep waterways, so we're pretty sure that the carepies will have been taken there."

"How will they get the carepies underground?" Ricky asked.

"Unless they've managed to hit on a really lucky find, my guess is that they've drilled a shaft. They'll attach the recording and tracking gear to them and simply lower them in."

"So what do we do when we get there?" Hal asked, perplexed. "We can't go down the shaft—and we'll be too late to stop them, won't we? And how could we anyway?"

They were good questions. Sherri and Ricky waited, bolt upright, for Lee's answer.

"Yeah, we wouldn't have much hope at the site, that's true," Lee said. Caro caught a glint of humor in his voice. "But there's a funny thing about Geology's new field camp," he continued. "It's really quite close to a little underground hide-out that you might remember—"

"The cave!" Ricky screeched.

Lee nodded, the glint flashing into a full grin. "I think it's time we found out just where the tunnel goes. And unless I miss my guess, we should be able to pick up the trail of the carepies from there."

"But—we can't all dive like Caro," said Hal. "And won't the tunnels be filled with water—how can we follow them?"

"Ah, Hal, Hal." Lee sighed, still grinning. "Don't you remember, we have with us, She-Who-Talks-with-Carepies. Now I'm not sure of her range—" Caro stared at him dumbly, open-mouthed. "In fact," he continued, "I'll hazard a guess that she's not sure of her range, either—but, I'll lay you any odds that if the carepies can come to her, they will. Also, Lutes' results at Main show that carepies have a decided preference for breathing air over using their gill apparatus. They're going to head for the shallows. And that's where we'll be. And I've got an inflatable dinghy." He added smugly, "Any more questions?"

"Only one," said Sherri. "Panic makes me hungry—when do we eat?"

"When we get to the cave," Lee answered. "We'll have to cook—we're mainly equipped with dehydrated food—and I'm not going to stop and set up a stove and hydrogen bipack unit for water now. I've got some squeeze tubes floating around, if you're that starving."

"That stuff is horrible." Sherri grimaced and gagged in an effort to get her point across thoroughly.

"Really?" commented Lee. "I'm rather partial to the artificial liver and onions—with a chaser of pureed turnip. Of course it's hard to tell which is which—I'm forever mixing them up." He glanced with one eye in the rearview mirror to catch Sherri's look of disgust.

"No wonder you eat us out of house and home when you visit," she said with a shudder. "You need a wife, Uncle Lee."

"Oh, I'm too young to get married," Lee quickly responded.

"That's what Mom says, too," Sherri pursued. "But she also says that marriage would be the making of you—it would settle you."

"Surely Miriam has something nice to say about marriage—" Lee mused to the dark night.

"But that's the whole point," said Sherri. "Marriage would be good for you—What, Hal!" She turned to Hal who was grinning over the conversation.

"Sherri," he began, "Can you think of anything less appealing than something that's 'good for you'?"

"And," Lee broke in, "why any woman with any common sense would decide a vocation on 'settling someone' is beyond me. Marriage must have something better going for it than that. Surely you want more out of life for yourself than that, Sherri?"

Sherri was staring suspiciously at both of them. "Well—yes, of course—I don't intend to get married at all—I'm going to be an artist."

"Then have the goodness to allow me to stay single too, okay?" Lee pleaded.

"Yeah, but you're a lot older than me," Sherri persisted, in utter illogic. "And besides, Mom was so disappointed when you stopped seeing Kay—you remember, Hal—white-haired Kay, the nurse."

"Sherri, it's not called 'white-haired,' it's called being blond—you make her sound like a grandmother. So this is what this conversation is all about. Let me ask you one thing: how could I have stopped seeing the poor woman? I never started seeing her!" Lee protested.

"Well, why not?" Sherri happily continued. "I think she's really nice—she can't help having blond hair. Why don't you sort of hang around her?"

"Along with a multitude of other reasons, I don't think that her fiancé would take kindly to me 'hanging around' her."

"You're kidding!" Sherri wailed. "And she was so perfect for you!"

Lee beat his forehead with his hand. Then he leaned forward, gripping the wheel with both hands.

He slowed the crawler and began peering out the front window as the treads pulled them over the rough terrain. He flicked on the raised searchlights and began focusing them in arcs beyond the range of the crawler's headlights. "Almost there . . . "

"I don't see anything," Caro said in bewilderment.

"Give it a second," Lee replied. "I've got the distance programmed in the crawler locate, but I still go very carefully here. The End chalk hills can be deadly—if you're going too fast, or not really watching, you can run smack into them."

And then Caro saw a solid wall of grey loom up before them. Lee turned to the left and followed the jagged mass of stone a short ways. Then a careful turn to the right, and it seemed as though they were driving head-on into the rock. Caro had the eerie feeling that they were somehow moving straight through it; she sat, unconsciously leaning back, waiting for the impact. Then they were through the narrow cleft and in an echoing hollow in the chalk hills.

"Whew," said Hal in a shaky voice. "That was the strangest feeling—are we still alive?"

"Yep," replied Lee. "I know because I'm starving. Let's get unloaded."

The four began stuffing their pockets with gear and food and then filled each other's suit backpacks while Lee hooked up the wind generator to keep the crawler from freezing. When everything necessary was out of the container, Lee switched off the crawler's bright beams and, in that second, the knowledge of where they were became reality. They left the niche of rock and traveled the short distance to the tunnel that led into the cave.

Tramping through the dark in single file, only their meter-range hood lamps for light, they remembered and were silent. It was the same asphaltlike soil that held the prints of their boots and slowed their progress. Once again their ears rang with the single note of the End forest wind. The same feeling of *smallness:* the uncomfortable, all-encompassing, dreadfully sure knowledge that they were the tiniest of ants crawling a cast-off rind of a mega-galaxy.

Caro felt her eyes strain with the effort to see past their paltry light range, to reveal the secrets lurking in the shadows. Reminiscent dizzying orange spots leapt across her eyes, wearied already with the struggle to see beyond light. The peal of the wind, the subdued crunch of the soil underfoot, the flickering spots, the white suits rising and falling rhythmically before her—nothing seemed real. The dark—over all and through all—swallowed realness and spat it back as nightmare. Caro abruptly left the row of white shadows before her; she had to see, to touch something that could connect her to its physical reality.

She walked a few strides away from the others to the edge of the forest. The eerie forms of the frontons rising into the night seemed to defy physical law, their sinuous trunks too slender to hold their malformed limbs. The wind whistled through them like one-toned organ pipes, but moved nothing; there were no leaves. Caro reached out and touched a trunk that climbed toward the dark sky, extinguishing in the night; she pulled her hand away. The fronton was soft and mushroomlike. As light as air. Nothing.

"Caro!" Lee's voice spun her around, a touchstone in the darkness. "Let's stay together—we've got to get settled in the cave as quickly as possible."

Caro watched, dazed, as the rock swallowed one white-suited figure after the other. Then they were all through the hidden niche and the chalky-grey walls and ceiling and floor curved around them like a cocoon, sheltering them from the alarming expansiveness of night.

"All present and accounted for?" Lee's robust voice further shut out the deep dark.

The tunnel curved in a slow, lazy S, ending in the cave that had housed the five of them a few short months ago. Those months fled now as they pushed through the ancient blanket that Lee had tacked up in the entrance as a windbreak.

The cave was almost perfectly round, about ten meters in diameter. It looked as though it had been crafted; the walls were smooth and the floor sloped at a consistent degree toward the center. The ceiling arched uniformly; at the apex it was perhaps three meters high. Opposite the entrance there was a smaller passage out of the cave; it appeared to run perpendicular to the outside tunnel. The chalky-grey of the cave camouflaged the smaller passageway, making it difficult to see unless viewed directly from the front. There was a large, natural firepit cut deep in the wall; a cleft above it drew the smoke neatly.

Lee had made the cave his hermitage. A pile of assorted kitchen gear—a heavy frypan dark with soot, several spoons and forks stuck tidily in a clean pot, a kettle as blackened as the frypan, and a large pot that tilted benignly to one side—rested against the side of the firepit. On the opposite wall was a healthy pile of Jonah wood and, neatly stacked beside it, several rolls of paraffin igniting caps. Leaning against the wood was a long-handled peavey, used for shifting the heavy logs. A sleeping mat was rolled up and laid across another pile of gear, which included a hydrogen bipack unit and small bucket, an extra Zero suit and second power pack, a wind generator and a light. Suspended above was a net containing a variety of dehydrated food packets, squeeze tubes, and a container of duck tea.

Hal stared in fascination at the light by the wind generator, lying with its cord curled neatly about it. "Caro, doesn't that remind you of the light we hauled from the container unit halfway here when we were lost last time?" he asked.

Caro and the others crowded around him, gazing at the light. Caro nodded. "Remember getting sick of carrying it around and dumping it on the side of the track—"

"—when Ricky found the dried fronton sticks," finished Sherri.

"Yeah," echoed Ricky.

"Funny thing about that light," Lee mused, squinting into space. "I was just wandering around one fine expedition, and lo and behold, just a meter or two from where I stepped from my crawler, I came across this light—covered in frozen nut butter, I might add. I said to myself, who would be so careless as to leave such a valuable piece of Community property in the middle of nowhere? And covered in nut butter? Who could be so disrespectful? I guess I should have known . . . "

"Really?" Sherri squealed. "This is our light?!"

"I guess so," he answered. It still works—in spite of the nut butter."

Lee put down the small, methane-powered stove he was carrying and gazed about him with satisfaction. "It's good to be home," he said. "And everything is as it should be. Now, I'll start a fire; Hal, you light the stove; and the rest of you take out of your packs and various pockets what you need in order to be comfortable. And spread out your sleeping mats to sit on. Oh—and fight over who's going to do the cooking."

"Well I know who's not going to do the cooking," muttered Sherri in an aside to Caro. "I nominate Hal and Caro," she said loudly.

"Seconded," Lee said hurriedly, working a length of Jonah wood into the fire pit. He stuck two caps of paraffin against the log and held the lighter to them. *Whuff!* The cave was shot with light for several seconds, then the flash from the caps receded into two modest, hard-working flames, licking intently at the Jonah log. "I love doing that," Lee said.

Hal ran enough water to reconstitute the food that needed hydration before cooking. Soon he and Caro were leaning over the small campstove: stirring and tasting, adding handfuls of dehydrated leeks to the soup pot, scowling over the blandness of the beef-substitute pasta sauce, and burning their fingers on the too-rapidly toasting cheese bread. A third pot of water was handed to Lee to place over the fire to boil for a mountain of dried pasta, and the kettle was ready for duck tea. They were determined to fill everyone with one good, well-balanced meal before they began the precarious journey through the tunnels to find the carepies.

"This is way better than the food at the End Base," said Sherri through mouthfuls of pasta. Ricky nodded vigorously, his chin dripping with sauce. Lee tried to agree and choked on a noodle that seemed determined to investigate his esophagus.

Bright red, he was viciously pounded on the back by Sherri, until he could, in an unreliable voice, call her off. "All right, all right, Sherri—I'm fine—that is unless you've cracked a rib," he gasped. "This really is wonderful, you two."

Over duck tea they began yawning. Lee was intent on explaining the new mapmaker function of his suit locater. "The locater really is a wonderful device. I haven't used it underground, yet, but it has revolutionized crawler travel out here. I'll activate the one on my suit when we leave the cave. It records every shift of direction we make—if the new direction is longer than five meters—and records changes in altitude. When we're ready to come home, it compiles the data and draws a map. You can even program it to blink if you move off the designated route."

"Wait just a minute," Sherri broke in after a fearsome yawn. "You mean to tell me this little thing draws a map for you—just like that?"

"Just like that."

Sherri and Caro looked at each other. "It can't be that simple," Sherri declared.

"I think that he's leaving out the part where you have to take the readings and apply post-calculus theorems to find points that you plot on a special graph—" Caro began.

Sherri continued, "—of which there is only one copy—located in a locked vault—"

"—on Earth," Caro finished, grinning. Hal laughed and Ricky snorted.

"And when you need it," Hal added, "the only Community official who has the pass for the vault is—"

"—at lunch," said Ricky excitedly.

"—in a meeting," Caro provided.

"—dead," Sherri announced.

Lee smiled wryly, shaking his head. "No, it really is that simple," he protested. "You four are too young to be so cynical about scientific technology."

Various howls, exaggerated coughs, and one gagging sound filled the intercoms.

"Ha!" exclaimed Caro. "We've all grown up in scientific communities! We know what goes on!"

"Yeah," agreed Hal. "We've had to learn the 'final' scientific finding on everything—again and again."

"Dr. Krisman," said Sherri in a deeply serious tone, "how many scientists do you think it takes to unscrew the lid off a jam jar?"

The others leaned forward expectantly, staring into Lee's half-smiling face. "I don't know, you cynic," he finally answered.

"One," she replied sweetly. "But it takes him thirty years."

"That's not the way I heard it," Hal blurted with unaccustomed abandonment. "It's three: one to research the jar, one to research the lid, and one to do the paperwork for the Community files."

"—all in thirty years, no doubt," Lee commented.

"Now you've got the idea," Sherri said, patting him on the back and nodding wisely.

Ricky yawned so loudly there was an astonished silence before everyone burst into laughter. "I can't help it," he said gruffly. "Hal keeps yawning, too."

"You all are," Lee said. "Even Caro—and didn't she sleep for thirty-odd hours or something?" He smiled at her teasingly.

"Not quite thirty," Caro protested, fighting a yawn that threatened to erupt.

"It's the lack of light," Lee explained. "Your system gets tricked inside the End Base building because of the extremely high levels of light they bombard us with. But here your bodies are telling you that it is definitely night-time. So you should all sleep. Even I'll crash in a while."

"I thought we were in a hurry—what about the carepies?" Caro demanded.

"The hurry was for me to duck out before I was given some absurd, goose-chasing order for the sole purpose of getting me out of the area. I had to leave before I was told not to," he said frankly. "But we're not going to get much further without sleep, and besides that, it will take the carepies some time to move down this way."

"Lee, tell me again why you think they'll come in this direction," Sherri said.

"Three reasons: the first is that Caro, the carepies' friend, is here; we're higher here than where they've been dropped, so the water table's lower here; and the third reason is that we're closer to the ocean—which is where they want to go. We're not all that much closer, I'll admit, but it should be somewhat of a factor."

Sherri had reached in behind her faceplate and was holding her eyes open while he answered. "Don't mind me; you're not boring me at all. They just feel better this way."

Lee shook his finger at her. "You're in sad shape. All of you are. Look—just this once, I'll clean up. You four spread your mats by the fire and sleep. Okay?"

"Thank you, thank you, sweet Uncle. I'll never, no never, say anything bad about you again," Sherri said, hauling herself to her feet.

"Sherri, I wouldn't recognize you if you quit badgering me," Lee replied.

"I'll wear a name-tag" was the weary reply.

Caro's last recollection before she sank beneath waves of sleep was seeing Lee add another log to the fire. He assured her—was it verbally?—that he would keep checking the fire while they slept and that she would wake to its light.

November, 2456
Actaeon—

I have discovered something about Lumini lupus *that is far more important than any behavior "tricks" or peculiar physiological adaptations. There is a bizarre, highly accurate communication ability between the different subjects that make up our End Base pack. I think that if I proposed a paper on it that I would be put away like Marchenko. For surely the Community must be responsible for his disappearance. What would it do for morale if it became known that a scientist went batty? But still, the* Lumini lupus *communication network is what I secretly study daily. Astounding that this, Actaeon, the most important research I ever do, cannot be published, but must stay within this private journal. Why is the Community so set against "nonmaterial" research? Do they fear it? Or is it simply unmarketable to the economic boards? Probably both. I fear it—yet this strange, uncanny phenomenon has become my reason for being.*

—Reginald

15

Lumies

When they awoke the fire was out and the pit ice-cold. Lee was gone.

"This is ridiculous!" Sherri kept repeating. "He wouldn't leave us. He can't be gone."

Ricky, sleep still in his eyes, was sitting up on his mat looking crabby. Hal was trying to restart the fire without much success. Caro's insides had melded into a frozen ball of fear and she sat, hugging her knees, staring blankly at the small circle of light from her hood lamp that illuminated the mat under her feet. Her nightmare was coming true; if Lee had deserted her, who was there left to trust?

"Caro," Hal called, "can you help me? When I pick up the log, can you shove a cap under it? That's what Lee did, didn't he?" She didn't even hear him.

"Caro!" he called again, straining with the weight of the Jonah wood in the peavey.

"Caro!" Ricky's cranky, little-brother voice crashed through the wall of fear. "Caro! Does she have her intercom on?! Caro!"

"What, what?" she gasped.

"Help Hal!" Ricky shouted, wanting to take out his anger on someone.

"Oh—sorry, Hal." Caro sprang to her feet and set the caps in place. "As if you couldn't do this, Ricky!"

The caps flared high and wide and then burned with steady passion, igniting the log.

"Look," said Hal. "We have to quit panicking and getting mad at each other. We've been in a worse spot than this—let's just have some breakfast and talk this out. If Lee's not back by then—"

"He'll be back!" Sherri exploded. "This is ridiculous!"

"Hal's right, Sherri." Caro tried hard to control the gravel-like quality of her voice. "Let's just try to stay together on this."

"You don't need to order her around, Caro!" Ricky yelled belligerently.

Caro gave Sherri a "see what I mean?" look.

"Okay, let's eat something and talk," Sherri agreed. "I'll get some bread out. Can we toast it or something?"

"Good idea," Caro answered, relieved.

"Do you want your nut butter, Ricky?" Sherri asked.

"Yeah. I'm starving," Ricky noted in surprise.

"So am I," Sherri admitted. "Emergencies and Strange Events make me hungry, I guess."

They sat in a circle before the fire, toasting bread over the flames, burning their fingers as their forks grew too hot to hold. Ricky and Sherri devoured piece after piece thick with nut butter. Hal and Caro melted strips of cheese on their forks and wrapped heated bread around them. There was enough water in the kettle from the last meal to make duck tea—after it had thawed and re-boiled.

Finally they gave up any pretense at stalling for time—they had finished their silent meal and Lee had not returned.

"So," Hal said, looking into the fire, "what should we do?"

"He'll be back," Sherri insisted.

Hal and Caro ignored her.

"What are our options?" Caro asked harshly.

"Well . . . " Hal swallowed. "I think we need to check whether or not the crawler's still here."

"And if it is?" Caro asked. Sherri stared horror-struck from one to the other.

"If it's there, we wait. He's got to be somewhere around," Hal said, jiggling his foot nervously.

"And if it's gone?" Caro persisted.

"Then—"

"It will be there!" Sherri interjected indignantly. "I don't believe either of you! Don't you know who you're talking about? Lee would never, NEVER, deliberately leave us here!"

"Sherri, you're exactly right," agreed Hal. "Lee would never leave us here *deliberately*. But here we are, and he's gone. We have to face up to that and make plans."

Sherri hunched down over her raised knee and didn't look at anyone.

"We have only one option—we have to find him." The words spoke themselves; Caro listened as they left her mouth. "We have to find him."

Ricky looked up, at first speaking calmly, then growing more and more heated. "That's right. Well, it's about time somebody made some sense in here. What did you think we were going to do, Hal—run off home and leave Uncle Lee here?!"

It was Hal's turn to become stubborn. "We can do him much more good if we go to the End Base and tell them—I can drive the crawler. We don't even have any weapons!"

"What if he's hurt?" Sherri's mouth twisted.

"All the more reason to go get help," Hal said, vehement. "How do you think we could even move him—he weighs nearly double what I do, I'll bet."

"I don't think there's time," Caro said. Ricky and she exchanged looks.

"We have to go after him now or we may never see him again," Ricky said. There was a flicker of indecision in Hal's eyes. "Look," Ricky continued, "he wouldn't leave by himself—we all know that. Either he is lying hurt somewhere nearby, or he's been taken. If you want to risk it, you go to the Base. I'm going to look for Uncle Lee."

Hal licked his lips. "I still think that Base personnel could handle a search much more effectively than us. Look—maybe we should split up—two of us look for Lee, and two head for help."

"No way," Caro said, her heart leaping, sticking in her throat. "We stay together!"

Ricky zipped his faceplate closed. He got to his feet and walked to the scattered pile of packaged food and began stuffing a bag of dried fruit in his front pack.

"Okay, okay," said Hal in resignation. "We'll all go look for him. Let's pack up. But first," he said in a louder tone, "we have to go check to see if the crawler is still there— Look, it's the logical thing to do, okay?"

"We don't need to," Caro said in a funny voice. She began trembling.

"What? What's wrong?" Sherri cried.

"Look at the entrance," she replied, pointing.

The old yellow blanket had a length of Jonah wood neatly anchoring it to the floor of the cave to stop drafts. It could not have been positioned there by anyone on the other side of the blanket. Lee could not have left the cave that way.

"I—I—I didn't even think," stammered Hal. "I saw him do that before I fell asleep—but I didn't even stop to think about it. There's no other way out!"

"Yes there is." Caro shone her light on the little passage on the other side of the cave.

"You can't see it unless you look right at it," Sherri said with a shudder. "It's so small."

"I can fit through easily," said Ricky.

"We all can, Ricky—Lee must have," stated Hal.

"Maybe he just heard something and went to see what it was, and it took him longer than he figured," Sherri said in a rush.

"Maybe. Let's pack up." Hal looked sober.

They each carried, attached to their suits, an emergency hydrogen bipack unit; they would take turns running these off their energy packs. Food was shoved into suit pockets: dehydrated soup mix, dried fish, substitute meat, fruits and vegetables, lentils, the rest of the flat bread, cheese. Then they each chose the kinds of "security blanket" foods that they felt they could not survive without. Ricky made a grab for the nut butter and crackers. Sherri stashed a bag of onion crumbles in her front pocket. Hal, shamefacedly, loaded a package of rice cereal in his suit. Caro pushed extra hunks of the leathery cheese in her pouch. Then she and Sherri as one reached for Lee's favorite: roasted prawb seeds. They looked at each other, smiled, and each took a small bag for him.

Essential group items were stowed in their suit backpacks. Hal carried the small campstove, cooking utensils and fuel, while Sherri carried two pots nestled into one another. They filled up the corners with first-aid equipment, although Ricky carried the balance of the kit. Caro stubbornly decided to carry the portable wind generator and the light.

"We know there's only so much power in our suits," she said. "And we know that the temporary generator in our suits doesn't work if—for any reason—one of us can't keep moving. We may really need the wind generator—and the big light." Sherri helped Hal load it into her pack without any argument. She and Caro stuck the telescoping extension for the light into Ricky's pack.

Ricky began climbing on his hands and knees through the small shaft out of the cave. Hal worked his way through next. "It's lots bigger than it looks," he called out in surprise.

Caro began leaning into the tunnel when she felt Sherri tug on her suit.

"What?" Caro asked, intent on following after Hal's rapidly disappearing heels.

"Wait!" Sherri cried.

"What, Sherri?" Caro asked again, fully irritated.

"I'm afraid," she whimpered, looking around. Caro felt the hair on the back of her neck stand up. The last thing she needed was more fear to add to her own.

"I'm scared of small spaces like this—I had trouble enough in the tunnel at the End Base. Really," Sherri said, rocking in fear. She still grasped Caro's suit.

"Well, you can stay here, if you prefer." Caro heard an unfamiliar icy voice proceed from her lips.

"No, no," Sherri whined.

"Look—I can't even see Hal anymore. They're leaving us," Caro said, her own fear driving her. She hated herself.

"Okay," Sherri said in frantic despair. "But please let me go in front of you."

"Just hurry up." The horrible voice spoke again through Caro's lips, and she was helpless to stop it.

As she climbed through the hole, Caro heard Sherri's teeth chattering over the intercom. After a short twist to the left, the passage widened into a tunnel that was high enough so that the girls, with heads slightly bowed, could stand up and walk.

The tunnel was a smooth, circular tube that had the same uniformly carved look of the cave. The concave floor sloped downhill and at first seemed precarious: Caro had the alarming feeling that if she yielded to the temptation to begin rushing down the slope, she would run faster and faster, out of control, and never stop. Sherri was already running heedlessly, unthinking in her anxiety. Caro lost her head and leapt after her, just as reckless in her wild panic at being left behind.

The tunnel continued turning. The girls, clutching at the wall in their frightened haste, rushed down the passage, and abruptly came to the end of the semicircle. They nearly ran over Hal and Ricky who were hunched down against the side, waiting for them with great impatience.

"Will you quit pushing me," Sherri said to Caro in a high, tense voice, breathing hard.

"I'm sorry," Caro gasped, leaning over and trying to regain her wind.

The passage had led them into a vestibule of sorts: the ceiling rose high above, and before them two tunnels split in different directions.

"Well, which way?" Caro asked, still panting.

"I don't know," Hal replied, rubbing his neck. "Do I ever have a crink. What held you two up? Ricky was ready to go back for you."

"It's a good thing I didn't," grumbled Ricky. "You would have flattened me." Sherri had run right over the toes of his boots before she could stop. He got up and peered down one tunnel and then the next.

"It was my fault we weren't right behind you," said Sherri, candidly. "I have a confession to make. I have this fear of enclosed spaces."

"Sure," said Hal, swiveling his neck about painfully.

"No, really," insisted Sherri. "I'm not too bad here where there's more room, but right at the entrance . . ." She shuddered. "I never would have done it if Caro hadn't made me go."

Caro, hidden deep in her hood, blushed in mortification. *Were enclosed spaces for Sherri what the lock had been for her?* "I'm really sorry, Sherri," she said tremulously. "I shouldn't have been so unsympathetic. It's just that I was scared to death to be left behind." She gulped at the horror of it.

Sherri nodded. "I know what you mean. I kept chanting to myself: 'it's worse to be left by myself, it's worse to be left by myself'! At least I made it this far—and as long as the tunnel stays like this, I'll be okay," she said bravely.

"How far do you think we've gone?" Caro asked, anxious to change the subject for her.

"I would guess almost a kilometer," Hal said. "I sure wish we had Lee's mapmaker. We're really going to have to keep our eyes open—especially at forks in the road like this. Okay—which way should we go?"

"To the right," Sherri and Caro said immediately. They looked at each other and laughed. "My mother has this theory," Sherri said, "that if you're ever lost in a maze all you do is keep taking every right turn and you'll find your way out."

"That's ridiculous," Hal said.

"No it's not," insisted Sherri.

Caro said, "You know, I never thought about it before, but she's right." Hal looked at her in disbelief. "Think about it a minute, Hal. Take every 'right' turn and you'll be all right. Get it?"

Hal laughed shortly. "Yeah, yeah."

Sherri looked wide-eyed. "You know, I'll bet you anything that that's what it is after all—a joke someone told Mom that she never got!"

"And I can guess who told her that joke, and laughs up his sleeve every time she mentions it seriously," said Hal.

"Her dear baby brother," Sherri said. "Well let's go find the bum."

"Okay—you two say 'to the right.' Ricky, what do you think?" Hal asked.

Ricky was kneeling on the floor of the right tunnel. "Quiet—be quiet," he hissed. "Turn your outside 'ears' on, but don't say anything."

They had been conversing through their intercoms, which intercepted signals only from each other's inner communication channel. At Ricky's urgent request, they switched over to pick up outside information. At this setting, their voices would project outside as well.

They heard the *hooo* of the wind and the soft rustle of their suits as they moved. Sherri's boot scraped along the ground as she squatted down.

Hal readjusted his intercom. "I didn't hear anything, Ricky," he said.

"Neither did I," Caro said, confused. She hadn't, it was true, *heard* anything, but she had felt a soft movement, a brushing of something or other, a presence moving away.

Sherri had her head cocked to one side. "I thought I heard something, but now it's gone," she said softly.

"Come over here." Ricky barely breathed. "Put your units right on the tunnel wall."

They shuffled over to Ricky, scared to breathe too loudly, bumping into each other, resembling white, rather lame, penguins, each vying for a spot against the wall.

"I still can't hear anything," Hal said, frustrated.

Sherri's head jerked up and she looked at Ricky. He nodded. Then Caro caught a faint, very faint sound. And again the feeling of some presence . . . *What is it?* She heard the sound more completely now; it had a regular rhythm. It reminded her of something—the dripping of water? No . . . Although it was similar, it was less intense. She tried to join in her mind the faint sound to the feeling it gave her. She closed her eyes and saw her old tabby cat that she had had when she was Becka's age. *Pad, pad, pad.* The picture in her mind changed, grew larger. Caro stiffened and sat up, her eyes wide and staring.

"It can't be," Caro spluttered, frantically adjusting her intercom so that she could talk freely. "They don't live here! We know that! They only naturally habituate the half-light zone—we're almost in the one-eighth—and headed deeper!"

"What, what," Hal was saying. "What did you hear?"

Caro looked at him, still sputtering. "It *can't* be them!"

Sherri glanced at Ricky again and he said one word: "Lumies."

Sherri held up her hand for silence and turned her intercom back. "I can't hear them anymore," she finally said, twisting around and facing the others.

"So they're moving away from us." Hal forced himself to speak calmly.

"But Hal, you read the paper I handed in on the lumies—'all research indicates that *Lumini lupus* inhabit the *narrow* niche of the half-light zone of the End region.' I got an 'A' on the paper," Caro wailed idiotically.

In spite of the tension—or perhaps because of it—they began giggling.

"Caro," Hal asked, "how many scientists does it take to unscrew the lid off a jam jar?!"

"Ha, ha," she responded weakly.

"Maybe they don't live here normally, and maybe they do. For all the papers written, nobody really knows much about the End region," Hal said, sobering.

"I know it was lumies," Ricky said. And Caro knew it, too.

"Maybe Lee heard them too and started out after them." Hal leaned his head against the wall, thinking.

"Probably he still is—he went further than he thought and doesn't want to give up the chase. After all, he knows we can take care of ourselves," Caro said staunchly, lying to herself. The last image of Lee stoking up the fire and assuring her he would keep it lit while they slept was too strong, too true. She knew in her heart that something was very wrong.

Sherri looked dubious. Ricky stated, "We have to follow them."

Hal admitted that the lumies seemed to be the only clue to Lee's disappearance. "We can stay a good distance away from them," he said. "Sherri, you and Ricky go first—with your ears on. If you hear anything, signal, and we'll stop awhile and let the lumies get further ahead. Hopefully, we'll start to hear Lee—and eventually catch up to him."

"Shouldn't we turn off our hood lamps?" Sherri asked hesitantly.

There was a brief pause while they looked uneasily at one other. No one wanted to walk the dark tunnel without a light.

"Let's have one light on only . . . " Hal began to say slowly.

"No," Caro said. "Let's just turn them to single beam right at our feet, then when Ricky thinks we're too close, we'll turn them off. After all, we need to be sure that we don't fall or something and make a noise."

There was relief at Caro's statement. Of course they needed their lights on—it would be disastrous to crash into each other, or the wall—or walk off some dark precipice.

The silent journey seemed to go on forever. Every step they took, anytime a boot scuffed against the ground, they would jump, startled, their nerves strung to agonizing tension. Every so often, Sherri and Ricky would give deep, emphatic nods, and the four would freeze where they were and wait until Ricky began cautiously inching forward again.

The tunnel had grown wide and high; no longer could Caro feel both walls with her arms stretched out at her side. And by the way the sound echoed through her intercom, she knew that the ceiling was high above her. She still had the sensation that the tunnel was continuing to slope downward, but she had lost her ability to tell objectively what was "up" and what was "down."

Suddenly Sherri was making frantic motions and Ricky's arms were waving wildly. He stopped himself so completely from proceeding in a forward direction that he slumped to the ground. Sherri squatted beside him, listening intently.

Against the continuing rush of the wind, Caro heard the soft, *pad, pad, pad* of the cushioned feet of the lumies. Her skin seemed to stand out stiffly from the rest of her, and she wondered, her mouth dry, how many there were in the pack.

"I can even hear them now," Hal whispered.

"I think we're very close," breathed Ricky. "Too close."

Sherri was silent.

"Wait," Caro whispered. "What are we so worried about? Remember, these are wild, normal lumies—not lab animals that were surgically sighted—these will be afraid of humans."

"Not if we walk in on their young," Hal answered softly.

"No, but we can always use the light—their eyes can only function at half-light levels. Our light will blind them," Caro persisted.

"What light, Caro? Our hood lights have about a meter range—that's not going to stop even one angry, or frightened, lumie," Hal argued.

"No!" said Caro, trying to keep her voice down. "I've got the big light—our old light, remember? And the wind generator!"

"Maybe we can use it as a weapon of defense," Hal said slowly. "Ricky—can you still hear them? I can't."

"Oh, yes," replied Ricky. "But they stop. Now they're going on—they're still moving away—I think."

"I'm not so sure," Sherri whispered. "I can't figure it out this time. They're definitely quieter, though. So they must be going further away."

Caro felt a vague uneasiness. She could hear the sporadic movement of the lumies, and it did grow quieter. Why then did she feel their presence so strongly? With an effort, she concentrated on the light.

"Okay," said Hal, making up his mind. "Let's rig up the floodlight and carry it ready to go. If we need it, I'll flick it on."

Caro turned around and Hal and Sherri hauled out the light and generator from her suit pack. Ricky and Sherri shone their hood lamps on Caro and Hal as they began hooking up the light to the generator. As the turbine was uncovered, the wind caught the small, bent blades and they instantly began humming.

"Look, before we harness this thing to me," said Hal. "Let's turn on the light—just to try it out—in the opposite direction, of course."

A chill ran through Caro. *What was the opposite direction?* She—like the others—had turned around a couple of times, adjusting this, moving that. She had totally lost all sense of direction.

"Uh, does anyone know what direction we are supposed to be headed in?" Hal voiced Caro's fears.

205

Everyone was silent.

"That way," cried Sherri and Ricky at the same time, pointing in opposite directions. They glared at each other, frustrated.

"Oh, wonderful," groaned Hal, beating his head.

"No, wait—it's okay," blurted Caro in relief. "All we have to do is listen, remember? We can tell in what direction the lumies are going—and that's our direction, too."

"Caro, you're a genius," exclaimed Sherri.

"Actually, we were all pretty stupid not to think of that," Hal said with a twisted, limp grin.

It was an obvious, simple plan that should have worked—but it didn't. They couldn't hear the lumies.

"I know why." Ricky spoke rapidly. "There must be a fork in the tunnel up ahead—or a turn or something. And that's why we were having trouble hearing them a few minutes ago—they've gone around a corner."

"That doesn't help us any," Hal said. "We still don't know which direction is the right one. I mean, we can walk one way and listen and not hear a thing in either case."

"Let's turn on the light," Caro said, frantic. "Maybe we can see paw marks or something—anything!"

"Why not?" Hal threw up his hands. "I just can't believe we were all so stupid as to get turned around like this."

"At least we don't have to worry about the lumies seeing our light," Sherri said in an odd, sobbing tone.

"Okay, I'm turning it on—it'll be pretty bright," Hal warned.

It was blinding.

"Yeow!" cried Sherri, throwing her arms over her faceplate.

"I can't believe this!" Caro said, shielding her eyes.

"Wow—just think what this would do to the lumies," Ricky cried gleefully, his head buried between his knees.

But it didn't do anything to the lumies. When Caro and the others' eyes adjusted to the brightness of the light she saw that they were pinned to the wall of the wide tunnel, surrounded by silent, motionless, unblinking lumies.

16

The Furred Man

L ee slowly opened his bruised hand, wincing as he attempted to move each rapidly swelling finger. At least all his fingers were still there . . . It had been a stupid thing to do—pulling out one small tranquilizer gun in the middle of a pack of twenty-odd lumies. He laughed shortly, massaging his hand.

The lumies had brought him here. Strange, so strange: the tremendous weight of the pack pushing against him, jaws clamped firmly on his hand until he quit resisting. They had maneuvered him along the tunnels to this cave, as tight as a jail, and now stood on guard just outside the entrance. The strangest thing of all was that they hadn't killed him.

Lee looked around the small, narrow cave, lit feebly by the blue-green flickering in the center of the floor. Dried fronton sticks were stacked within arm's reach of the fire. Several thick-furred lumie hides were heaped up like a couch. A smoked haunch of what looked like lumie meat hung from the low ceiling. Lumie teeth were festooned on crudely spun fiber. Bones and teeth lay in piles on a rough shelf of rock carved from the side of the cave. There was a second shelf under it with a stack of what looked like notebooks, papers. Lee took a step toward them, playing his hood lamp across the pile.

Journals. Scientific Circulars from the End Base. *Lee's own unpublished paper on lumie behavior.* His hands began shaking as he held it, because there was no explanation for its being there. More journals. Several of his reports on the lumie clean-up.

Lee sat down on the hides and held his head. He reached out and touched the rock that edged the firepit. It was solid, tangible, warm from the fire. Lee walked to the entrance and took one careful step out. *Whumpff!* The teeth missed his throat by millimeters. He picked himself up off the ground from where he had hurled his body backwards: the lumies were real enough. Lee looked around the small cave again. And so were the journals.

Lee pulled several bound volumes off the uneven shelf, carried them to the pile of lumie pelts by the fire, sat down, and began to scan through the entries, seeking some kind of answer.

Most of the entries were written as letters: to Actaeon from Reginald . . . He looked at the binding. A faint, gold imprint . . . Lee held the journal up to the fire. His hood lamp was too bright; it washed away the color of the letters. *R.A. Coleney.*

Lee sat up. Coleney was something of a legend; a veterinarian with a double doctorate in molecular genetics and animal behavior, he had been an early leader in the field of genetic behaviorism. Coleney was a pioneer in lumie research; it was he who first proposed that *Lumini lupus* could physiologically be made to see in full-light conditions. Coleney had not lived long enough to see his proposal first become general procedure, and then, under Lee's efforts, be banned by the Community.

The journals began ten years earlier—while Coleney was still in a research unit on Earth. Lee flipped through the pages written by this brilliant, widely read man. How tragic that an innocent research proposal had turned nightmare—and cost him his life. Lee shook his head, a smile flickering—he would have liked this fellow scientist who labeled the Community's dictatorship of Clytie "a circus" and the Community's officials "grinning half-wits who delighted in trained monkeys."

Lee rubbed his hand over his face. He got up and walked restlessly around the small cave. He paused and listened by the entrance. First, nothing, then a familiar mewling grumble. Lee threw a few more sticks on the fire with impatient force, then settled back down on the hides and picked up another journal.

He flipped through the next volume idly. He was getting sick of Coleney's theories about the lumies; he was getting sick of lumies, period. Almost immediately something caught his eye and he sat bolt upright.

The writing had changed—that is, the handwriting became crude, childish, and, instead of normal, everyday pen ink, the entries had been made with the thick phosphorous ink that scientists used when writing notes in the dark. The ink would glow briefly and fade out gradually, leaving a raised, green script while the writer was recording his observations.

Lee stared at the writing, comparing it to earlier entries. At times the letters crossed into the previous line, running on an angle. Had Coleney had a stroke? Were these entries made by Coleney? The wording in certain respects was the same, yet different: terse, fragmented, as crude as the letters that formed the jarring phrases.

A third difference: the entries no longer were formatted as letters. Lee paged back and began reading from where the changes occurred.

November 17, 2456
It's been three days since I left Blake and Wolnichuk
chasing the odd, eyeless creatures that dart across the
tundra. Blake named them "queechies" from the noise
they make. He and Wolnichuk were under my orders
to tag a random sampling of the rodentlike animals.
Am sure that the Lumini lupus live off them—what
else is there is for such a large mammal to survive on
in this frozen region? No L lupus sighted yet.

November 19
Have noticed myself thinking out loud. Must be a
reaction to total withdrawal from human voices. Any
voices. No one for my intercom to pick up. Strange,
strange, to hear nothing but the infernal whine of
wind. Still no L lupus.

November 20
Reached the cave where I stored my gear and not a
minute too soon. Near exhaustion—air and energy
depleting rapidly from this suit—quite light-headed
and cold for some time . . . New energy pack in place
and have just finished eating. Now I'll sleep.

November 23?
My timepiece stopped. I have repaired it, but must
guess at the date. Found a tunnel in the cave yesterday.
Began exploring it first thing. The tunnel is like a mine
shaft—round and smooth, as if it had been drilled. It
slopes down, easy walking. Been walking 6 hours, no
end yet.

November 25?
I'm lost. At about 20:00 yesterday, I decided to give up
exploring the shaft and head back to the cave where

my supplies are. Must have missed a fork—I've been
walking, on and off, for 14 hours, trying to find my
way back.

November 29?
Still lost. My hood light is very faint. Not much more
energy left in this suit.

December 1?
Cold. Bone-bitter cold. A killing cold. I'm already dead.
If by some absurd twist of fate I survive, it will be
because I will have become a different creature . . . man
does not belong here and never will conquer this harsh,
dark realm.

December 17?
I'm still alive. L lupus down here. Came across an old,
lone one—probably turned out of the pack because it's
lost its usefulness. I killed it and am wearing its smelly
hide next to my skin. Nothing to cook the meat over; it's
like chewing soggy leather. The blood will keep me going.

December 23?
Can only tell what "day" it is by my wake-sleep cycle.
No more energy in my suit. Am still cold, but the fur
helps. No light but for this briefly glowing ink. If I write
too slowly, the word ahead disappears before I get the
next one down. But I can read it by feel.

Christmas, December 25?
Have attached myself to a small pack. They seem to be
traveling. Possibly a group of hunters or scouts?
They're puzzled by me, but so far not aggressive. I think
I smell like one of them because of the fur I'm wearing.
Am noticing flashes of light periodically—green spots

above me, beside me, dripping all around me. Could be physiological—low blood sugar? Dehydration? Malnutrition? Or maybe psychological.

December 28?
Discovered that I can breathe down here. Not sure why—I'm warmer, too. Opened up my hood and can hear better. There's a draft in the tunnel with a monotonous whine. One animal limps.

January 1, 2457?
Happy New Year to me? Still following the pack. One older animal is obviously limping more and more. Could they have chosen this underground route because it's less difficult than outside? Can't figure out if they can see in the dark, or just know this trail by smell. They never falter—but I can hear the old one laboring. Almost bumped into it once. Still seeing shooting light out of the corners of my eyes. Highly irritating.

January 3?
I killed the old one. Tied the hide around my head and shoulders and got rid of my hood. Shared the meat with the rest of the pack.

January 5?
Noticed that the trail is starting to move upward—getting colder. I may be able to survive underground, but I know that I'll never make it outside. Not sure yet what to do.

January 9?
Have made my decision. I must stay underground. I

214

turned around when we woke and headed back down the tunnel. One of the animals has stayed with me.

January 11?
Have been walking with one hand trailing the wall and have found a side tunnel. We're following it. The green spots in my eyes are driving me crazy. The animal that stayed with me never bumps into anything. Why? It can't know this tunnel; I chose it randomly.

January 16?
Constant green spots before my eyes. They dance and glow in the distance and almost seem real. I think they are caused by my involuntary straining to see. I must guard against following the light-spots blindly—surely that is the way of madness.

January 17?
Have made an interesting discovery. The animal that stayed with me is blind. It is perfectly adjusted to this underground darkness—never falters. Perhaps the other senses, such as hearing and smell have compensated, but I think there is something here beyond that.

January 20?
I've made a crucial decision. In order to adjust fully to my new environment I must be a new creature. I cannot conquer this overwhelming forced-staring to see light where light can never be. The only way to stay sane is to put out my eyes.

January 22?
Will place several drops of topical anesthesia in my

*eyes. Will follow through with an injection of —— in
each.*

February 1?
*. . . the habit to write and read is so strong. I've taught
myself to read the thick, phosphorous ink with my
finger tips. The green spots have disappeared.*

Lee began intently paging back over the entries, trying to pinpoint the year they were entered. He found what
he was looking for: 2456, the year Coleney disappeared.
But the entries went on. And on.

There was a rush of fur at the entrance of the cave and
Lee leapt up, startled.

"Is it Reginald," asked Lee, "or Actaeon?"

17

Green Pearls

H al and Caro stood as if turned to stone, still bending slightly away from the light, holding their arms up as shields from the blinding rays. Sherri and Ricky had instinctively scrambled backwards, flat against the wall. All four pairs of eyes were riveted on the lumies forming a barrier before them.

The lumies silently, steadily hemmed them in, the space between them shrinking tighter and tighter. They gazed steadfastly at the four, their white-ringed eyes and dark lashes unblinking in the bright light. A voice within Caro screamed indignantly, "This is crazy! They should be running! They're supposed to fear light!" But her mouth remained firmly closed. Not one of the four dared to move.

Still the lumies moved in on them. Hal shuffled against Caro, stiff with fear, as a large lumie reared above him, baring his teeth and moaning. Caro sidestepped into Sherri, still adhering firmly to the wall.

Then the lumies surrounding Ricky fell back. Mewling, they turned their backs on the four and stepped forward, ears twitching backwards. The lumies by Hal were pressuring him to move; he was white with panic, pushing against Caro, who, in turn, pressed harder than ever upon Sherri.

A second lumie reared up and whapped at Hal with his paw. That did it. Hal, driven by utter panic, a salt-white ring around his blue lips, shoved so hard at Caro that the desperate force of their combined weights caused Sherri's limpetlike hold on the wall to be broken. She fell into Ricky, who took a step forward. And then another. And then a third. The four moved in a petrified unit, Caro working hard to free her heels from the toes of Hal's boots.

The lumies in front of Ricky began giving ground, while the ones at Hal's back drove them on. The realization of what was happening penetrated Caro's frozen brain: the lumies were taking them somewhere.

There they were, marching along, underground, deep in unexplored territory, being herded by lumies probably to their deaths, and Ricky whispered, "I knew this was the right direction, Sherri!"

"I don't think that matters now," she answered in a strained, breathy voice.

Caro realized, to her surprise, that her mind was operating with diamondlike precision. She rapidly saw that Lee must have been captured in much the same way, and that it was likely that they would be taken to the same place as he. Were the lumies doing this on their own? she wondered. Was there a more intelligent force directing them? Perhaps there had been a central intelligence with whom they had communicated all along.

She watched them: their heavily pelted, muscular backs moving before and all around her. They marched in military precision but flowed with natural grace. Three mahoganies, two chestnuts, three black-and-whites, a dusky brown one with irregular white splashes, and an ugly red brindle beast; there were ten lumies forming the unbroken circle around them. All seemed to be in prime age and condition. All ten pairs of round ears stood out from their broad heads and twitched and quivered, as sensitive as geigers, as adapted to the environment as the grey walls on either side of them. *How could they have hoped to sneak along behind them unheard?*

The lumies moved as a unit. There was no hesitation as they neared a fork in the tunnel; they swept the four humans into the left arm without a break in stride. Yet each animal was an individual. For instance, the red brindle had an itch in its back; it sent a deep quiver through its skin, then twisted around in a mighty arc and bit into its deep fur fiercely. Sherri looked ready to collapse; the red brindle was on her right side.

The tunnel began to close in. Occasionally Caro could feel the top of her hood brush against the ceiling, and the lumies at their sides began to fall back behind Hal or move in front of Ricky. Sherri began breathing heavily, and Caro prayed fervently that she would be able to handle her fear.

There was loose rubble underfoot here. Caro kicked something hard and let out an agonized "Ow!" before she realized it. Ten pairs of ears registered the sound, but the lumies did not pause.

Then Ricky stumbled. Sherri, moving by sheer force of will, couldn't stop in time and fell headlong over him. Caro stopped dead and remained upright, until Hal barged straight into her. They collapsed in a heap, the lumies behind Hal actually crashing right into them.

Caro's cold, clear mind said, *This is it. We are dead.* But nothing happened.

The lumies seemed uncertain at first. Hal picked himself off the top of the heap and helped Caro and Sherri to their feet. Ricky was furious with the others for falling on top of him. He was panicked and shocked by his hard fall, and it burbled forth in anger.

"You didn't need to kill me, too! It's bad enough that the lumies are! Now you've scared them!" he shouted senselessly. "I'm sick of you stepping on me, Sherri! Quit pushing me—all of you!"

"Look!" called Sherri, ignoring Ricky. "Look at the wall! It's a *painting!*"

"Rock pictures," Hal corrected, still keeping his voice down, as if the lumies couldn't hear him. "Look—they're up higher, too. They must be from minerals or something . . . "

The pictures were childlike in their intensity. Swirling, shooting flashes of oranges, blues and reds upon clouds of green. They made Caro think of fireworks.

The lumies had re-grouped. They began to crowd the four humans again and the strange cavalcade resumed walking quickly down the passage. The realization of their near escape hit Caro and she began trembling. The lumies had been given a prime excuse to attack and had not taken it.

Hal voiced Caro's thoughts. "Can you believe it? They could have thought we were trying to escape—or even launching an attack—but they didn't do anything. One fell right on top of me, but he just scrambled off right away. This is really strange."

"Yes," said Caro. "Look at their ears when we talk— but they don't even hesitate, they just keep us going."

"They remind me of giant guard dogs," Sherri added.

"That's it," Ricky said. "They've been trained. They aren't wild at all. They're taking us somewhere."

"All right," Sherri joked nervously, "who was the idiot who said, 'take me to your leader'?"

"Don't look at me," Hal answered, trying to grin. Every once in a while he still trod on Caro's heels and she knew that it must be very nerve-wracking to have five sets of lumie jaws and claws right at your back.

Sherri continued, "Maybe their leader is a reclusive artist . . . "

"Yeah, maybe he just wants some new models," Caro added wryly. "What I can't figure out is their eyes. They had absolutely no reaction to the big light—we were blinded; they didn't even blink!"

It didn't make sense. Either the lumies' eyes had been physiologically altered to withstand full light, or these animals were a genetic variant of the "normal" lumies in the half-light zone. *But how was it that they could also march so unhesitatingly through the dark?*

The tunnel had been banking to the left. As they rounded the curve, they saw a greenish glow in the distance. As they drew closer it grew brighter, larger. Unmistakably, there was light ahead. Caro fixed her eyes on the green vividness emanating from the top of the tunnel about twenty meters away.

They came closer to the green glow. Then it was over them, gleaming from the ceiling as the tunnel abruptly widened into a cave. They were marched through the cave and ushered down a small side passage to the right that led into a smaller cave. The lumies did not all enter the side passage, and the three that did turned around and left the four dazed humans staring after them as they padded back up the small shaft toward the larger cave.

Hal and Caro looked at each other, then at wide-eyed Sherri and Ricky. Without a word the four began to walk out of the small cave. Snarling wails filled their heads and they backed up hurriedly, each stepping on the one behind in their haste.

"Well, I guess we're here!" Sherri exclaimed in a shaky voice.

"Yeah—but where's 'here'?" Hal asked.

"And why?" Caro said, somewhat absently. She was fascinated by the green glow. This smaller cave was even more vibrantly lit than the expanse of the tunnel-room.

Ricky had approached a lighted area and was staring up at it. Caro joined him, mystified at the translucent glow that seemed to drip from the ceiling and walls. The light emanated from tiny green beads that were joined together in ornate, weblike strands. Their rich gleam made Caro feel thirsty.

"Look!" she cried. "They move!" The beads seemed to stretch out and, amoebalike, move in fingerlets along the wall.

Ricky turned. "No! Over there!" he yelled excitedly and dashed across the cave. He pointed up at a rock column that stretched from the ground to the ceiling. The green gleam dripped in webs off the ceiling and down the pillar. Before anyone could stop him, Ricky jumped up and touched the edge of the drip. His glove glowed green.

"Wow!" he marveled. Ricky reached out and touched his sister with it. Caro's suit gleamed where his hand had been.

They began playing with the light. Whatever they touched with the beads glowed and gleamed and lit up the darkness. Soon they were covered with them. Sherri turned off her hood lamp and stood there in the dark, radiating neon-green. The others immediately switched their lamps off and looked at one another.

"Like a black-light," Hal commented, waving his arms around.

"I wonder if the light wears out?" Sherri asked, flitting about the cave. She danced around, pirouetting with her arms out. Ellipses and entwining circles cut through the night.

Ricky spun madly around and the green sprayed from him, forming a gleaming cloud around him. The beads did not fall from him; they seemed to string themselves together and cling tight to their own intricate pattern.

"I don't think it can wear out," Caro said, her eyes shining. "I'm sure that they're alive—like some kind of luminescent bacteria or something." A strand of green beads moved slowly off one arm and Caro caught it in her palm. Holding her hand high, she let the strand slip from it down into her other hand. The web remained connected, the pattern reorienting itself to this new size and position.

"Hey! They go back up, too." Hal held a handful of green pearls to the wall. They watched the smaller pattern lose itself inside the larger web above it.

Caro moved beneath the pillar until the dripping heap of green flowed onto her, spilling over her head and shoulders. She gasped as the green covered her faceplate and then slid down. "I love it," she said, utterly thrilled.

It was Ricky who called them back to their situation. "This isn't getting us any closer to Uncle Lee," he blurted.

"What do you suggest, Ricky?" Caro retorted. "Shall I shoo the lumies away for you?!"

"We have to do something! We've come all this way!" he yelled.

"You mean we've been taken all this way," Caro corrected him sarcastically. "There's a tiny bit of a difference, you know."

"We could look over the cave to see if we can get out any other way," said Hal the peacemaker.

They turned their hood lamps back on and began to carefully inspect the walls for any possible way out. The green beads flowed from them, or over them, forming small webs, or rejoining the large pattern along the walls. There was no sound but the scrape of boots on chalky rock and the scratch of gloves on the walls of their prison.

"Look—" Sherri said hesitantly.

"What!" demanded Ricky, crowding into her.

"That thick patch of green," she pointed. "Right there—it's not solid—"

"None of it's solid," Ricky returned in disgust. "It's all tiny beads in long stretchy strings."

"No, no," Sherri murmured, still staring. "There—did you see it?"

Caro nodded; there had been an almost imperceptible wave in the beads just above their heads to the left of the pillar. The green patch undulated again, like a waving curtain, or a spider web in the breeze.

"There may be a draft behind it . . . It may be too small, though," Hal said, trying to keep his excitement down.

"Boost me up, Hal," Ricky demanded. He scrambled onto Hal's shoulders and stuck his hand right through the mass of gleam and swept it partially aside. Sure enough, there was a dark hole behind it.

"I'm going in there!" Ricky scrambled over Hal's head and pushed through the green curtain. The others saw the soles of his boots gleaming green as he disappeared.

"Ricky! Come back!" shouted Hal. "Give us a report!"

Ricky's head burst through the beads. The imp within Caro laughed at the incongruous picture of the gleaming light surrounding his head; he resembled a grubby cherub with a green halo.

"It's perfect!" he exclaimed. "There's a shaft here, not just a hole! It goes up and to the right. There's plenty of room to crawl."

"Can we all fit?" asked Hal, worried about his larger frame. Ricky popped back in. "Hey, Caro," Hal said, "let's boost you up next—see if I can fit, okay?"

Caro was hoisted high onto Hal's shoulders. She swam through the green beads, so thick that for a second she couldn't see where she was going. Suffused with light, her faceplate glowed. Then she was through.

The small, round shaft sloped gently up. The ceiling, past the entrance, was high enough for Ricky to stoop; Caro saw that she and the others would have to travel on their hands and knees. There were small heaps of the green beads here and there festooning the ceiling and walls of the chalky rock.

Hal asked anxiously for a report.

"Ricky's right, Hal," Caro called to him over her intercom. "It'll be fine for all of us. The beads are in this shaft, too. Sherri, the tunnel up here is wide enough to easily turn around in," she added.

Sherri was next to come through the beads. She burst through the curtain and lay sprawled along the floor with a dazed expression. Caro looked at Ricky, frightened for her. "It's okay," Ricky said. "You looked like that, too, just at first."

Sherri scrambled the rest of the way through and got up on her hands and knees. She looked around, her chin trembling. "Well—the good news is that the lumies are down there. Maybe I like small spaces after all." Caro looked at her in admiration. Sherri's courage warmed her completely.

"What about Hal?" Sherri asked. "Who's going to boost him up?"

Ricky slid carefully down to the opening. "I've got a rope," he announced. "I can pull him up."

"Right, Ricky," Caro said. "We're on a slope here; he'd pull us all down."

"Hey, Hal . . . " Ricky began, his head through the curtain. He started laughing and backed up hurriedly, scrambling over Sherri. Hal's arms shot through the green curtain, scrabbling and clawing along the rock floor of the shaft.

Sherri and Caro grabbed him, trying to help pull him in. His feet still stuck out the hole; in one hand he clutched the end of a rope.

"How did you do it?" Caro asked in amazement.

"He stood on the stove!" Ricky chortled. "It was great!"

Hal dragged the rest of his long frame into the shaft. He sat up with a sigh and smacked his head on the ceiling. "Ow! Going through the green light—that was incredible," he declared, trying to rub his head through his hood.

"What's the rope for?" Caro asked.

"To haul up the stove," Ricky interjected. Hal nodded. He maneuvered himself around and began to tug on it; immediately his body began sliding towards the opening. They grabbed at his legs.

"Forget it!" Caro shouted, clutching his boot. Ricky, in turn, was hanging on like a bulldog to Caro's leg. But Hal did it. Slowly but surely the campstove made its way through the shimmering curtain and into the shaft.

Hal collapsed. "I was scared it would leave too clear a trail for someone to follow." He lay flat on his stomach and Sherri and Caro loaded the campstove back into his suit pack. They hit his head with it trying to slide it through the opening of the large pouch. "Sorry, Hal," Sherri said remorsefully as he clutched at his head in silence.

"Okay," announced Ricky, "We're off!"

Hal finished nursing his head and started to rise from the floor onto his hands and knees. His backpack crashed into the ceiling, knocking him down flat.

"I don't believe it," he moaned. Poor Hal received several fresh bruises as the girls removed the offensive stove.

"I can take it," said Caro. "I've got nothing in my backpack—remember, I was carrying the light and generator."

"It's pretty heavy," Hal warned.

"It can't be heavier than the generator."

"You're probably right. But this is bigger, more awkward," Hal replied.

Caro lay down flat on her stomach while Hal and Sherri battered her head with the stove, trying to load it into her pack. "Sorry, Caro," they chorused in sympathy with each skull-resounding clonk.

Caro rose slowly to her knees, carefully balancing the wide load, and found that her pack just cleared the top of the tunnel.

"If it gets any tighter up ahead, we'll have to dump it," said Hal.

They were off. Ricky led the four, with Sherri smack on his heels and Hal following her. Caro found herself last, to her escalating horror, but sheer exhaustion soon numbed fear. Crawling on the hard rock became torturous. Caro glanced at the winking red light on her wrist; the carepies seemed a distant warmth, belonging to another era, a different Caro.

The shaft seemed to stretch on eternally; there was nothing by which to measure their progress. The green beads with which they had played gradually slipped from their suits, and the webs in the shaft were fewer and further apart. Caro searched for them as for precious pearls, living from one glimmering heap to the next.

Their rest stops grew more and more frequent. They stretched flat on their stomachs, or lay across the shaft, breathing hard, tenderly stroking aching knees and hands. Hal ran his hydrogen bipack and Caro mixed up some juice. They swallowed deep draughts, experiencing a cooling renewal from the vitaminized drink mix. They snacked on Sherri's onion crumbles and Ricky's nut butter and crackers. Caro handed around thick slices of leathery, aromatic cheese. Then they began the journey on their bruised knees again.

They rounded a slow curve and Ricky let out a faint cheer. A familiar, cool gleam of green emanated very near. And almost immediately, the tunnel grew higher and wider and Ricky was able to walk.

Caro heard Sherri's muffled prayer of thanksgiving when she could stand and stretch her aching legs. Then Caro staggered to her feet, drunkenly trying to walk while balancing the heavy campstove in her backpack. It was awhile before Hal could walk, and then it was with bent neck, shuffling along, stooped like an old man.

Then Ricky stopped dead and flattened against the wall. He began signaling frantically. Hal stiffened, smacked his head on the ceiling, and sat down in disgust. Caro and Sherri crept forward and joined Ricky at the mouth of a vast, green-lit cave. They heard men's voices. Without a word between them, they flicked off their hood lamps and crouched down.

"I'm sure one of them is Uncle Lee," Ricky whispered. "But there's another man—talking to him. Down there."

Hal joined them. Ricky peered around the opening into the large cave. "They're below, I think," he continued. Ricky motioned to them and got down on his stomach.

Sherri softly moaned, "Here we go again." Hal nodded painfully.

Creeping forward on their bellies, they discovered that they were on a wide ledge high on the wall of a cathedral-like cave. Strings of beads hung like chandeliers from the high, arched ceiling, and garlanded the walls and edge of the balcony where they lay. Directly below them, as if meeting in a royal hall, sat Lee and a tall, heavily furred man across from one other at a natural stone table. Beside the table, a rounded fire pit glowed purple and green, sending curling whiffs of green-tinged smoke through the air.

Lumies lay like great dogs about the room. Some slept in undulating heaps around the fire; others watched, as still as sphinxes, the two men at the table. The lumies' mewling wails and the thuds of their bodies dropping to the ground echoed in the hall.

Lee looked comfortingly familiar, but tense, wary. His faceplate was unzipped and, sitting on a pile of hides, he leaned away from the strange man, observing him with watchful eyes. His Zero suit, in the light of the beads, looked as though it had been dipped in neon-green dye.

The stranger was suitless. He seemed taller, larger than Lee, but perhaps, thought Caro, that was because he was shrouded from head to toe in thick lumie-fur pelts sewn together in long robes. Even his turbanlike hat, gloves, and boots were made of the fur. His face was older than Lee's, and the uncovered portion of his skin resembled darkly etched leather. He had a stiff grey beard that stretched from ear to ear. Was he a man? Caro wondered. He relied on no oxygen pack that she could see.

One giant black-patched lumie lay close by the stranger at the table. Occasionally, while he talked, the furred man would reach down and stroke him, never pausing in his speech.

He spoke in smiling tones, with careful diction. His voice ran up and down the scale: melodic and graceful. And although he spoke the same language, his words had a foreign ring to them, as if the pronunciation were slightly off, or the emphasis placed on the wrong syllable. By comparison, Lee sounded young, unfinished, abrupt. The man addressed Lee by his full name.

"So you see, Levi, I have everything a scientist could hope for—time, adequate quarters, and," he added, emphasizing the next three words with fond slaps to the lumie below him, "very willing subjects."

"Subjects?" echoed Lee.

The stranger looked up inquiringly.

"You still haven't explained what it is you're researching, Dr. Coleney. Nor why you disappeared so many years ago," Lee said. "Or why you have records of my research—including two papers that I never saw fit to publish."

Dr. Coleney threw back his head and laughed. "Yes, yes," he said in delight. "I have many questions of yours to answer, of that I am most positive. My dear Levi," he added seriously, leaning across the table, "you are the right man for the job—you know this? I have done my homework here."

"I don't recall applying for any job," Lee replied brusquely.

"Ah, come now," Coleney said, shaking his glove at Lee. "You are an animal behaviorist born and bred; you prefer to work in the field on your own; you have read and studied my research until you know it inside out. And you say that you have not fitted yourself for this position?"

"Just what is it that you're researching?" Lee demanded again.

"Why my friends, of course," replied Coleney with an expansive gesture that embraced the twenty lumies lolling about the cave.

"You do know that your proposal to sight *Lumini lupus* surgically was carried out—and was subsequently banned?"

"But of course, Levi. I am well aware of the limitations associated with laboratory research—particularly in the field of behaviorism."

"Just what 'limitations' are you referring to? Surgical sighting of lumies was banned because it made them killers—127 men and women died—I'm not talking about what it did or did not accomplish in allowing us to observe lumies in full light—that, Coleney, is a little beside the point."

Dr. Coleney leaned toward Lee for a minute and then roared with laughter, slapping the stone table with a heavy hand. Lumies leapt up. When no further demonstration was forthcoming, they began, with mewling grumbles, to settle their large bodies.

"Ah, my Levi. You are delightful. But it is the whole point, as you say. I quite agree. *Lumini lupus* put the Community to shame, eh? And that was valuable to learn." He relaxed, leaning back on the hides. "Now, let us return to the subject of limitations in behaviorism. Haven't you wondered what pack behavior is really like—what your subjects are really capable of doing? I don't mean in a paltry lab experiment, I mean in their world—the real world."

"You mean field research—any behaviorist worth his salt goes into the field."

"Oh, my young friend; is it that you are so naive—or so loyal to what you know to be outdated science? I know from your work that you are far from stupid. Must I spell it out? This is far more than sitting behind a tree with an aud-vis recorder. Levi, *I have become one of the pack.* I am a 'lumie,' as you so charmingly call them. I live where they live, I eat what they eat."

"That's ridiculous," Lee said flatly. "You're a man, not a lumie. Simply by being here you are creating an unnatural situation."

"Ah, but in your youthful passion to prove me wrong you have overlooked the most fundamental level determining behavior: emotions, drive, guts—whatever you choose to call it. At that level, Levi, I have chosen to act, think, feel, and behave according to pack law. Anything that I do within the framework of their government, their custom, is permissible. The consequences that follow are merely according to selection principles. If something works, it may or may not be added to pack vocabulary and tradition. If not, it may simply be dropped, or I might be chastised. Of course as leader, that happens rarely." Coleney ran his glove along the hides, smiling. "Levi, you know that logic, intellect, reason—whatever you may choose to call the cognitive process—is helpless before *behavior* itself. We feel and react long before we think."

"You're saying, 'we react, therefore, we are.' "

"Exactly. Mankind's increased ability to think only allows him a better chance of forecasting whether or not a new behavior will work, and, in the aftermath of that behavior, judging whether or not he should adopt it. Or adapt it." Coleney laughed noiselessly at his wordplay.

"What about the supernatural?" Lee asked abruptly. "How does the supernatural fit into your theory?"

"But that is precisely what I'm after, Levi! I knew you'd be the right man!" Coleney exclaimed.

"No," replied Lee. "I agree with you when you say that outward behavior, plain gut reactions, are an outworking of something very deep within us, and it often bypasses our thinking processes—although, thank God, we humans can often temper and overrule, to some extent, our guts. But that's not all there is. You would redefine 'supernatural' to be a material process; I believe that it is beyond the natural, beyond the material, beyond man himself. There is a vast difference in what the two of us believe."

"Oh, semantics, lad—words and more words. It is what I have *not* missed in becoming the leader of the lumies. But, as we used to say, the proof of the pudding is in the eating. Look at me—perfectly adapted to and at home in my surroundings. Look at you—more frail than the youngest cub—relying on that suit and oxygen pack and helpless in the dark." Coleney settled back, smiling patiently.

"I wouldn't exactly call this the dark," Lee replied, looking around at the green beads showering him with their cool light.

"Well, at the mercy of your suit light—and the fire—then. The point is, as a pack member, I have no longer any need of all that paraphernalia."

Caro, listening breathlessly up on the ledge with the others, gazed puzzled at the scene below. Lee didn't have his hood lamp on—he didn't need to, so suffused in light was the cathedral-cave.

"You're blind in more ways than one, Coleney," Lee said tiredly.

"Only in the light, Levi," Coleney replied, laughing. "It had to be done, you know. *Lumini lupus* used to occupy only the half-light zone—they relied on their eyes far too much. Now we can occupy any zone. We have developed senses far beyond sight."

"First you gave them the ability to see full light, and now you're taking their sight completely away . . . "

"Odd, isn't it?" Coleney said genially. "Odd that my initial premise would center on increasing light capacity. Out here light is simply a barrier to freedom. Who needs barriers, eh?"

Caro looked at the others. So that was it; the lumies had been blinded. No wonder they hadn't fled from the big light.

"I noticed their hyper ear action right away," Lee commented. "I wondered about that—now I know—their ears are compensating for their loss of sight."

Coleney hesitated a second and then replied, "Yes, their ears are keen. Of course it's more than that."

"Pheromones?"

"A part of it."

"Pack communication by signal?"

"Oh, the rudiments."

"Extrasensory perception?"

"You are a little closer." Coleney laughed. "Yes, yes, undeniably you are the man for the job. But I can't relieve your curiosity with words, Levi. You must experience it for yourself . . . "

"It may be a little archaic, but I'll keep my eyesight, thank you," Lee said firmly.

As Lee was speaking, two lumies bounded into the cave. The pack sprang to its feet and gathered around them. Coleney rose majestically and stepped into the center of the milling beasts. Lee watched them closely.

Several of the pack, in great leaps, disappeared down the tunnel. The rest stayed grouped around Dr. Coleney who returned to stand before the stone table. "Well, Levi," he said pleasantly. "It seems our conversation must be terminated for a time. And I was just going to show you the laboratory—but never mind—there will be time enough. Your four young companions seem to have disappeared."

Lee started to his feet and stepped toward Coleney. The black-and-white lumie reared up, rumbling. "You have them, too?" he ground out.

Dr. Coleney's lips parted in a smile. "Not at the moment." He turned, sweeping his robe behind him, and disappeared with the large black-and-white lumie still at his side. The remaining animals, ears flickering, began pressuring Lee toward a smaller shaft, under the ledge.

"Uncle Lee!" called Ricky through his intercom. Lee jumped. "Where are you?" he hissed, looking around. "What are you idiots trying to prove—get back to the crawler and go to Main—*go home!*"

234

A chestnut lumie reared and bared his teeth, swiping at Lee. "Okay, okay, I'm going," Lee said to it. "Did you hear me?!" he repeated to the four. "Are you all okay? All four of you?"

"We're fine, we're fine," Caro and Sherri exclaimed. "Are you okay?"

"What can we do?" asked Hal anxiously.

"Oh, I'm fine, just fine—can't you see? Get back to the crawler and go home—home to *Main,* not to the End, if you can at all avoid it. If you must, talk only to Lutes."

"We're going to rescue you, Uncle Lee!" Ricky yelled.

"Don't do me that privilege—really—you're all wonderful, but GET OUT OF HERE!" And Lee was gone from sight and intercom range.

18

"You Have Thrown Me Down"

t least he knows we're okay . . . " Sherri said.

"He didn't seem too pleased to see us," Ricky said squiffily.

"What did you want him to say, Ricky?" Caro asked in a low voice.

Hal looked upset. "Well, at least we know a little of what's going on here and can tell Lutes about it. I sure hate to leave Lee here, though."

"What do you mean?" demanded Sherri.

"We're not going anywhere without Uncle Lee," Ricky bellowed, near tears.

"Shut up, Ricky," Caro said wearily. "Hal—we can't go back—for the simple reason that we never marked a single tunnel. We'd be hopelessly lost in minutes."

"I don't know," Hal said. "I'm pretty good with directions—"

"Forget it. I'm not going to end my days squeezing through tighter and tighter tunnels. I'd rather be eaten by umies. I MEAN IT," Sherri said, totally distraught.

Hal stared unhappily from her to Caro to Ricky. "Well—here we go again. What are our options?"

"Find out where Uncle Lee's being held," Ricky blurted.

"Then what?"

"Distract the lumies so that he can get away," said Caro.

Ricky looked admiringly at her. "Yeah!"

"That's not bad," murmured Hal.

"Great!" exclaimed Sherri. "How are we going to distract them, Caro?"

"Well—"

"We can run across the tunnel and when they chase us yell for Uncle Lee to make a break for it," said Ricky all in one breath.

"I was thinking more along the lines of tossing some food down the tunnel—sort of as bait," Caro said.

"Good, real good—good idea," Hal and Sherri hastily agreed, nodding emphatically at Caro.

"I guess," said Ricky, looking disappointed.

"Okay," Hal reflected. "We know that the lumies have taken Lee down a shaft underneath this ledge. I wonder—do you think that the side passage just a little ways down the tunnel we crawled through would take us down to a lower level . . . to an entrance into the cathedral-cave?"

"What side passage?" asked Caro.

"Just a few meters before the tunnel opens into this ledge. Didn't you see it?" Hal said.

Caro shook her head.

"I did. It's *small*." Sherri grimaced, working to control her quivering lip.

"It's either that or go back to the cave where we were held, Sherri," Hal said in sympathy. "And from now on let's mark tunnels," he emphasized.

In a very short time the agony of crawling on their hands and knees through the downward sloping side passage drove everything else from their minds. It was as i the cathedral-cave had never happened; everything outside this torturous shaft had receded into faint, far-off dreams.

There were no green beads in this shaft; Caro began concentrating her gaze on the blinking red light on her wrist, still picking up signals sent by the equipment the carepies carried. She had given up all hope of meeting them now; even her heart-memory of the carepies had grown fuzzy in this painful journey. In front of her, Hal's heels were moving out of sight, but she could hear him struggling along with the others up ahead.

Caro winced, trying to shift the campstove in her backpack to a slightly new position. It wouldn't budge, and she dropped one shoulder, trying to inch it off the sore spot under her shoulder blade. Then it tilted, sliding from her back, tipping her sideways. Caro tried to compensate by throwing her weight the other way, but she lost her balance and began to flip onto her back. Instead of hitting the wall, Caro found herself slipping down a hole, moving faster and faster.

Her body gained speed by the second. Too shocked to scream, she tried to grab the sides of the small channel. The friction heated her gloves but did little to slow her headlong fall. The beam of light from her hood leaped crazily off the sides, the floor, the ceiling; she lost all hope of control. Caro was free-falling, speeding through the black, hypnotized by the bouncing beam that poked random holes in the dark shaft.

She heard the thud of her body as it hit the ground, and in that instant, darkness velveted her mind.

Lee prowled about the small cave restlessly. He would pick up a Circular, flick through the research article, trying to find another piece to the puzzle. He strode back and forth, throwing one paper down for the next, and on and on. There seemed to be no end to the pile of possible clues, and no way out. He viciously kicked Coleney's journal against the wall but it did not diminish his rage.

There was a rush of fur and Coleney swept in, throwing back his long robe, smiling affably. Lee set his teeth in disgust. "Look, Coleney," he began, "it's one thing to hold me here; it's quite another to be pursuing four children around the tunnels."

"My thoughts precisely, Levi—let's just forget about them and get on to business, shall we?" Coleney said graciously. "I'll take you to my laboratory."

"You're insane." The words meant nothing; Coleney's pleasant expression remained undisturbed. *"There are four children out there,"* Lee phrased deliberately. "I'm going to go find them and take them home. I will be back, Coleney—don't fear that I won't—I will be back."

Lee pushed roughly past the furred man. An odd expression slipped across Coleney's face as he staggered.

Lee made four strides; the big black and white lumie rose up, knocked him down and clamped his jaws around the back of his neck. A second and then a third lumie leapt noiselessly into the cave. Lee was pinned; heavy jaws like vices gripped his arm and leg. He couldn't breathe.

"Now you see," Coleney said, readjusting his robes. He sighed. The lumies released Lee, who cautiously sat up. His head bent, Lee drew several long, rattling breaths.

"Now—let us proceed to the lab, shall we?" Coleney announced when Lee stood up. "And already a thorough lesson in pack behavior, eh?" he added playfully.

Lee, escorted by the three lumies, followed Coleney out of the cave and down a short, curving passage that ended in a long, low room. He stopped, heedless of the mewling snarl behind him, and stood rooted, gazing at Coleney's laboratory. It was filled with up-to-the-minute technology: computer terminals hummed, tracking equipment circled slowly, digital readings pulsed and spoke in monotones. A stack of just-published papers stood beside an audio computer reader.

"The Community does know you're alive," Lee said.

"Welcome to your new assignment, Levi" was Coleney's hearty reply, his gesture wide and warm.

"Among other things, you're monitoring the carepies."

"Oh, we have many interests for you to pursue, lad, many interests—but you must be one of the pack." Coleney smiled roguishly.

"And if I don't choose to be 'one of the pack'?" Lee spoke quietly, lethally.

"But you will—when you come to know us. And, just think, your four little friends would be so distressed—"

Lee caught him a direct knockout blow to the jaw that sent him reeling against the regulation Community lab table chock-full of regulation Community lab equipment. The table rocked violently, meters spinning and glassware sliding and shattering on the stone floor. Coleney slumped to the ground, out cold, bleeding from his mouth, and Lee waited to die.

Out of the corner of his eye Lee saw a blur of black-and-white, chestnut, and mahogany fur as the three lumies flashed noiselessly through the air and landed, ripping, grinding, tearing the hide off their downed leader. Lee, his fury spent, and helpless to stop what had already happened, watched with tears beading up in his eyes. In a matter of seconds, lumies of all descriptions raced in, eager to join the fray, and still Lee stood, heedless of his own certain death. He mourned the loss of this bent bit of humanity. When the snapping and crunching of bones registered in his brain, Lee bent over in a sudden spasm, painfully vomiting up bile. Then he turned and stumbled out of Coleney's laboratory, unpursued.

19

Hoverlight

aro came to consciousness slowly, feeling thick blackness like a presence leaning upon her battered body. She was lying with her face against the rocky floor, her arm curled uncomfortably under her, and her leg numb and twisted against the wall. Slowly she straightened out her limbs, reaching around with an arm to move her cramped leg. Her eyes were squeezed shut with pain and terror; as the blood began to flow and awaken the deadened limbs, her lids flew open with the startling agony.

Caro's eyes strained wider and wider, frantic to see. Gasping sobs tore from her throat; she was in her nightmare, in the deep dark and all alone.

Caro slid back into semi-consciousness.

She woke again, lifting her head stiffly, again straining to see something, anything. Caro rested her swollen face back down on her arm and realized, with renewed anguish, that she had lost the disc that monitored the carepies. The little red light was gone. Her last connection with the carepies had been severed.

Eventually it became too painful not to move. Caro tentatively stretched out one arm and touched the wall.

She struggled to rise to a sitting position; her head whirled sickeningly, and her stomach churned. Flooded with nausea, she gagged, propped up on her elbows. As the giddiness began to pass, she rolled to the side, setting her back against the wall of the tunnel. A small part of her registered thankfulness that somewhere in her mad rush down the side shaft, the campstove had been dislodged from her pack and had disappeared.

Caro stretched her legs out in front of her. Every square centimeter of her was bruised, but her legs and arms worked, and her head, although it throbbed with every pulse, was rapidly beginning to process the situation.

She reached up and fingered her hood lamp; it was hopelessly smashed. Fighting a rush of panic, she began going through her pockets, taking stock of what she had left with her. Her cheese had become a mashed lump. The flat bread had ceased to have any resemblance to anything edible. The small bag of roasted prawb seeds she had brought for Lee was still with her. Her drysuit was there, untouched in her deep inside pocket. The packet of nuts and dried fruit remained in the pocket where her mother had placed it. The nuts seemed ground to a powder, but Caro chewed several pieces of the fruit. She still had the diving knife that Lee had given her, safe in its ankle sheath. There was a short length of cord. A flat package of dehydrated fish had been caught in the folds of her tattered backpack. Everything else was gone.

The most frightening discovery was that her small emergency hydrogen bipack unit had become a bewildering, bent piece of tubing and canisters. Caro had no idea whether or not it was still functional; in any case, she could not hope to operate it without seeing which valve released hydrogen and which one controlled the oxygen mix. She immediately began to feel horribly thirsty.

A loose wire swung with every motion, and Caro put up her hand to trace it to its source. Her intercom rattled as she touched it. "Hello," she tentatively said, but her voice stayed buried in her suit. Her hand shook as she tried to feel where the wire should go.

Then she realized that there might be bigger problems with her suit than a broken intercom: what about the energy pack? How long had she lain there, unmoving? The generator would not recharge the pack unless she began walking; she must start moving.

But how could she? Caro had no idea where she was, what surrounded her. She might be on the edge of a dark precipice for all she knew. She unzipped her faceplate, trying to hear, to receive some clue about her surroundings.

The cool wind struck her face, fresh and bracing as ocean spray. But except for its ceaseless rush, she heard nothing. She leaned first to her left, and then to her right, sending her fingers across the ground like antennas to bring back news of her environment. Rock on both sides, rock as far as she could feel through the toes of her boots. Caro jerked clumsily, painfully to her feet and stood, slumped against the wall. She felt as though her head had continued its upward motion and was circling dizzily far above the rest of her body.

Willing one foot in front of the other, in shuffling steps, hugging the wall, she began walking. It was all she could do in her fight for life, and she set her teeth and did it.

She continued along the dark, silent path, her shoulder touching the wall, walking with one arm out in front and the other chasing through the thick night to her left. Caro never knew how long she journeyed; the surrounding black swallowed up all signs of progress. Her mind had set her to walk and walk her body did, dumbly, faithfully, choosing life.

Caro rested, sitting down against the comparative safety of the wall, her fingers running again along the smooth, unyielding floor, sending her no messages of alarm. Unbidden, her thoughts drew a picture of Dr. Coleney: tall, smiling in his clipped grey beard, leathery skin, a strangely melodic voice, deep and—not warm. *Not cold, either,* she mused. *Just—not warm. So pleasant, so smoothly pleasant, but . . . un-human,* came a voice within. She shivered, blasts of cold traveling through her as she recalled how he had patted the large black and white lumie at his feet. She could see him with the same genial smile skinning the lumie and eating its flesh.

Yet Coleney saw himself as a good scientist—and was he really so different from the many other scientists whom she knew? Was he different from her parents? Tears welled up as she suddenly saw a picture of her dad tenderly bent over a cocoonfly who had become entangled in a spider's web. His look of distress at Ricky's "This is a quicker way to rescue it, Dad!" and the abrupt stomp of his young son's eager boot on the hungry spider. Not that her dad never killed any insects . . . but, yes, he was different. Very different.

Different from Dr. Lutes? Caro smiled involuntarily. The contrast was hilarious—Coleney and Dr. Lutes?! Lutes with his rumpled lab coat, courtly manners, and bright, light-filled eyes? Caro's eyes overflowed and the tears rained down her face. Yes, kindly, gentle Dr. Lutes was very different from this man who was clothed in the hides of his followers. Lutes loved his work, he loved the children he taught, he loved the carepies, *he loved her.* Dr. Lutes would look for her, and Uncle Lee, of course, and Sherri, and Hal, and Ricky; they all would do whatever they could do to find her because they loved her, Caro, the odd, silent, sensitive one. At least she was easy to recognize, she sobbed in hysteric relief—just look for the one with the funny face!

She sniffed, reached inside her hood, and tried her best to wipe dry her runny nose. She laughed, picturing what she looked like after all this weeping. And then Caro felt the carepies call.

She sighed nostalgically, missing them utterly, not realizing that she was not just recalling a fond memory, but actually hearing them from somewhere so deep inside of her that it was beyond her. But the call gave her the strength to rise again and begin walking along the dark path, unseeing, and sure that she was just as invisible.

Caro was very thirsty. So thirsty that when she opened her eyes again after a lengthy rest, scrunched firmly against the wall, all she seemed to see was a bright, light-filled fountain hovering in the dark, a short distance away.

The light-fountain came closer. Caro blinked her eyes, then pushed against them, trying to clear them of visions. She looked up again, moving her tongue against her dry lips, wondering.

It came still nearer—hovering in the velvet, moving up and down, but straight ahead, straight toward her. As it grew yet nearer, Caro heard not the sound of water, but a strange clicking noise. A comforting noise; a "be of good cheer" reassurance of good things forthcoming. Caro, warmed and watching, nevertheless coolly reminded herself of the physiological symptoms of dehydration and oxygen deprivation.

The light-fountain grew nearer, shooting energetic radiance in a magnificent flood, cheerfully chasing the dark from the tunnel. It came, and it sat at Caro's feet.

And Caro drank it in. The creature—for creature it was—had a warm-glowing cylindrical body the color of golden sand. From out of its body, in every direction, shot a rainbow of hair, each fiber lit from within. The hair waved wildly on end as if charged with static electricity; some of the individual strands were nearly as long as Caro's arm.

It had two rows of five round, black feet on short, black legs. It was the feet that she could not see in the dark of the tunnel that gave the creature the appearance of hovering in the air. Its three black eyes shone like mirrors. The creature's face was difficult to see under the flickering hair, but Caro saw the movement of its mouth as fresh chirps and clicks filled the tunnel. Three antennae stiff as black braids stuck up like a coronet.

Caro held her hands flat on the ground, palms up, before it. The hoverlight-creature climbed happily into her hands, fitting its ten, suctioned-cup feet neatly onto her fingers and the heels of her hands.

Caro lifted the hoverlight onto her lap. She laughed out loud. "You wonderful thing!" And then she grew silent with the mystery of it.

Her journey was lit now, for the hoverlight stayed with her, riding on her shoulder, clinging to her head at times. Every once in a while it would go off on a short scouting mission of its own. But it always came back to her, and she never lost sight of the sparking, clicking creature hovering in the night.

By the light of the creature, she saw that she was in a broad, smooth tunnel as safe and wide as any of the passages the four had been on. When the knowledge that she had no idea where she was going threatened to send her into a panic she would remind herself why she needed to keep moving and fix her eyes again on the hoverlight.

Caro now knew that her hydrogen bipack was incapable of providing her water. She had examined it carefully under the sparkling glow of the hoverlight, but although she tried to reshape the twisted tubing, not a drop of water trickled out. The insulating factor of her suit slowed dehydration somewhat, but Caro knew that she must have water soon.

It was then that the hoverlight, on one of its forages, disappeared. Just for a second—then it popped back in sight. Caro, after her heartbeat returned to normal, realized that there must be a passage off to the right of the tunnel she followed.

She quickened her pace and came to where the hoverlight sat at the junction of the two tunnels. The hoverlight began to move down the new tunnel, weaving in sporadic bursts from one side of the passage to the other. Caro followed.

This tunnel was much smaller; Caro could reach out and, with her arms straight out at her sides, graze the tips of her gloved fingers on each wall. The tunnel curved and turned back on itself, but the hoverlight, and Caro chasing after, kept following its kinks and twists.

Caro began to be aware of a background noise building as they journeyed through the tunnel. It was a large, living throb and it filled Caro with fear. But the hoverlight seemed unconcerned, or unaware; it continued its wobbling trek across the tunnel or rode like a flaming porcupine on Caro's head.

They rounded another curve and the sound rushed into Caro's ears. Ahead, there was light emanating around another bend in the passage. The hoverlight scrambled down from its perch, hurried along the short length of tunnel, and disappeared around the corner.

Caro hesitated before chasing after the creature. The roar overwhelmed her, the familiar feeling of dread rising from her stomach. She paused, hoping that the hoverlight would come back. It didn't. Caro set her teeth and stepped around the corner.

Water. White-rushing, tumbling, fiercely laughing water surged from channels cut high above her head. It was a vast wall of waterfalls. Eternally the water dove, escalating its wild roar, melding with the deep-green swelling pool at Caro's feet. The cavern shimmered with bioluminescence; blue-green rainbows danced in the spray. Caro waded through the rainbows, drinking in the light-drenched spray with her faceplate off and her mouth open and laughing. The hoverlight sipped decorously from the lip of a puddle of spray; it looked up as the girl walked past and chortled a greeting to her.

Caro walked along the edge of the pool under the shooting rivers. The water was a tumultuous, lacy froth, churning with white waves. Caro followed the slow curve of the pool around a wide rock pillar, frosted with bioluminescence, to where the water was serene, deep, and so clear that Caro saw the movement of a small, scurrying creature across its bed. Here Caro knelt and drank. The hoverlight came and joined the girl, and lipped softly at the water beside her.

20

"Fish Stew"

al, Sherri, and Ricky continued crawling down the passage, unaware that Caro had disappeared. They were aching and near despair. The unyielding stone walls gave no hint of ending; the three could not escape the awful knowledge that this tunnel, instead of leading down into the cathedral-cave, might go nowhere.

The shaft grew smaller and tighter, and Sherri's panic began to communicate itself to the others. Ricky felt Sherri's gloves on his heels and forced his limbs to push harder, faster. Hal was left behind as Sherri drove Ricky on.

Just as Ricky sobbed "Cut it out!" he dropped through the end of the shaft into a wide tunnel. Sherri, gasping in thanksgiving, fell on top of him. Another minute and Hal's head emerged from the passage.

"That was horrible," he said with passion. "The worst experience of my life." He pulled his long frame out of the tunnel and stretched painfully.

Ricky was already on his feet, hopping with impatience. "This is great," he enthused, trying to keep his voice down. "Look at the green light coming from around that bend—I'll bet you anything that's the cathedral-cave entrance. We have to move really quick—and quiet, too. Lumies all around, I'll bet. We better know to make a run for this shaft—it's too small for them."

"Ricky!" hissed Sherri. "Must you say things like that? I don't appreciate feeling like teeth are going to chomp into me at any second—remember, *these* lumies are like big guard dogs—they won't hurt us. Right, Hal?"

"That's right, Sherri—at least not right away," answered Hal mildly. "They'll just take us to the madman who will hurt us."

Sherri was speechless. "Look," she finally said. "I know as well as the rest of you that we're in pretty deep here, but there's no point in rubbing it in, okay? Now—what's keeping Caro? Let's get going on our plan. The sooner we free Uncle Lee, the sooner we're out of here."

"Look, maybe we should get the bait ready now," said Hal. "Right here, by this shaft, so that we can duck in it if anyone comes." His face clouded. "Yeah—where is Caro?"

"Caro?!" he called, peering back into the shaft.

"Caro!" Ricky's impatient voice shocked the others.

"Do you mind, Ricky?" Sherri exclaimed, starting to get worried. "Caro!" she called, even more loudly than Ricky.

Hal turned around exasperated, his ears ringing. "There is no point in yelling," he said. "With these intercoms you can hear a whisper just as well as a shout. You know, I'm wondering whether maybe that campstove in her pack got her wedged against the ceiling of the tightest part of the shaft." He started sweating, pushing at his glasses through his faceplate. "But why isn't she answering?" he asked no one in particular. "Caro!" he bellowed, then glanced at the others, shamefacedly.

"Look—one of us is going to have to go back and find out what's wrong," Sherri said, white about the mouth.

"I'll go," said Ricky. "She's always making trouble," he grumbled, trying to hide his fear.

"Just keep talking to us, Ricky," Hal said urgently. "Don't leave us in suspense here, okay?"

Ricky nodded importantly and slipped into the shaft. He began the long, arduous journey through the dark, all alone, his knees rubbed raw.

"Ricky?" he heard Hal call.

"What—I'm a little busy, you know," he panted.

"I know, I know—but just say something every once in a while," Hal pleaded.

"I don't see anything yet," he announced in fury. "Caro!" he called again and yet again.

"Still nothing?" Hal asked desperately.

"Nothing," Ricky said, his voice beginning to tremble.

"I can't believe this!" Sherri exclaimed in a high, thin voice. "She was right behind you, Hal—didn't you ever talk to her?"

Hal didn't answer Sherri. "Ricky," he said, his voice cracking, "are you to the point where the tunnel gets really tight yet?"

"I'm past that," Ricky stammered. The signal was fading; they could no longer hear him clearly.

"Ricky—don't go any further. We're coming, too—we can't hear you anymore," called Hal. He and Sherri climbed back into the shaft.

They found Ricky huddled up, sobbing by the tiny side shaft that no one had noticed in their earlier pass through.

"She's gone down there," Ricky wailed. "There's nowhere else. She got lost!"

"Caro couldn't have got lost, Ricky," Hal said. "That little passage is so small that there's no way she could mistake it for the one we were following. Besides, she was right behind me."

"Maybe she went back for some reason," Sherri said, trembling.

"No way," said Hal. "She couldn't turn around with that campstove in her pack—don't you remember, at our last break, I had to help her maneuver against the wall?"

"She's gone down there!" Ricky wailed louder, pointing.

"Look, Ricky," Hal said. "It slopes down—maybe she did think that this was the right way . . . Hey—I'll tie my rope around you—you go in—just a short ways, and call for her—maybe she's out of range."

Hal tied one end of the rope around Ricky's waist and the other end around his own. "Okay," he said.

Ricky slid through the shaft and immediately began skidding down the rapid decline. *Smack!* Hal saw stars as the force of Ricky's weight pulled him straight into the wall. The rope held, and between him and Sherri yanking on the rope from above, and Ricky scrabbling for any toe and finger hold, they pulled him back out of the deadly shaft.

Ricky was wholeheartedly sobbing. "It goes straight down—and there's a curve—but I couldn't see to the bottom. Caro's gone down there!"

"Where were we when we took our last break?" Hal asked in desperation. "Was it before or after this point? Does anyone remember? Because—that's the last time we saw her."

"It was after—I think," said Sherri. "She couldn't have gone down there! She's not stupid!"

Ricky began shooting off down the shaft. "Where are you going?" Hal yelled, clutching at his boot. Ricky kicked out and caught Hal full in the stomach. Hal abruptly let go and rolled into a ball, wheezing and gurgling. "I have to go get Uncle Lee and tell him," Ricky said in a rough staccato. "Uncle Lee will find Caro."

Sherri lost her head and scrambled over Hal's twisting, rocking body, and after Ricky.

When he could breathe again, Hal carved a large "X" on both sides of the shaft and another in the floor of the passage at its opening. Then he flung himself after Sherri and Ricky, sliding and scooting on their stomachs, clawing their way down the passage in their panic to go tell Lee.

Ricky shot out the shaft at such a pace that he landed flat out on his stomach in the large tunnel. Sherri scrambled out after him, gasping, trying to catch her breath. "Are you okay?" she asked. He answered by jumping to his feet.

"Look—there's no time for that food bait idea to distract the lumies," Ricky said. "See the green light? That's got to be the cathedral-cave around the corner. That's where the lumies hang out. This is the plan: I'm going to run around and attract the lumies, and then make a break for this shaft. I'll wait in there for you. You go find Uncle Lee when the lumies are busy with me." Sherri nodded, already green with the horror of it.

Ricky and Sherri, clinging to the wall, cautiously made their way around the curve in the tunnel. Sure enough, they were at a lower entrance to the cathedral cave. The firepit still glowed with purple and orange coals. The green light from the beads emanated from all around, but high on the ledge it had been far easier to see just what was in the cave. From this perspective, here by the entrance to the large hall, they saw only blurred, moving shadows.

Ricky eyes were horror-filled. By the pillar, there— were those three lumies crouched still and watchful? Or just a shadow cast by the ledge up above? The stone table was shrouded, the green light eclipsed by bumps and ridges in the rock all around. The fire sent green-tinged smoke playing across the heaps of hides. They moved. Or did they?

Ricky swallowed hard. Sherri was peering through the shifting light under the ledge. "I think I see the passage where the lumies took Uncle Lee," she whispered. Ricky nodded.

Hal stepped silently out of the shaft and moved quickly around the bend of the tunnel. There were Ricky and Sherri standing still, clutching the wall. He stiffened. *Coleney and the lumies must be right there*. He soundlessly moved up behind the two and placed his hands on their shoulders. Ricky let out a piercing wail.

Sherri didn't look back. She began running, heart pumping, mouth in a frozen grimace, racing toward the passage under the ledge.

Then Ricky tore off—around the cave screeching like a banshee, waving his arms in a wild dance, leaping upon the stone table and off again, madly dashing near the edges where the shadows lay as ugly and horrifying as lumies. Surely packs and packs of lumies were at his heels; one final wild cavort in the center of the cave, and then, the final sprint out of the cave, past the shocked Hal, to the safety of the small shaft. *Hal, run!* Ricky's mouth tried to form the words but it was still locked in a high, wide scream.

Hal's legs received the message even if his brain did not. Hal was off and running, his long stride catching Ricky in four great leaps and then—on. It eventually penetrated into his panicked consciousness that he had no specific idea why he was running. True, there were many general reasons to run: Coleney, the lumies, Coleney with the lumies. Just who was chasing him?

He heard nothing as he scrambled into the small side shaft; Ricky pushing impatiently against his long legs, popped in as neatly as a rabbit. And they waited, Ricky envisioning the hordes of slavering jaws, blood-red tongues and claws as thick as sabers.

"Where's Sherri?" Hal wheezed, drawing sobbing, frantic breaths.

"Gone to get Uncle Lee," panted Ricky. "We did it, Hal," he added soberly.

"Did what?" Hal choked out. He adjusted his oxygen mix feverishly.

"Distracted the lumies!"

"What lumies?" Hal gasped.

"What do you mean what lumies?!"

"I didn't see any lumies," Hal insisted, beginning to draw more normal breaths.

"They were chasing me! You ran, too, don't you remember?!"

"I didn't see any lumies. I ran because, well, because you and Sherri ran," Hal said, overcome by the shame of it.

"They were so chasing me!" Ricky raged.

"I think I would have seen them, Ricky. Where did Sherri think she was going?" Hal demanded, fearful for her. "Come on, Ricky—we'd better go find her. Likely she's the one who's being chased by lumies while we hide here."

"I wouldn't go out there, Hal." Ricky still clung desperately to the vision of foam-dripping teeth, but had reduced the hordes to two or three lumies, on the smaller side.

Hal, drenched in chagrin, roughly climbed over Ricky, pushed his head out of the shaft, and smacked into Sherri on her way in.

"Hal—are you crazy!!" Sherri blurted in pain, fireworks popping and fizzing in her brain.

"I'm sorry!" Hal yelled, holding his head and rocking. "I was just leaving to look for you!"

"Where's Uncle Lee?" Ricky demanded.

"I couldn't find him," she wept, feeling sick to her stomach. "There were two passages; the one I took didn't go more than a few meters."

Hal looked at the two of them. "I think you two were just lucky that there were no lumies in the cave. They must be guarding Lee in the other passage—the passage you didn't take, Sherri. You two were taking an awful risk doing a crazy thing like that. I think that the food idea is way safer. For one thing, we just have to plant it—we don't need to be anywhere near them. And it will keep them busy longer. You see, Ricky? Sherri wouldn't have had time to find Lee anyway—even if there had been lumies chasing you."

Ricky was red with rage at being so deceived by the lumies. "Let's do it, Hal," he said fiercely. "At least we know where the lumies are now—good work, Sherri. What food have we got to use?"

They climbed out of the shaft again. Hal made up a thick concoction of re-hydrated fish in the big cooking pot that Sherri had been carrying in her backpack. "Fish is good because it smells," Hal explained.

"Quick—let's spread it in the cathedral cave," Ricky said, panicked. "We don't want them to smell it and come looking for it here."

As one they hurried to the entrance of the green-lit cave. Too late; lumies were roaming in, throwing themselves down on the stone floor, mewling and moaning among themselves.

"My rope," Hal said, neurons firing like lightning. "And—something solid—and long. Quick, think! We've got to swing this pot along the other side of the cave so that this tunnel and the one under the ledge is clear."

"The extension," stuttered Sherri, clutching at Hal's arm "for the big light—Ricky's carrying it! In his backpack—Caro and I stuck it in!"

The collapsible rod was perfect. When fully extended they had five meters length from which to dangle the fish pot. Hal's fingers flew as he took out his rope and tied the pot onto the end of the rod. Then he went to pick it up. He couldn't. The leverage was so great that he couldn't budge the heavy pot from the ground.

It took all three of them to lift it. They staggered into the cave and toward the area by the stone table.

"Okay, turn!" Hal directed, lips tight. "No! The other way, the other way, Sherri!"

The lumies smelled the swinging pot of fish. The aroma would arc high above their heads and then swoop down again tantalizingly. They heard a scraping sound as the pot grazed along the ground a short ways. Ears stood out, quivering. Up high again, whirling wafts in small circles over their heads. The lumies sat up and took notice.

The ugly red brindle, his nose following the fish pot unfailingly, launched himself into the air and batted at the teasing smell. The three humans at the other end of the rod began to quake.

Other lumies joined in the fun, gaily leaping and whapping the air where the pot had just been in its zooming course up and down and over their heads. One lumie received a heavy clunk on the side of his wide face from it. It shook its head violently and crouched down, preparing to leap again.

"What are you idiots doing?!" Lee's voice boomed over their intercoms. He stood in the far entrance to the cave, one eye warily watching the lumies, the other gazing in horror at the three.

"Run, Uncle Lee, run!" Ricky shrieked, holding with a death grip to the torturous rod.

"We're saving you!" Sherri screamed, furious at his utter stupidity. "Don't just stand there!"

The pot made a violent swoop across the pack, sending several lumies back on their heels, shaking their ringing ears.

"Let it go!" yelled Lee.

"I'm not sure we can," Hal muttered, grim as death.

"Just let it go—and run out of the way!" shouted Lee. He edged cautiously around the enthralled pack, avoiding the lethally swinging pot.

"Okay—at the count of three," Hal said. "Everyone drop and run—one, two, three!" The pot made one last wild whirl and then hit the ground, rolling into the center of the lumies, scattering the pack momentarily. The red brindle sprung upon it with a moan of pleasure and the other lumies closed in around him.

"You, you . . . " Lee glared and shook his fist at them. Then it hit him—only three. "Where's Caro?"

"She's down a hole!" sobbed Ricky. Lee looked at Hal.

Hal gulped. "We think she—took—a side shaft by mistake. It goes almost straight down. We'll need a longer rope, or something."

Lee grabbed the three of them and began running toward Coleney's laboratory.

"Hal, can you take me straight to the hole—do you know how to get there?" he tersely asked.

"Yes—we've marked it—it's not far," Hal replied.

Lee paused in the entrance to the lab, blocking the three, and looked frantically about for Coleney's body. But there was no sign, other than the chewed, cast-off robes, that he had been there. The stone ground yielded no clues.

"This is amazing," said Hal, shocked by the technology displayed.

Lee went to a terminal. "Hal—check the back wall—I'm sure you'll find robes, harnesses, whatever we need.

And keep your eyes open for a tranq gun. All of you—load up." He began feverishly to enter commands into the entry board. Soon he tore off three sheets from the dataprint.

Hal, carrying a bar across his shoulder, handed Lee a round canister of tranquilizer darts. He shrugged. "That's the best I could find."

Lee grimaced. "Okay—let's go."

Sherri and Ricky, swathed in ropes, ran toward him.

"Maps?" said Hal, racing beside him back down through the tunnel. Lee nodded. "I'm not sure what good they will do us," he muttered. "Maybe show us a quicker way out—"

They paused at the entrance to the cathedral-cave. Lee drew a dart from out of the canister, looked first at it, then at the pack of lumies lounging at the far end of the cave, and shook his head. "Come on," he said grimly. The four scuttled along the wall of the cave. The lumies barely stirred; the red brindle rolled over and licked his fur.

They were through. But not safe until they entered the small shaft. It was a tight fit for Lee and the extra gear, but they made it in record time to where Hal had carved the three crosses.

"Down there," Hal pointed unnecessarily, wretchedly.

Lee rigged up the bar across the opening of the shaft and tumbled the rope down its dark depths. "You know how these harnesses work?" he asked Hal, as he fitted himself into one. Hal nodded.

"Okay, then," Lee said. "I'm going down. Hal, here's one of the maps. When I get to the bottom I may be out of range and won't be able to tell you this so I'm telling you now. If I'm not back in twenty minutes, take the shortest route to our cave—get into the crawler, go to Main and tell your parents." He added roughly, "Shut up, Ricky—listen to me—you will be helping Caro and me much more if you

261

do this. Now, Hal—look at your watch. Remember, if you don't hear me, leave in twenty minutes."

Then he was gone, slipping down through the darkness, bouncing gently against the rough-cut ridges, watching for any signs of Caro's descent.

Lee soon began to find them. Although the slope was initially very steep, there were pockets of smooth, even passages. Here, nestled in the turns of the shaft, he found spilled packages of food: a trail of crackers here, scatterings of dried fruit. He reached down and scooped up from its niche the monitoring disc for the carepies, its red light still blinking.

The final few meters were a straight drop. Lee landed in the lower tunnel, turned, and flashed on his extra hood lamp, looking for what he did not want to find. He saw only the campstove, skidded up against the opposite wall, mangled.

He stared through the dark of the wide tunnel, "Caro! CARO!" he called in mad hope.

The three waiting silently, counting down the minutes, heard him call. Hal turned limp with relief.

"Lee!" he said. "Can we come down?"

There was no answer.

"Lee!" Hal tried again.

"Uncle Lee!" Ricky's ear-splitting shout raised nothing. Yet they could still hear Lee calling for Caro. But his voice was growing fainter.

"He said that if we couldn't hear him we were to wait twenty minutes and then leave," Sherri said suddenly. They looked at her. "Don't you see?" she continued. "We CAN hear him . . . "

"Let's go down," said Ricky, catching on.

"Look—you all know what he meant," Hal argued feebly.

"No—you look!" Sherri retorted. "When he finds Caro she may be hurt—how can he make it back up the shaft carrying her, all alone? Besides, she doesn't have a harness," she added, making no sense.

"Let's go down there," shouted Ricky.

They went.

21

Navigator

Caro, with the hoverlight mounted on her shoulder as a living torch, padded softly under the airborne rivers of the waterfall rock, and around the deep green pond. She paused for one last look, then turned and entered the roaring mouth of the large cave through which the pool emptied.

A small channel, etched out in earlier times, stood out like a shelf edging the fast-flowing river. Caro walked along it, her feet shining with the bioluminescence lining the rock ledge. Occasionally she knelt by the water and scooped some up in her gloves, quenching her long thirst.

The underground river gradually widened and slowed. The water lazily looped around the pillars that rose like flat columnar islands, or jagged like ice floes. Caro marveled at the depth of the river. Although here, as in the quiet section of the pool, the water was as clear as emerald, she could not see to the bottom. The water seemed to go on and on, down and down, a pristine, liquid universe.

And she heard the carepies and wondered at the clarity of their call. So Caro was not surprised when she followed the hoverlight around a slow bend and saw, suspended in the limpid depths, the round, living islands with outstretched, welcoming beaks. *Hello, carepies. Hello, Navigator.*

Hal, Sherri, and Ricky made it to the bottom of the steep-sloping shaft with only one minor mishap: Hal's glasses got dislodged from his nose and he, blind as a bat, traveled down the entire length of rope with them uncomfortably wedged in the neck of his suit. Hal was the last one down the shaft, and it was sheer bad luck for Ricky that he happened to be standing right where nearsighted Hal came to land.

"You—you, stupid!" yelled Ricky, tears of pain starting to his eyes from a boot caught in the ear.

"I'm sorry, Ricky," Hal exclaimed. "Couldn't you see me, either?"

"Never mind, never mind," said Sherri impatiently. "Come on—Uncle Lee's way ahead—let's hurry."

Lee was a good distance down the tunnel, bending over what he guessed were the remains of some flat bread. The thought that Caro must have stopped and eaten something here cheered him immensely.

Then he heard the three. Lee straightened up abruptly and roared, "You *idiots!* What did I tell you?!"

"Shut up," Sherri shouted. "Just shut up! I'm tired of being called an idiot—do you hear *me?!* We're here—and that's the end of it!"

Hal felt her shaking with rage. He waited beside the dumb-struck Ricky for the tunnel to collapse.

Lee opened his mouth—and closed it again. He looked away—and he looked back. "You must get that awful temper from your dad," he finally said mildly. "I know it can't be from the Krisman's side of the family."

They ran all the way to join him.

Caro had left, every so often, an encouraging pile of crumbs; they would rise up, heartened, whenever any one of them found the next lunchbreak point.

However, they nearly missed the smaller tunnel to the right. With their hood lamps trained on the ground, Lee, and then Hal and Ricky walked past the dark passage. It was Sherri, trailing her hand along the wall, who, pausing to lean against the side, fell sideways in the shaft. "Hey!" she yelled— and then saw something odd. "What's this?" She scrambled to her knees and pointed to a small, silky pile of multi-colored strands. They were of various lengths; each one, when caught by their hood lamps, richly reflected the light.

"There's a whole pile of it," Lee muttered, examining the strange fibers. "Look how they glow—how did we all come to miss them?"

Sherri shook her head, mystified. "I fell almost on top of them, or I wouldn't have seen them either."

"Look!" Ricky cried. "There's more in this little tunnel—maybe Caro left it as a sign that she went this way!"

"Hal," said Lee, trying to make a decision, "let's you and I go down the wide tunnel, say, another kilometer or so. If we don't see any clues that Caro stayed in this tunnel, then we'll come back and all head down this one. Sherri and Ricky, we need you here to mark the spot for us. If we lose sight of this little tunnel God only knows when we'll find it again. So DON'T MOVE."

They nodded, awed by the seriousness of his tone. Sherri sat down and leaned against the side of the small tunnel. They ran some water and ate the last of her onion crumbles and several of Ricky's crackers with nut butter. Then Ricky stretched out across the wide tunnel and promptly fell asleep.

When Hal and Lee returned, both Sherri and Ricky were dead asleep. Lee sat down with Hal and they had a brief meal of dried fruit and water.

"How are you doing, Hal?" asked Lee. "Are you okay for a bit longer, or do you need to sleep?"

"I'm absolutely wiped," admitted Hal. "But I don't think I can sleep yet. I just keep thinking that if for some reason her bipack goes out, and she doesn't have water—well, I think we should go on."

Lee looked at him and then nodded. They woke the others.

"I feel way better," said Sherri sleepily. "Except that now I can't move my legs, they're so stiff. Did you find anything?"

"No," answered Lee. "It's down the little tunnel we go." He fingered the silky strands and placed them in his inner chest pocket. "Ricky—ride on my back a ways, okay?"

Ricky gave Lee no argument. Hal helped Sherri to her feet.

The winding, narrow tunnel yielded up no clues for a long time. Everyone had grown anxious, silent, their eyes glued to the ground. Sherri trailed a hand along the wall, just in case they missed another new passage.

It was Hal who found a few scattered roasted prawb seeds. He held them up wordlessly and they circled him and stared at the black seeds, smiling broadly, mist filling their eyes. "I've never been so happy to see those awful things!" Sherri exclaimed.

"What do you mean, 'awful things'?" said Lee, almost his old, cheerful self. "Caro's got good taste—they're wonderful!"

"The pointy shells get stuck in my throat and I gag," explained Sherri.

"Oh—that explains it," said Lee smoothly. "Anything that threatens your speaking apparatus you view with horror."

"Ha, ha," replied Sherri.

Sherri and Ricky first heard the throbbing roar resonating deep in the walls. "Like a geoquake," Ricky said, his voice trembling.

"Like a lion," Sherri said, eyes round.

Soon they all heard it and grew accustomed to its deep pulsing tones chiming with the ring of the wind.

When they followed the twisting tunnel to where the white light emanated from around the bend just ahead, Lee let Ricky slip to the ground and run on ahead.

"Hey—it's incredible!" came back his excited voice.

The waterfalls made them all a little crazy.

"Well, at least Caro has had enough to drink," shouted Hal, waving his arms ecstatically.

Sherri and Ricky cavorted madly through the flashing rainbows and mist. Ricky lay flat on his back at the foot of the waterfall rock, watching the airborne rivers high above him shoot from the cliff and begin their graceful arc to the green pool. Lee drank deeply from the emerald-clear waters.

They rested there: drinking huge draughts cupped from the waves, eating nuts and dried fruit and Ricky's ever-present nut butter on crackers, and fell asleep, lost in the almighty roar.

When they awoke and ate and drank again, they followed the river through the mouth of the cave, walking joyfully along the gleaming ledge beside the water.

Caro pulled on her drysuit over her Zero and slipped into the water with the carepies. She greeted each adult, and played with the babies; she paid her respects to the older two. *Navigator, oh, Navigator, it's so good to see you.*

The babies, a little more solemn in these waters, nevertheless vied fiercely for her attention, bucking and cavorting through the emerald sea, bumping into the girl in careless joy. Then Caro saw the tracking equipment held by rivets through their circular fins and grew sick. *I'm sorry, babies, so sorry.*

They seemed puzzled by her distress, tugging gently on the ripples in her air-filled suit, wanting her to dive and play with them. But Caro could only just duck below the water in this suit covering.

While Caro was with the carepies, the hoverlight beamed and sparked and clicked from the glowing ledge. It ran busily up the wall a short ways and down again, sending out encouraging chirps to itself and to the girl in the water.

So it was, when Lee and the others came around the bend in the river, the first thing they saw was the hoverlight. Lee unconsciously patted his chest pocket where he had placed the strange, light-reflecting hairs.

The hoverlight went to them, sending out light like a fountain, and filling their ears with welcoming clicks and chirps. And when Caro looked up from the water, there they all were, surrounding the hoverlight and holding out their hands to it. She couldn't hear them, enclosed in the dry suit with her useless intercom, but she swam to the ledge and pulled herself up, and then they saw her.

And ran to her, mouths moving frantically. Caro, laughing and laughing, tugged off her drysuit, but before she could unzip her faceplate they had descended upon her.

"We thought you were dead!" sobbed Ricky, clinging tightly to her arm. Sherri and Hal clutched at her, exclaiming equally unintelligible remarks to her.

"Can you breathe?" cried Lee, hugging her so tightly that if she could have heard and been heard the answer would have been "No!"

Hal realized her dilemma. He pushed past Lee, reached up and twisted two wires together; shrieks and static burst in her ears.

It finally penetrated through to Lee. "You can't hear us," he shouted at her. "Nod your head—are you all right? Are you getting enough air?"

Caro finally freed herself and unzipped her faceplate completely. "I'm fine." She laughed.

Lee grimaced at those words. "Really?" he asked.

"Really. Really, truly," she said, eyes shining, and started to cry.

Lee pulled on his drysuit and slipped into the water. While Caro stroked the carepies, he clipped off the rivets attaching the tracking equipment to their fins.

"Throw them far away, Uncle Lee," Ricky ordered.

"No," commanded Sherri. "Drop them right here—all the way to the bottom of the river. Let's see how far we can see them before they disappear."

"I'd line them up on the ledge and stomp on them," Hal said in a fit of violence.

"Nope," said Lee, grinning at all three of them. "I think we can come up with a more creative way of disposing them." But he wouldn't say what he was planning to do. "I think it's time to start thinking about going home," he said, when they persisted.

"Oh," groaned Ricky, "I forgot—we've got to do the whole thing over again—only backwards."

"What!?" snorted Lee.

"We've come all this way and now we have to go the same way again, but in the other direction," interpreted Sherri.

"Let's hope not," replied Lee, looking dazed.

"Won't your mapmaker have us going back the same way?" asked Hal.

"Not if I can help it," he replied. "That's one of the reasons I printed the maps—what there are of them—from Coleney's computer. I thought that we might have to make an emergency exit. Happily, we only have to make an exit," he said, smiling at Caro.

The hoverlight walked about on all of them as Lee worked on the homeward journey. Caro gathered the creature into her arms and leaned back against the rock wall. The hoverlight's clicks filled her ears and she watched the round backs of the carepies bopping and dipping, and the occasional benign beak checking out the situation above the water.

"They'll have to stay here, won't they," Caro said softly.

"Well, we can't carry them out, sweetheart. But that doesn't mean they won't find their own way out," Lee replied. "Your 'Navigator' seems to be doing fine."

"If they found the right route out," asked Caro, "how long do you think it would take them to get back to the ocean?"

"Oh—maybe three or four weeks," Lee said. "Maybe less. Who knows?" Lee leaned back and nodded in satisfaction. "Yes, this looks quite possible. We're going out by boat! As far as we can, anyway."

"Yeah—my legs thank you and your mapmaker, Uncle Lee," Sherri said, lolling back against the wall.

Caro smiled. At least she wouldn't have to say goodbye to the carepies quite so soon.

The polymer dinghy was pulled out from Lee's backpack and inflated with suit air. It stood, bopping on the water, bumping up alongside the ledge while Lee fixed the small, extendable mast in place.

"Okay—ready to go," he finally said.

They crowded in, five humans and one hoverlight slowly sailing along the emerald river with the seven carepies diving and circling around them. Caro laughed at the astonished expressions on the babies' faces and the amused paternalistic looks of the adults. Navigator swam alongside the boat with a strong wave pattern.

"You'd never know it," Lee said, looking at the old bull, shaking his head in amazement. "I can hardly believe it's the same carepie."

Caro never forgot the feel of that journey home: the silver gleam of bioluminescence layering the walls of the tunnel, the odd, jutting islands of rock, the rich emerald of the water, the stir of the wind in the tiny sail. And, of course, the hoverlight, busily running over the five humans, sipping daintily from Caro's palm that dripped with the icy water.

They left the carepies at a branch in the river. Ricky was soundly sleeping, curled up on the bottom of the boat. Sherri, half asleep, was leaning her head back on the air-filled side. Hal was alternately staring into the distance and watching the hoverlight mounted on Lee's shoulder. Caro was trailing her hand through the silky water, smiling at the babies' outstretched beaks.

Lee steered the rudder to the right and Navigator slowly gave ground, dropping around behind the boat, coming up on the other side. The other carepies joined him, closing in like a unit, following the river to the sea.

"Oh, stop, Uncle Lee," Caro called, anguished.

Lee shook his head. "They're going, sweetheart."

"I never said good-bye!"

"Say it now," Lee gently said.

Oh, good-bye carepies. Thank you. Thank you, babies. Oh, carepies, will I see you again? And the rich warm flow back, *"When it is Good, and for Good . . . "*

The little boat began turning, leaving the rest of the river to flow on. The backs of the carepies dipped one by one, sending rings rippling across the still, emerald surface. *Good-bye, Navigator. God speed.*

The right branch of the river broke again, a short ways down, into two smaller streams. They took the left fork, following the blinking instructions of the mapmaker. The stream flowed cold and dark; they had left the bioluminescence behind them. But it was here that the four who had never seen the hoverlight in the utter dark gloried in its light-showering splendor.

Lee kept one hood lamp trained on the water ahead and the rest they turned off, delighting in the creature whose body seemed to pulse with greater energy every passing second.

The stream grew darker and more sullen; Lee began to feel the rudder scraping the bottom of the shallow channel so he pulled it up as high as it could go, relying on the narrowness of the tunnel to keep them straight.

It grew more shallow, until the bottom bulged at times with smooth protruding stones, and they barely slid from one to the other. Lee flashed on all the lights and there was dry rock ahead, the oily water licking against it.

"Okay," said Lee. "We're about as far as we can go."

"Oh," Sherri moaned. "I never thought I'd say this, but it will be good to stretch my legs. But, wow, that was truly wonderful—every second of it."

Caro sighed, picked up the hoverlight, and stepped out onto the rock.

Soon they were walking through the passage, the chalky grey walls of the tunnel closing in around them as if the river had never been.

"Believe it or not, it's not all that far now," Lee said. "It is, however, uphill all the way. Caro, you're not going to be able to keep your faceplate unzipped too much longer; it's going to get colder by the meter, and you'll have real trouble breathing with it open. The problem is, you're not going to be able to hear us, right?"

"No, I can hear you—but I can also hear multiple squawks, shrieks, and tons of static," Caro said. "Hal fixed it for me," she added, grinning at him.

"Well—we'll just tell Sherri not to talk—that'll cut out a lot of the static, at any rate," Lee said cheerfully.

"Wait," called Sherri, not hearing him. "Look, look, look! More pictures—do you remember, we saw those pictures on the wall when the lumies were kidnapping us? There are more here!"

They stopped and stared at them, awestruck, shaking their heads at the mystery of them. Were these a series of pictures, or was there only one continuous craft, spreading in vast, explosive splendor across the grey expanse? At any rate, one or many, the pictures were alike; the same brilliant shooting colors from soft, light globes, and deep green clouds all around. It was the pattern that varied, sometimes thrilling with the firework explosions, and sometimes a subdued brilliance cloaked by the green.

Hal, Ricky, and Caro speculated on their origin and wondered over their meaning. Sherri was silent. She stayed before the wall, entranced, mesmerized. Caro, glancing at her, knew she was burning them deep in her mind and heart so that sometime she could recreate their startling message.

"Do you think that it's a natural phenomenon?" asked Hal.

"You mean, from a natural source, as opposed to a supernatural source?" asked Caro. "Why not a supernatural origin?"

Lee glanced at Caro. "That would be my vote," he said.

"What do you mean? A ghost did it? Or an angel?" Ricky looked baffled and alarmed. He took a step back from the wall.

"I'm not saying that the pictures weren't placed there by a natural force," said Lee. "Be that force animal, vegetable, or mineral. I'm talking about the cause of it being there—which, I somehow feel, is supernatural."

"That's the same thing," said Ricky, puzzled.

Hal looked thoughtfully at Lee. "You mean like a religious symbol?" he asked.

Lee shrugged. "Only if by religious symbol you include, along with your religious writings and icons: flowers, Jonah trees, waterfalls, families, frontons, stars, and carepies, and hoverlights, too, of course," he added, smiling at Caro. " 'All things fearfully and wonderfully made.' "

"Even lumies?" Ricky demanded.

Lee paused and then laughed. "Hmm. Well—I guess they would come under the 'fearfully made' part. Yes," he added, a little sadly, "even the lumies."

They moved on up the tunnel, away from the pictures. Sherri was silent for a long time after, wrapped in the wonder of them. But the chalk walls closed in again and seemed to say this is all there is and was and will be.

The hoverlight stayed with Caro most of the way back. During one of their rest stops, it hopped off her shoulder and began running around clicking and chirping busily. Caro's brow wrinkled; something was different about its behavior. She watched it, leaning her back against the wall, and called, "Turn off your hood lamps."

And then it was like she and the hoverlight were back in the dark, pain-ridden tunnel where she had fallen. The hovering effect of its black feet in the night, the sparking explosion in the air, floating, floating. She wordlessly watched it click and whirl and flame; the living light seemed super-charged, spraying color through the night.

And then it paused. The golden glow of its body increased in intensity, in thick pulsating waves. Then, gleaming, green pearls began to appear around it. String upon string in intricate network formed all around the creature. The hoverlight began to move slowly from wall to ceiling to wall and back again, and everywhere garlands of glowing green pearls streamed from it. The tunnel began to quiver into light and radiate with the living greenness.

It went on forever; it was over too fast. Caro, tears streaming down her face, watched as the hoverlight buried itself in a heap of green and its light began to fade. Slowly, slowly, the orange, red, pink, blue sparklers dimmed; then the warm body began to flicker. It went out.

For the rest of the journey home, Caro mourned the hoverlight. Her heart recalled how the faithful creature had come to her when she hadn't known of it, how it had stayed with her in her wanderings, how it had lit up the night. She wished that she could be there when its gleaming eggs hatched out: to see the tunnel full of sparking hoverlights, to hear their cheerful clicking.

22

Home

A month, almost to the day, after Caro and the others returned home from the End region, it was her sixteenth birthday. Caro's mother, with Sherri's assistance, planned a family party to be held at Caro's favorite beach. Of course any "family" outing was not complete without Sherri's family, Hal and his dad, as well as Dr. Lutes—who arrived with long-handled net and bucket in hand.

Lee, who had finally worked himself back into all the respective parents' good graces, brought a lab boat with him and soon he, Hal, Sherri, Caro, Ricky, and Dr. Lutes were sailing about, bucking the solid incoming waves of the Pantropic coastline. It was the first time since their arrival home that they had gathered together as a group and the conversation naturally veered around to the End region and Dr. Coleney.

"Did the lumies kill Coleney because he was mean to them?" asked Ricky abruptly. "Or just because they are mean themselves?"

Lee, looking out over the foam-mauve waves, said, "Well—Coleney would have said that both were the same thing. That is, because he 'became' a lumie, he was just treating them as they treated themselves. I'm not so sure about that—the lumies didn't blind themselves."

"Was he crazy?" Ricky asked.

"There are lots of different kinds of crazy, Ricky," Lee replied. "But yes, I think it's crazy to think that we humans can have a healthy, non-crazy life by renouncing our human-ness. Unfortunately, Coleney wasn't, or isn't I should say, alone in thinking that way."

"Yeah," said Hal. "I asked my dad about that—I mean, about the Community knowing about Coleney all these years and giving him equipment and everything. He said that he'd never heard of such a thing." Sherri laughed, and Caro knew immediately that she was picturing Hal's dad's easily read face. She could just see the look of utter horror, red and heavy, remolding his features.

"There were only three people in on it," Lee said. "All three, I am very happy to say, have been reprimanded and lowered in rank. I also hear—unfortunately for that planet—that they are being restationed on Earth."

"Dr. Lutes," Caro asked, "did you know Dr. Coleney—I mean before, when he was working at the End Base?"

Dr. Lutes looked out over the bow. "Yes," he said. "I knew Reginald when he was new here from Earth. A promising scientist and a sensitive man. One who was very alone and very lonely. I was there at the End Base when he disappeared."

They were still for a while.

"Dr. Lutes," Caro shyly began again, "do you remember telling me one time that it was okay to fear the dark—as long as you didn't forget why you feared it?"

The old man's silver head nodded slowly. He smiled at her encouragingly.

"Dr. Coleney . . . he forgot, didn't he? I mean, he forgot who he was—and that's what the dark tells us, isn't it? That that's really the way we always are—wandering in the dark until a hoverlight comes along, or a carepie, or your friends, and they point you along the way awhile longer—" Caro paused, embarrassed, uncertain if she had made any sense at all.

But Dr. Lutes beamed. "Yes, yes, my dear," he said softly. "The paradox is that it is in the dark that we can see most clearly . . . "

Lee nodded solemnly, gazing into the horizon. The others were silent; Sherri's face mirrored her attempt to touch the mystery of it. Finally she said, "Well, Hal, aren't you going to say it?"

"What?" He looked up, startled.

"I think," she began, signaling to Caro, who joined in, grinning, "—that this is something beyond the realm of material science!"

Hal reddened till his ears glowed.

"That's true," protested Lee on Hal's behalf, not understanding the joke.

"You never finished about the blinded lumies—what's happening to them?" asked Ricky.

"Nothing," replied Lee promptly. "They tried to saddle me with the job and I would not take it. Told them I was experiencing the ever-handy disease known as 'space fatigue.' I figure that those lumies will be wonderful guards for keeping out nosy scientists from tagging hoverlights."

"They wouldn't!" Caro and Sherri exclaimed.

"Sure they would," Lee said. "I'm kidding," he admitted. "I am doing the clean-up operation for this one, too. Actually, I meant to talk to you about the hoverlight. I don't think anyone but us has ever seen one. And yes, I do think that somebody will eventually be following the hoverlight around with an aud-vis recorder. But—to hold off that evil day as long as possible—let's keep quiet about it, okay? Or is this coming too late?"

"We've only talked among ourselves, haven't we?" Sherri asked the others. Caro and Ricky nodded.

"I didn't want to tell anyone about it," Caro said.

"Neither did I," said Sherri with a puzzled look on her face. "You'd think that that would have been the first thing we'd tell everyone, but, somehow, I didn't."

"I didn't think anyone would believe me," Hal admitted.

"It's nobody's business but our own," said Ricky grandly. "What are you going to do with the blinded lumies?" he persisted.

"Not much, actually," said Lee. "They don't pose an immediate danger to anyone, and it would be impossible to relocate all of them. I have a feeling that the lumies will take care of the lumies—without much help from me."

"They sure liked Hal's cooking," said Sherri with a straight face.

Everyone laughed, recalling the wildly swinging pot of fish-concoction. Lee ground his teeth, "It's funny now, but was I ever furious with you three. It was like you had this giant fishing pole and were fishing for lumies . . . What if you'd caught one?"

"Oh, well, dear uncle, we survived," Sherri said, reaching over and patting him on the back.

"I missed that!" Caro exclaimed. "I missed a lot of fun stuff!"

"Well, you were a little busy yourself," said Lee dryly.

"Remember the tunnel pictures?!" Hal exclaimed.

"Yes," answered Sherri, a dreamy look settling in her eyes. She had drawn her own re-creation of the rock pictures and was waiting for Caro to open a large, scrolled parcel in her pile of birthday presents on shore.

Lee turned the rudder and the boat jigged across the waves, changing direction, running parallel with the shoreline. He sighed in satisfaction. "You know there are compensations for being in Marine biology, aren't there?"

Dr. Lutes, leaning over the edge and trailing his net in the water, beamed. "That there are, Levi."

"And to think—I've got this boat for a month," Lee gloated. He smiled at the purple flashing waves and then at the others. "A whole month."

"How come—do you mean you're going to be here, at Main, a whole month?!" Ricky's voice escalated.

"Yep," answered Lee, looking—if possible—more pleased with himself.

"I thought you said you'd taken the post of cleaning up Coleney's mess," Hal said, bewildered.

"Yes, well, I've got a month's reprieve on that," Lee answered. "All the folks at the End Base are having an unexpected few weeks off while Aquatics and Geology tear up the water system . . . "

"Aquatic *Biology*? Geology? Shouldn't it be the engineers that fix any water source problem?" Hal stared at Lee, perplexed.

"Yeah, usually. Oh, don't worry, Hal, I'm sure they'll have one or two engineers hanging around—I pity their luck. No, Aquatics and Geology are pretty excited. They seem to think they've got a pod of carepies under the water treatment center . . . "

"What?!" said Caro, unable to believe him. Lee was almost doubled over, trying to keep from laughing outright. "No, you didn't—" Caro said with a dismayed look on her face.

"I didn't mean to—entirely," Lee said earnestly, a huge grin erupting on his face. He laughed then.

"I don't get it!" said Sherri. Hal looked mystified.

"What??" Ricky demanded.

Caro answered, "I think he disposed of the carepies' tracking equipment at the End Base—in the water system."

"No, no, no, Caro! I simply flushed them down one innocent toilet—I really didn't think they'd survive the bacterial recycling. It sure makes you think...it's probably a good thing they're overhauling the whole system," he added with a grimace. "And in the meantime . . . " He gestured at the boat and the sea.

Everyone laughed in delighted horror.

"Can you see their faces when they don't find a single trace of a carepie?!!" Sherri exclaimed.

Caro leaned back, smiling, watching the distant shoreline. They were passing by their "own" stretch of beach; Caro saw the crawlers perched high on the rose-rock cliffs and the tables and chairs set up on the thin stretch of pink sand. Becka and Meggie were playing in the gentle waves of the cove.

"Hey—" Sherri said, leaning forward and squinting at the beach. "They're all watching us—they're staring at us through viewers!"

Hal laughed. "You're right, Sherri! I suppose they think that we're going to disappear—be carried away by a tornado or something!"

"More like, 'be carried away by that awful Lee,'" Lee said with sudden passion. "As if it were all my fault—I don't KNOW how many times I told you to GO HOME." Dr. Rokmanoff had been the only parent who had seen his side—but unfortunately, Hal's dad was a quiet ally.

"Never mind, Uncle Lee, never mind," Sherri said consolingly. "We promised our parents never to let you lead us into danger again." She started waving gaily to the shore. "We're here! We're alive!" she called. "Uncle Lee hasn't killed us yet!"

"Sherri!" Lee roared.

But Caro wasn't watching either them or the line of concerned parents on the shore. She was looking, staring out to sea. She lifted her sun shades and squinted into the flashing waves. *There!* She leapt to her feet and ran to the bow of the boat, leaning over, eyes scanning, intent.

"Hal—grab the rudder," Lee called urgently. "She's going to go over in a second—and right before her mother's eyes—" He ran over, tilting the boat, and grabbed Caro.

"It's them, oh it's them—don't you see?!!" Caro cried out in sobbing laughter.

Lee looked, deep into the horizon, and saw the rounded backs of a carepie pod dipping and bobbing in the distance. Was that a knobby head peering back at them? Lee watched, eyes straining to see. "Sweetheart . . . maybe it was, I couldn't tell," he said gently. "They were awfully close to shore, though, weren't they, Dr. Lutes?"

Dr. Lutes had risen to his feet and was standing, one hand clutching the side of the boat, one hand shading his eyes. "Yes," he said. "Carepies do not usually come this close to shore."

Caro leaned over the bow, looking longingly into the distant waves, knowing, feeling *it was the pod.* They had made it back home. *I'll see you again, carepies. I'll be back! Oh, Navigator—thank you.*

If you have enjoyed this book, or have any comments to make, the publishers would be delighted to hear from you. Please write to:

Meryl Doney
c/o Hodder & Stoughton
47 Bedford Square
London
WC1B 3DP

GOLD BOOKS

A goldmine of excellent fiction for young adults, combining international award-winners and exciting new writers.

ALL ABOUT JAS

Millie Murray

Who wants to go to a foster home, never mind be apart from the family while Mum has an operation? Jas is not keen but stays cool – until she meets her temporary foster family. Not only do they all go to church, but Judy Fenton is white and her husband Aubrey is black! How is she to cope with this on top of everything else, especially when she is preparing for an important rap competition and romance is in the air?

DARK IS A COLOUR

Fay Lapka

Caro is sure she'll never get used to the ice-green sky on the new planet. Her best friend Sherri is no longer speaking to her. And to crown it all, her scientist parents are being whisked away to deal with a crisis at the research centre deep in the End Zone.

What will they find there? Uncle Lee has a disturbing theory about the beautiful "lumies" — enormous, gentle creatures with soft eyes and silky fur. But no one is prepared to believe him. Until, that is, Caro and her friends begin a nightmare journey into the dark, to bring the truth to light.

GOLD
BOOKS

THE BOOK OF THE DUN COW

Walter Wangerin, Jr.

At a time when the sun turned round the earth and animals could speak, Chauntecleer the Rooster ruled over a more or less peaceable kingdom. What the animals did not know was that they were the Keepers of Wyrm, monster of Evil long imprisoned beneath the earth. And Wyrm was breaking free . . .

'Belongs on the shelf with ANIMAL FARM, WATERSHIP DOWN and THE LORD OF THE RINGS.' *Los Angeles Times*

'A beautifully written fantasy . . . a book in which there is adventure and humour, betrayal and despair. But most of all there is hope.' *Washington Post*

GOLD
BOOKS

THE BOOK OF SORROWS

Walter Wangerin, Jr.

The terrible Wyrm, incarnation of evil, was struck a mortal blow in *The Book of the Dun Cow*. The animals, led by Chaunticleer the Rooster, fought with every weapon they possessed. He was defeated by the courageous action of Mundo Cani the dog. Wyrm was dead.

Or was he? In this sequel the enemy returns, more insidious this time and more deadly. Will the animals be able to stand against him? Can evil be overcome with good? The fate of Mundo Cani is revealed. But who is the mysterious Dun Cow?

'This is a beautifully written yet demanding book, in which strong language and telling images combine to weave a fable of immense power. Not for the faint hearted!' *Meryl Doney*

JUST FOR THE SUMMER

Karin N Mango

Jenny Smith is spending the summer as a lifeguard at a lake in beautiful New Hampshire, USA. She is trying to forget her problems with Alec, the boy next door at home, when she becomes intrigued by her new neighbour. After two weeks, Rollo's only words have been a curt, 'Leave me alone,' and she wants to know why.

Jenny finds herself falling in love as the mystery surrounding her strange neighbour is slowly revealed. And, in an unexpected twist, she learns how to deal with her own worries.